"Don't go too far," he said.

Cynthia raised her chin, sniffed, and turned away. She took two steps but failed to look where she was going and inadvertently stepped in a hole. She found herself pitched forward right into the creek. Once again, she landed face down—this time in water—and her feet were up the incline of the bank, only slightly higher than her head. The flounced skirt and petticoats ballooned forward, almost covering her head and exposing her white lawn pantalets, trimmed in several rows of dainty lace.

Immediately, Cynthia panicked and began to flail her arms and attempt to right herself. The position was so awkward she couldn't find a handhold or foothold. Strong hands gripped her shoulders, lifting her once again to a sitting position in the creek bed. She was soaked and her long mass of curls now hung in wet, limp clumps.

She flew into an uncharacteristic rage. "Can't you get me out of this water? Why am I sitting here? Do something!"

With little effort, Ricardo picked her up and carried her to a level spot on the bank. Instead of gently setting her down, he leaned over, lowered her bottom to within half a foot off the ground, and released her.

Cynthia literally bounced on her rump. "You...you...!"

Ricardo had turned away to retrieve his boots, but he paused and looked over his shoulder with one raised eyebrow. "Yes, Miss Harrington? You wish to say something?" He had such a regal air.

"Ohhh, piddle!"

As he walked away, she heard him laugh out loud, a deep rumbling sound of pure joy. He was *laughing* at her.

All My Hopes and Dreams is a sweet story of young love. Ms. Yeary has done an exceptional job creating a strong, embraceable hero and a heroine. Both grow and change, as they fall in love and struggle to meet the challenges of family. Ms. Yeary has penned a fantastic debut novel!

~Mallary Mitchell, author of Roped and Tied, and The Last Promise

All My Hopes And Dreams

by

Celia Yeary

All My Hopes And Dreams

Cover Art by *Angela Anderson*

The Wild Rose Press
PO Box 708
Adams Basin, NY 14410-0706
Visit us at www.thewildrosepress.com

Publishing History
First Cactus Rose Edition, 2008
Print ISBN 1-60154-369-7

Published in the United States of America

Dedication

For my husband, Jim

Chapter One

Nacogdoches, Texas, 1880

If I'd known running away would be this hot and this dirty, I'd have stayed home. With her dainty lace handkerchief, Cynthia Harrington dabbed the perspiration from her upper lip. She sighed heavily for the one-hundredth time today and impatiently brushed the dust from the skirt of her best lavender day dress.

But she could not stay home, where she would much prefer to be right now instead of in this unbearable heat. Her father had made peace between them impossible with his idiotic demands and lectures about her place in society. Society, indeed! Nacogdoches was not exactly the social center of Texas, so she made the decision to leave home and drive her one-seat buggy to Austin or San Antonio. All she knew to do was go west. Either city would do. She hoped she would be there in one day, because she had brought only one change of dress and one other bonnet. The one-hundred dollars tucked in her reticule would surely be enough to live on for a while.

She snapped the reins lightly on the back of the horse, just slightly, because she couldn't bear to hurt the sweet thing. Of course, she would need to feed and water Little Dixie, but she believed livery stable fees were reasonable.

A sound of pounding hooves brought her out of her thoughts. A rider approached behind her, and he was already close. Fleetingly, she thought of

1

highwaymen and unsavory characters that might be out to harm her, but she'd never heard of such things in this civilized part of Texas. She guided her mare to the side of the road and stopped to allow him to pass. Surely, he would ride by, and not throw a swirl of dust all over her. She sat very still beneath the bonnet of the little buggy and pressed her back to the seat.

The horse, however, seemed to slow its gait, and yes, it was brought to a halt beside her. She ventured a peek and blew out a breath. *Ricardo Romero. That...that ne'er-do-well.* He'd escorted her home once from her friend's house and had acted as if he were the master of all he surveyed.

She stiffened her back and held her breath. *Go away; go away.* If she pretended not to see him, let alone recognize him, maybe he would take the hint and ride past.

He touched the flat brim of his gaucho-style hat. "Miss Harrington. Good morning."

Why doesn't he wear a western hat like all the other men in Texas? Why does he have to wear those tight, brown pants with the silver conchos down the outside seams? Why must he wear those fancy-stitched boots, instead of nice, serviceable ones like everyone else?

Land sakes alive; he was so different. Even his skin was dark, and his eyes resembled shining pieces of obsidian. *And oh, such arrogance and haughtiness.* He literally looked down his long nose at everyone, including her father, as if he thought he was better than most other men.

That was another thing. Why in the world would her father, the local banker and one of the richest men in town, admire him and be so solicitous?

"What do you want, Mr. Romero?" she asked as coolly as her shaking voice would allow.

"Why, to accompany you, Miss Harrington. I am

2

to be your escort," he answered.

His rich, foreign-sounding voice made her even more nervous.

"What?" She jerked her head toward him. "What are you talking about?"

She leaned forward to get a better look at him. The big, black stallion danced around—his powerful body demanding to unleash its power and race down the road. With expertise and ease, Ricardo handled the beast with one slim hand holding the reins. His other rested on his own firm thigh. The animal seemed to recognize the man's superiority.

"Your father asked me to find you and bring you home. However, if you insist on continuing your journey, I will take you to your destination. Where do you wish to go, Miss Harrington? I am at your service." His smile revealed blinding, white teeth.

"Where I wish to go and where you wish to go will not be the same. Do you understand? We will not be traveling together, not now, not ever. So turn around, go back, and tell my father I'll travel on my own. I will not return home. Thank you very much." She lifted her chin and looked straight ahead once more.

"But he is worried about you, Miss Harrington," he replied. "Are you running away?"

"*That* is none of your business. Now, go." She waved a hand toward him as she might shoo chickens from a yard.

Without looking at him again, she made kissing sounds to her mare and resumed her journey west to find Austin or San Antonio.

After ten or fifteen minutes, she turned around and peeked through the opening where the buggy bonnet didn't quite reach the back of the seat. She had to bend almost double, but what she saw infuriated her. He still followed. For a couple of miles, she stewed and fussed, trying to formulate a plan to rid herself of the officious man.

As Little Dixie clip-clopped along, Cynthia daydreamed of living in the city. There she would be free of her father's restraints and watchful eye. If she had a mother, brothers, or sisters, perhaps he might have turned his attention to one of them, but every ounce of protective instinct he had, he directed at her. Now he had gone too far. He'd selected a husband for her and a full-out campaign had begun to see them married. The so-called beau was one-hundred percent in league with her father to win, woo, and wed her as quickly as possible. *Oh, the nerve!*

Out of the Piney Woods, a deer dashed across the road in front of her, causing poor Little Dixie to sidestep and toss her head. Cynthia was on alert instantly, but it was too late to control the mare.

Over went the buggy, and Cynthia fell to the side with it. Her rib cage jammed into the iron arm on the seat. Her head hit the edge of the buggy bonnet as she was propelled forward by the momentum of the small carriage. She found herself face down in the dusty road, with her feet caught in the upturned buggy higher than her head. The little horse neighed, whinnied, and screeched in fright, as she strained to be free of the twisted traces.

Cynthia heard a deep soothing voice. "There now, there now, little girl. You're fine. Calm down, now. Shhh. That's a good girl."

Cynthia gritted her teeth in frustration. *The man is rescuing the horse first.* She tried to turn to her back, but she found her feet were caught in the armrest. She managed to disengage one, but now her legs spread-eagled in an entirely inappropriate way. In a futile attempt to turn to her back, her straw bonnet came loose from her head and ended up partially over her face. Now, her entire body resembled a twisted piece of licorice.

4

Ricardo squatted on one heel beside her head. She quickly averted her eyes. *How utterly gauche for him to be in such a position.* She clenched her jaw.

"Are you hurt?" he asked without touching her.

She sighed heavily with her eyes shut. "Will...you...please...help...me?"

"Why, certainly, Miss Harrington," he replied in a calm voice. "Remember, that's why I'm here, to be your escort."

"You've already...said that."

"What should I do first?" he drawled.

She opened one eye to peek at him. "What happened to your accent? You just now sounded like all the other Texans around here."

Ricardo chuckled. "Hold still so I can free your foot. That sure looks like an uncomfortable position."

"That's an understatement if I ever heard one," she snapped.

Once she sat up, she removed her bonnet. Her thick hair that had been on top of her head in a secure coil of curls now fell askew to one side. She lowered her chin to remove the remaining pins. When she looked up, her eyes connected with his for an instant. She leaned her head back and shook her hair as a horse would a mane.

Next, she stretched her legs straight out on the ground and wiggled her feet. Then, she gingerly touched her left ribs and winced.

"Hurt?"

"Mmm, just a little."

"Maybe I should check. Make certain you don't have anything broken."

"No, no, that's all right." The thought of his dark hands on her body sent shivers along her arms. She wasn't certain if the feeling was aversion...or anticipation. *Uh-uh, not anticipation.*

"Raise your arm just a little. I really think I should see if you're hurt. Won't take but a minute."

He knelt beside her.

She obeyed him and sat as docilely as she could. He placed one palm along her right ribs, just under her breast to hold her still, and used his right palm to cover her left ribs. His long-fingered hands almost spanned her rib cage. He pressed slowly, more and more, until she sucked in a breath. Next, he moved his fingers over each rib, and satisfied, he withdrew his hands from her tiny waist.

Ricardo sat back on his heels and placed one hand on his thigh. With the other hand, he pushed his hat from his forehead. His dark gaze roamed over her face, pausing longer on her eyes.

With her face free of any expression, Cynthia returned the look. She studied his handsome face, with its chiseled cheekbones, aristocratic nose and cleft chin. He was all angles and masculinity, but long, black lashes that any woman would envy softened the effect.

"I don't think anything's broken or even cracked, but you'll probably have a nasty-looking bruise there. Your whole body may be a little sore. You took quite a tumble. Can you stand?"

"Of course." She answered more curtly than she intended, and before she knew if she actually could.

"Let's get you under that tree over there, in the shade. I need to see to your mare."

In an attempt to stand, she stepped on the hem of her dress and stumbled a little. Ricardo caught her elbow, and once she was upright led her to the tree. When she sat and leaned back on the big trunk, he walked away in that swaggering manner similar to her friend's husband and his wranglers. She propped up her knees and carefully pulled her skirts and petticoats over them, down to her toes.

****

Ricardo Romero was an expert at handling women and horses. The little mare watched him

6

with big, baleful eyes, as if she dramatically and silently willed him to touch her.

Women often looked at him the same way. This woman, though... This one was different. She was one reserved lady, and he knew without a doubt in his mind no man had ever laid a hand on her.

He'd previously made her acquaintance or at least had been in contact with her a few times. Once, his friends, Robert and Roxanne King, asked him to escort her back to town from their ranch. As he'd moved onto the buggy seat beside her, she'd been as haughty as Queen Isabella, and as cold as water from a spring well. He chuckled to himself as he remembered the command to leave her presence. Her father would be quite angry if he saw them together.

He also knew she and Buck Cameron had been an item in Nacogdoches for a year, until Marilee Weston came to town. Then, Buck dropped Miss Cynthia Harrington like a rock. Ricardo had made a mild attempt to interest her. However, she would have none of it.

He soothed the mare as he unhitched her and led her to the green grass in the shade. The buggy looked unharmed, but he studied it from all sides, especially the underside which was now fully exposed. These little one-seaters were lightweight, but they were generally sturdy. If he could push it upright, he might be able to determine any real damage. Right now, all he could see was a slight dent in the iron support of the bonnet.

Every so often, he slid covert glances at Cynthia. She kept her eyes on him as he moved back and forth. Was she wondering why he came to retrieve her? Was she angry he had touched her ribs and had even brushed the undersides of her full, firm breasts? Maybe she studied him as a male specimen.

Whatever she was doing, it unnerved him.

Women usually did not make him nervous, so why was he tense and too aware of her? She had a way of calmly smoothing errant strands of hair away from her face with her small, elegant hands. Her movements were slow and easy, as though she performed a private dance. So far, she hadn't lost control or become hysterical, and for that, he was grateful. That was where he drew the line. He couldn't stand high-strung women.

Ricardo knew her father was a tyrant in a way, but it was obvious he loved Cynthia with every fiber of his being. He was overly protective and demanded the best for his little girl. What had Mr. Harrington done to make her run away? There was the one crack in her facade—she was as clueless about the outside world as she was about men.

The bright summer sun was past the halfway mark. Noon had come and gone maybe three hours ago. There would still be several hours of daylight, and he needed to decide what to do. He should have already had her back to her father, but now, he wasn't certain he could accomplish his mission before darkness fell.

****

Cynthia sat beneath the oak tree and fanned her face with her wide-brimmed hat as best she could. *Gracious, it was hot out here.* This time of the afternoon, a person should spend time indoors, with dress and petticoats off and only a lightweight chemise covering the upper body. One should read a book of poetry or one of those novels her father had forbidden her to touch because of the "racy" contents.

So far, she hadn't been able to read the one she had past the first chapter, in which the heroine had only just encountered the hero. Every time she'd been able to buy one of the books, it had disappeared from her bedroom, no matter where she hid it. She was highly suspicious Maria, their housekeeper, found the books each time and turned it over to her father. Next time she managed to obtain one, she must find a more secure hiding place. She simply had to discover what the heroine would do when the tall, muscular, extremely handsome hero touched her.

Her gaze wandered to Ricardo Romero. Why did he follow her? He said he was to be her escort. What on earth did that mean? Did her father expect Ricardo to stay with her?

The subject of her musings walked toward her with a loose-jointed saunter so indicative of most Westerners, but he was Mexican. For the life of her, she couldn't figure out why he often appeared wherever she went. She'd thought he worked as a wrangler out at Robert King's ranch on the north side of Nacogdoches, but he didn't fit the profile of a ranch hand. Something was definitely mysterious.

"Miss Harrington?" His deep drawl startled her from her reverie.

"What?" she asked.

"It's about your mare."

She came to attention. "Oh? What? Tell me."

He hunkered down and sat on one heel, and said, "Your horse has a small gouge in one hoof wall, probably from a sharp pebble, and she has stiff leg muscles, maybe from overheating. I'm going to lead her and my stallion to the creek down there." He jerked his chin toward a stand of trees down the hill. "Both could use a drink, but I want your mare to stand in the water. What would you like to do?"

"Me?" she asked and glanced around the area. "Well, I suppose go with you." She began to push herself up, but found she, too, had stiffened from the fall and sitting still so long.

Ricardo stood, reached down, placed his hands around her waist, and lifted her to her feet as easily as he might lift a feather pillow. For a heartbeat, he

9

held her in place until she regained her footing. As soon as she could breathe normally, she stepped back and clasped her hands in front of her.

"Lead on, Mr. Romero. I'll follow."

He gathered the reins of both animals, one in each hand, and turned toward the creek. Cynthia trailed behind, not wishing to be too close to the horses. Nor did she wish to be too close to that man.

As they made their way down the slight slope, she studied Ricardo's long, lean back and, well, his rear. She stumbled on her own thoughts and had to catch herself before they spun completely out of control. Her musings could only go so far, since she knew nothing of the male population.

Oh, there had been Buck Cameron, but he had to go off and marry that little miss nobody with the illegitimate daughter. Cynthia knew other people said b-a-s-t-a-r-d, but she couldn't bring herself to say the word, let alone think it. He'd hardly ever kissed her, and even then, she had to initiate the contact by leaning back her head, closing her eyes, and puckering her lips. His kiss was so-so, as she recalled, because it had never generated any kind of feeling, but she loved when he cupped her shoulders to give her brief, light kisses.

His big hands were warm and solid, a working man's hands, even though Buck was from a well-to-do family. She had tried everything in her limited knowledge to entice him, but she succeeded only to receive a gentle smile and an offer for a stroll.

As long as she was thinking, she wondered why her father had chosen Ricardo to come after her. Her father knew many men much better than he knew Ricardo. Any one of them would have been happy to perform the task.

The creek was not wide and certainly not deep, but it bubbled clear and pure over pebbles and a sandy bed. The horses followed Ricardo right to the edge and drank their fill of the cool, clear water.

Ricardo sat on the grass, removed his boots and socks, and rolled up his tight pants legs. He ground-tied his stallion and the horse immediately began to eat the sweet, green grass under the shade of a willow tree. Then he led Little Dixie into the water. Obediently, she followed and stood docile as a statue while he rubbed her legs, up and down, up and down.

The motion caused Cynthia to become a little sleepy, so she wandered upstream to find a soft place to rest.

"Where are you going, Miss Harrington?" he called after her. He stood next to the mare with his arm slung over her back and his hat hanging down his by the cord. He looked young with his inky hair mussed and errant strands falling over his forehead. He wasn't as old as she'd thought.

"To find a place to sit, that's all."

"Don't go too far," he said.

Cynthia raised her chin, sniffed, and turned away. She took two steps but failed to look where she was going and inadvertently stepped in a hole. She found herself pitched forward right into the creek. Once again, she landed face down—this time in water—and her feet were up the incline of the bank, only slightly higher than her head. The flounced skirt and petticoats ballooned forward, almost covering her head and exposing her white lawn pantalets, trimmed in several rows of dainty lace.

Immediately, Cynthia panicked and began to flail her arms and attempt to right herself. The position was so awkward she couldn't find a handhold or foothold. Strong hands gripped her shoulders, lifting her once again to a sitting position in the creek bed. She was soaked and her long mass of curls now hung in wet, limp clumps.

She flew into an uncharacteristic rage. "Can't you get me out of this water? Why am I sitting here? Do something!"

With little effort, Ricardo picked her up and carried her to a level spot on the bank. Instead of gently setting her down, he leaned over, lowered her bottom to within half a foot off the ground, and released her.

Cynthia literally bounced on her rump. "You...you...!"

Ricardo had turned away to retrieve his boots, but he paused and looked over his shoulder with one raised eyebrow. "Yes, Miss Harrington? You wish to say something?" He had such a regal air.

"Ohhh, piddle!"

As he walked away, she heard him laugh out loud, a deep rumbling sound of pure joy. He was *laughing* at her.

Cynthia calmed herself. All her upbringing and tutoring had completely flown out of her head. She took deep breaths with her eyes closed, until she once again felt normal.

She gathered her hair into one twisted rope over her shoulder and wrung it free of excess water. Next, she removed her high-top, lace-up shoes but stopped at the stockings. They fastened above the knee with a ribbon, so she could hardly remove them in the presence of a man.

And her dress. The layers and layers of wet fabric were quite heavy and she wasn't certain she could stand under the weight. She really should remove the garment to allow it to dry. She couldn't go around in all these wet clothes. Unfortunately, the dress buttoned down the back—two-dozen small cloth-covered buttons she could not reach. Worse yet, her wet corset felt like rough canvas, even through the fine lawn chemise. It had to go.

Oh, what a predicament. Perhaps Mr. Romero

would unbutton the dress, even though it was not at all proper. She could go from there.

As much as she hated to ask, she needed his help. He had replaced his boots and now sat under a tree some distance away. His hat was on the ground, and she had another look at his shining, ebony hair. It seemed to be the same glossy black of his eyes, and now most of it fell straight back from his forehead, just past his collar.

He leaned back on the trunk of the tree and rested his head there. One knee he bent up, with an arm across and relaxed over it, and one finger crooked around a cheroot. As she watched, he slowly brought the cigar to his fine, chiseled lips, and drew on it. He never opened his eyes.

Something fluttered in her stomach. She jerked her head away, afraid he would catch her watching.

After several minutes, Cynthia was still quite uncomfortable. Not only were the clothes chafing her skin, she needed to relieve herself.

"Mr. Romero?" she called.

Silence.

She cleared her throat as loudly as she could, but asked in a normal voice, "Oh, Mr. Romero. Are you awake?"

Lazily, he rolled his head toward her. One side of his mouth quirked up, and to Cynthia, it certainly appeared to be a smirk. She ground her teeth. "I require your assistance, Mr. Romero." He returned his head to the original position and closed his eyes once again.

Cynthia was furious, and she rarely lost her temper. Why ever be angry when she had her way all the time? After contemplating her problem, she rolled to the side, placed her hands on the ground, and managed to get to her knees. After struggling with the wet clothes, she was finally able to stand.

In a huff, she strode as fast as she could in her

hampered condition and reached his side. She lifted one almost bare foot, but before she could kick his leg, he caught her ankle, quick as a timber rattler. Unbalanced, she fell once more—the third time today—but this time she had a softer landing. Ricardo had grabbed her skirts and pulled her forward so that she fell over him.

Her arms flailed. "Let me up! Let me go! Don't touch me, you...you scoundrel!"

She stilled when she noticed he had his hands in the air, as if he surrendered. Even with the cheroot clamped in his teeth, he still managed to grin around it. One deep dimple appeared in one cheek. Her stomach dropped.

With as much grace as she could, Cynthia sat up and smoothed her hair back from her face. Without thinking, her shoulders slumped in defeat. She clasped her hands in her lap and closed her eyes.

"Are you all right?" he asked in the soft drawl.

She opened her eyes. "Do you have anything to eat?"

Now he sat up straight. "Are you hungry? You did leave real early this morning."

"Just before daybreak."

"I don't have anything. I thought we would be back at your house long before now."

Casually, she studied him. His eyes glittered like black diamonds. They were the most fascinating eyes she had ever seen.

"Oh!" she said. "I have a picnic basket in the buggy. Did you see it?"

"I saw something with a red checked cloth over it. It fell in the dirt."

"Maybe it's okay," she said. "Everything was wrapped. And there's a Mason jar of spiced peaches."

"That sounds good. But varmints probably have it by now."

"Would you mind looking?"

14

"I suppose not." He stood and held out his hand to help her stand. "Listen, before I go. I really think you should get out of those wet things. Turn around."

Obediently, she did so, and he began to work on the buttons.

"I don't suppose you have any extra clothes in that buggy."

"I do, actually. I have one extra dress in a small valise."

"I'll bring it."

While Ricardo was gone, Cynthia removed her petticoats and spread all three on nearby bushes, as much out of sight as she could manage. After she removed the corset, she was clothed on top only in the chemise. She giggled a little. How wanton she must look.

Chapter Two

The day was almost spent. The sun lowered and the air cooled when darkness descended. The mare and the stallion stood nearby at the edge of the water, content to lazily munch grass and stomp a foot to occasionally remove some annoying insect.

Cynthia continued to sit under the tree where Ricardo had leaned. She wasn't frightened, really, maybe just minutely edgy. How long had he been gone? She had no sense of time out here. The forest was so quiet and still. One thing she did know, however, was she was tired and hungry.

She dozed a while and woke with a start. A little daylight still filtered through the trees, creating dappled patterns on the grass, but it was waning quickly. Where was Ricardo?

A little shiver of fear ran down her spine. Suppose he didn't come back? That was silly. Of course, he would, because his stallion was still here. But what took him so long?

Then she saw him striding down the hill toward her, and her heart sped up with some sort of strange feeling. He angled around the small bushes in his path, when at last he stood in front of her. Silently, he offered his hand and pulled her to her feet.

"Are your clothes dry?" he asked, as she blinked to clear her mind. She expected him to tell her what he found, but he asked about her clothing.

"Not quite." She fingered the neckline of her bodice to determine, that yes, it was still damp.

"Well, you know we're going to have to spend the

night here. It's too dark and too late to start back to Nacogdoches. I was wondering if you might want to change into something a little drier. You could have my shirt."

Ignoring his offer, she asked, "Didn't you find my valise? I have an extra dress."

"No, I looked all around, everywhere, but there was no valise. Are you certain you brought it with you?"

Cynthia closed her eyes and tilted her head back. After a moment, she lowered her chin, and told him, "Now, I think I must have left it on my bed. It was packed, but I don't really remember placing it in the luggage boot."

"So here's what I did find." He held up a small parcel. "Some of the food, at least."

She sat on the ground with her feet to the side, and he hunkered down and, as usual, sat on one boot heel. They examined their loot.

"The spiced peaches! I'm surprised the jar didn't break. The boiled eggs aren't cracked. That's good. Where are the cheese and bread and ham?"

"Varmints got it. Could have been anything. Anyway, the packages were torn open and food was scattered about. A few pieces of cheese and ham were here and there, but you don't want those. This'll have to do."

She sighed. "I'm so tired. But let's eat and then decide what we're going to do next."

"Can you wait until I build a small fire?"

"I suppose. A fire would be quite nice. May I help?"

Ricardo looked at her as if he hadn't heard correctly. "You would like to help build a fire?"

"Well, I've never made one, indoors or out, but I could gather sticks or something."

"You know, I think I should do it. Sometimes a surprise hides under a stick or log."

"A surprise? Such as?"

"Snake, lizard, spider…"

"Oh, all right." She laughed.

****

When the fire cheerily crackled and popped, Cynthia sat near him, and they delved into the food. The peaches presented a problem, but he easily solved it. He retrieved a slender bone-handled knife from the inside of his boot. With it, he speared a peach half, brought it out of the jar, dripping sweet, sticky syrup and offered it to her.

Carefully, she held the knife with the fruit on the tip, leaned to the side, and bit off a small chunk of sweet peach. The juice ran down her chin, but she daintily wiped it away. Again, her delicate, feminine lips wrapped around a bite, and once more, she wiped her chin with her fingers.

Ricardo held his breath each time; his eyes riveted on those lips and mouth. His heart beat hard and heavy in his chest, something it had never done before in the presence of a beautiful woman.

"Your turn."

"Umm?" Her words bewildered him for a moment, but his casual air quickly returned. "Thanks," he said as he took the knife from her fingers. He held it in midair while she carefully and precisely licked and sucked each finger clean. Then she folded her hands in her lap and smiled at him.

"Well, go on," she urged. "Eat your peach."

And in turn, Cynthia watched as he speared a half, leaned his head back, and dropped the entire piece into his mouth. When the last morsel was down, he swiped the back of his hand across his mouth.

He smiled to himself when he saw Cynthia gulp as unobtrusively as she could. Surely, sometime in her life, she had seen a man wipe his mouth.

While they took turns eating a peach half, they

exchanged few words. In short order, the jar was empty, save a few sips of juice.

"Here," he said as he handed the jar to her. "Drink this."

Obligingly she did so by turning the Mason jar upside down to drain the last sugary drop into her mouth. Again, she blotted her lips with her fingertips, as if she was at a society luncheon and she held the finest linen napkin. Her manners were impeccable, even when she had no proper utensil and had to use her fingers.

Cynthia peeled the boiled eggs while Ricardo added more wood to the fire. He watched her over the small fire as she precisely removed each piece of eggshell and formed a little pile beside her skirt. With the first peeled, she looked about, as if she wondered where she should place it. After brushing a spot clean on her lavender muslin dress skirt, she carefully laid it there and proceeded with her task. She held the second one between two fingers until he rejoined her on the grass.

While they nibbled on their meager dinner, the moonlight washed over them and with the glow from the fire, soft light shimmered and danced around them.

Cynthia's chestnut brown hair turned copper, and her skin looked translucent. He studied her briefly but turned away in chagrin.

"Why did my father send you after me?" she asked in a subdued voice.

"He was worried. Remember I told you before?"

"Did he know I ran away?"

"Yes, I believe so."

"How?"

"I don't know the details, but I think when you didn't appear for breakfast, the truth came out, somehow."

"Maria."

"Yes."

"May I ask how is it that you speak in a precise aristocratic tone one time, and at the other, you drawl as if you're a Texan?"

Ricardo chuckled as he shifted to lay on his side and prop himself up on his elbow. He looked up into her pretty face. "The way I was reared, I suppose. Formal speech for polite occasions; regular drawl for casual ones. Something like that."

"Excuse me, but you're Mexican. No Mexican I know speaks nor dresses as you do."

Patiently he answered, "I am not Mexican. I'm a United States citizen, born in Texas where I've lived my entire life. I've never lived in Mexico and only traveled there once."

She cocked her head in bemusement. "I don't understand."

Now, he sat up to talk earnestly to her. It was important to make her understand. "I am Spanish, descended from the early Spaniards, two-hundred years back. My father traces his ancestry all the way back to Spanish royalty. My mother is half-Spanish. Her father was a Comanche warrior."

"What!" She placed her hand to her breast. "Your mother is half-Indian?"

"Yes, and proud of it. She loved her father very much and grew up on a huge ranch and hacienda in far South Texas. He gave up his native ways and lived as the Spanish did, running cattle and sheep, and farming."

"Oh my," she said.

"So, you see, a Mexican is a citizen of Mexico, just as an American is a citizen of the United States of America. Either might be of various ancestries, though, such as Spanish or Indian from Mexico or the U. S."

"So, you're an American?"

"Yes, of course. Most of the Spanish migrated to

California a hundred years ago. They didn't do well under their own rule in Texas, but they've been highly successful on the West Coast."

"But your family stayed."

He nodded. "My father's family had some land, so they toughed it out, as they say."

Ricardo saw her open her mouth to speak, so he spoke first. "So, Miss Harrington, I answered your questions; now you must answer mine."

"What about?" she asked.

"Just why are you running away? You have a perfectly good home, a father who obviously loves you, and you want for nothing."

He waited and watched as she looked down where she was forming little pleats in her now quite wrinkled, soiled dress. Small lines of concern, mimicking the pleats, furrowed her brow. At last, she looked up to him. "Do I seem terribly spoiled and ungrateful? You needn't answer that, for I believe that's what you think. Yes, I suppose I live a privileged life, but it doesn't come without its restraints. My father and I have been alone most of my life. I don't remember my mother. He loved her so," she said with a sigh, "and I filled the void, I think. All his attention turned on me. I should like to stop now, because I'm betraying my father and he means everything to me. Truly, he does."

Ricardo nodded. "We should get some sleep. We need to be up very early to ride back to Nacogdoches."

"Fine," she said.

"Where are your petticoats?"

She pointed. "Over there, drying on some bushes."

"I'll get them. I'll help you make a bed of sorts."

"No! No, a...a gentleman must never touch a lady's petticoats."

"Tsk, tsk, Miss Harrington," he said with a grin.

"After what we've been through? You're worried about my seeing your underthings?" He leaned close to her face. "When you were upside down—twice today—I saw your pantalets both times."

"Ohhh! You're horrid. I can't spend the night with you. It isn't seemly."

"But you will, Miss Harrington, you will," he said with that dimple appearing in his cheek.

****

Before the sun was quite up, the weary pair made their way back to Nacogdoches. Cynthia had taken the time to plead with him to take her to San Antonio. He argued her father would come after them, and both would regret their actions in the long run. Many obstacles were in their way, he had added, such as, no food, no adequate transportation, and no place to spend nights. The only alternative left was to return home.

The buggy suffered damage, not so much that someone couldn't repair it eventually, but it was out of commission for now. Ricardo had pushed and pulled until he had it off the road and hidden as much as possible. Little Dixie had a sore foot, but she could walk. The idea Cynthia could ride her was out of the question.

That left only one way to return home. They could ride double to Nacogdoches and keep Little Dixie in tow. The arrangement was almost intolerable for Cynthia, for she had to either sit across his lap or ride behind the saddle. Both ways were uncomfortable. Besides, her body was far too close in contact with his.

Finally, they came to an agreement to switch off—one rode and one walked, but Ricardo had too much pride and was too much of a gentleman to allow her to walk while he sat astride. So, much of the time, both walked or only Cynthia rode. When Ricardo tired, they rode double but only for a short time.

In the middle of the afternoon, the pair dragged into town. Ricardo suggested they skirt the business section and try to stay on back streets and alleys to avoid detection by any citizen. Cynthia couldn't agree more.

Oh, how she dreaded walking into her father's house. He would absolutely explode at this chance to chastise her. He could work up anger as no one else she knew. How he would punish her, she couldn't imagine. Except she knew with all certainty that he would not strike her.

No other recourse remained. Now, her future would be to marry Harris Newton.

Just as Cynthia feared, her father met them at the back door. Word had spread through town they were on their way, so the plan to enter unseen had gone awry.

"Romero, what the hell happened? Y'all look like something the cat drug in!" He turned to Cynthia and continued. "Get in here, young lady. Go to your room and stay there. I'll give you time to rest and eat and clean up. Then we'll talk. Romero, follow me. Maria!" he bellowed.

"Yes, sir?"

"See to Miss Harrington. Then rustle us up some food. We'll be in the study when you have a meal on the table. Make it quick."

Ricardo followed the wild-eyed man into the study. He sat across the room in a large tan leather armchair. Mr. Harrington went to the liquor cabinet and poured two glasses of bourbon.

"Here. Drink up. You look like you need it."

What Ricardo needed was a bath and food, but he politely took the drink and sipped. "You ready for me to tell you what happened?" Ricardo Romero did not "sir" the man, because he was neither his employee nor relative. In fact, he should be the one addressed as "sir," but he let it pass, for now anyway. While he waited for Harrington to calm down, he loosened his collar by unbuttoning the top button and removing the string tie. No need to try to look presentable. His attire was well past that, anyway.

"What I want to know," Mr. Harrington began, as he settled his oversized frame into the other armchair, "is why you didn't return immediately with my daughter?"

Ricardo sipped his drink before forming an answer. "An unforeseen accident occurred. I caught up with Miss Harrington about fifteen, sixteen miles out, but unfortunately, a deer darted across the road in front of her buggy. The mare shied, and the apparatus turned over."

Now, the other man leaned forward with his arms on his thighs. "Was she hurt?" he demanded.

"Not really, but she hit her ribs on the iron arm of the seat as she went over. Nothing seemed broken, but she winced when I probed."

Harrington surged to his feet and pointed his drink toward Ricardo. "*You touched her?* By gawd, man, you'd better not tell me you took liberties with her! No man on earth has touched her, and you better not be the one!"

Ricardo stood slowly and deliberately, tugged down the cuffs on his sleeves, one at a time, all the while intently studying the fabric. Casually, he flicked an imaginary speck of dirt off one sleeve. At last, he raised his narrowed eyes to the big man. "What are you implying, *Mr.* Harrington? That I am a despoiler of young, innocent women? That I am not *Anglo*, as most people are around here? That I am not worthy to *touch* her, but certainly good enough to fetch her home on your request? Tell me, Mr. Harrington, before *I* lose *my* temper."

He cleared his throat. "I implied nothing of the

sort. If you are offended, you simply mistook my meaning." He spread wide his hands. "I'm only concerned for my daughter, as you might well imagine. She's all I have in this world, and I have to protect her on every corner. The simple fact is that as her father, I guess I got my dander up. Now, how about another drink?"

Ricardo had already placed his almost full glass on the table, so he merely shook his head. "I should go. I have business to attend to, and now, I'm running behind."

"Could I have one more moment of your time, Romero?"

"Five minutes."

"Can I rely on your discretion in this matter? Can I trust you not speak of it at all to anyone in this town?"

"As only a gentlemen would do, Mr. Harrington. Of course, I would not sully Miss Harrington's name for all the money in your bank."

"Humph." He nodded, as he tugged down his silver brocade vest over his ample stomach. "Shall we shake, as friends and fellow businessmen?"

Ricardo held out his hand and firmly shook on the agreement. Then he turned on his boot heel and walked regally from the room, looking neither right nor left. Nor back.

****

"Cynthia? Cynthia, answer me."

She sat on her bed, dressed for dinner but was reluctant to go downstairs. She had no stomach for food or listening to her father, because listening is what she would do. He would pay no attention whatsoever to anything she might have to say, so why bother? However, she knew he would not go away, nor leave her alone, so she rose and walked to her door. She opened it and faced her one formidable parent whom she loved with all her heart. At this moment, however, she was very angry with him.

She stepped out without speaking and walked past her father. Down the stairs, she went to the dining room, which was very formal and silent. Two places at the table were set with the finest china, the most elaborate sterling silver, and expensive crystal stemware in Nacogdoches.

Her father was before her, pulling out her chair, and solicitously seating her as if she were royalty. Oh, yes, he adored her, and why not? She was the perfect daughter, never caused any problem, nor posed the least discomfiture. Was this to be her destiny? Being a model daughter? Never having a thought of her own, nor yearning for something beyond the walls of this house? Even to marry one Mr. Harris Newton, she would still be under the thumb of her father, for he had chosen a man who would not take a breath unless his father-in-law, Mr. Harrington, said so.

"So, Cynthia. How are you feeling this evening?"

"Oh, I'm fine, Father," she answered with her hands folded just so in her lap. "And you?"

"Fine, fine. I should tell you that I spoke with Ricardo Romero, and he's given me the particulars of your little jaunt. He said that your ribs were slightly injured. Are you well, or should I fetch the doctor?"

Cynthia paused a moment, her eyes unfocused, as she remembered Ricardo's warm hands on her rib cage, and his slim fingers probing one by one to determine injuries. Her body involuntarily shivered at the thought. Then she recalled the time at the campfire when his dark lean cheeks appeared painted in gold, and she could barely keep her eyes off him. They had eaten the spiced peaches with the knife. Oh, she had seen men eat in such a manner; it was just that his way held such allure. Her stomach clenched, and she wondered if she could eat anything at all.

She took a deep breath and exhaled slowly. "No need. I'm quite well, thank you."

"Fine," her father continued. "Harris will arrive in the morning at nine sharp to discuss the wedding. He's quite eager to marry you, my dear, and the three of us can discuss the wedding date."

"Father..." she began.

He held up his big beefy hand. "Now, Cynthia, let's not start with the objections, because this wedding will take place. You and I only need to get on with the planning of the actual ceremony."

Cynthia drew in another deep breath and spoke as firmly as she could to her father. "No." She said the one word, knowing that was the only way she would gain his attention.

"No? Didn't I just say...."

"I said no, and I mean it. I don't even know Harris Newton very well, and from what I've seen, he's not the sort of husband I want."

"What the hell is wrong with him?" he roared.

She began to stand, but her father raised his voice once more. "Sit down!"

She sat, always the obedient daughter. She saw he was not going to drop this subject. He was determined to see her married and that was that. Since she had not procured a husband on her own, he took charge in his indomitable way and found one for her.

"Will you give me a chance to voice my opinion, Father? Can't you listen to me, for once?"

The man eased his bulk to the back of the chair and fingered the stem of his wine glass in agitation. He heaved a great, long-suffering sigh. "All right, all right. And forgive me for cursing in your presence. That was uncalled for."

"Thank you. I much prefer to discuss this as two adults."

"You're my little girl," he said.

"Yes, I know, Father, and I love you dearly. But I do not want to marry a man whom I do not know, let alone love."

"Fine." He leaned forward. "I'll tell you about him. Harris is the best accountant I've ever seen. Right now he keeps books for Grayson's Mercantile, but he does accounting work on the side for extra income. He really should be set up in his own business."

"And you're going to help him accomplish that."

"Maybe." He looked down at his still empty plate. "Maria!" he yelled.

Cynthia grimaced at her father's occasional uncouth ways. He knew how to act in polite company and in business dealings, but his early years of toiling in the cotton fields and then running a gin among rough men ingrained coarseness. When he became angry or agitated, he invariably reverted to the language and actions he learned in those lean, brutal years.

When Maria had filled their plates with the light dinner of fresh green salad, baked chicken and roasted new potatoes, the pair ate in silence. He forked his salad and cut his chicken with purpose and gusto. She picked at the tomatoes and pushed the chicken back and forth on the beautiful plate.

"Now," he announced, "let's continue. Harris will make you a good husband. He's reliable, honest, and a good Presbyterian. He's an elder, you know, and he takes all his responsibilities seriously." He paused as if to wait for her interruption. When she didn't, he continued with even more enthusiasm. "I know he's not quite the dashing figure of a man but don't let his height fool you. Dynamite comes in small packages, you know," he said with a wink.

"But he's bald," she stated flatly before she could stop herself.

He waved his hand in the air. "Nothing, my

dear, nothing. Believe me; you'll be proud to be the wife of an upcoming businessman in our fair city. You'll live in a fine house very soon, not quite as grand at this one, but a wonderful, roomy home. All yours. Now, how about that?" He finished with great satisfaction as if he'd just pulled off the business transaction of the decade.

"I'll meet with him in the morning, just as you ask. However, I can't say now I'll marry him. That's the best I can do."

"Cynthia," he began in a warning note, "you will do as I say. You're already twenty years old. How many men do you think will take a wife much older than that? You've got to do this. Besides, I need grandchildren."

That was the last straw. First, she was on the shelf at twenty, and now she was required to produce babies to sit on his knee regardless of what she—or a theoretical husband—might wish.

"May I be excused? I'm very tired."

"Will you do as I ask?"

"Yes, Father. I'll do my best."

"That's my girl."

Chapter Three

Once again, Cynthia Harrington sat on the edge
of her bed and procrastinated. She did not want to
leave her room. This had been a private haven her
entire life. Here she had the freedom to arrange and
decorate any way she desired.

As a little girl, she asked for a white wrought
iron bed she had seen in a catalog at the mercantile.
She wanted pink ruffles on her spread and curtains,
a fluffy, pink rug at her feet, pink roses on the walls.
She had been cured once and for all of owning
anything pink. As she grew up, her preferences
changed to more sedate surroundings, all the while
remaining quite feminine.

A slight hitch in her breath accompanied the
thought she would be giving up her freedom very
soon.

If only she could have succeeded in completing
her journey to Austin or San Antonio, whichever
came first. She still didn't know. Ricardo had been
no help at all when she begged him to take her
there. All he could say was she should go back home
and have a discussion with her father. Discussion,
indeed. Her father didn't really know how to have a
give-and-take conversation, at least not with her.

A light rap on the door brought her out of her
reverie. "Yes?"

Maria entered and immediately began to scold.
The diminutive woman had taken care of the
Harrington household for most of Cynthia's life, and
that included her. She walked a fine line between

the role of a servant and a surrogate mother.

"No, no, no." She shook her head, causing the thick, black braid to swing back and forth across her back. "Why you have a gray dress on? Gray? That is color for mourning, not for young lady who will meet future husband. And the sleeves! Oh, *yi*, such bad choice. Too tight, and neckline too high, and..."

Cynthia took two steps away. "Okay, Maria. Stop. I want to wear this."

"But you must look very beautiful. You should wear the silk rose with the ruffles around shoulders. And your hair! No, no. Here, turn around and let's get you in another dress. And I will fix your pretty hair. You'll see."

Cynthia actually stamped her foot, something she had rarely done her entire life. But enough was enough. She would not dress to impress a short, bald man who had no will of his own. No.

"Stop, stop, Maria!" She swatted Maria's hands away from her dress. "I am wearing this, you understand? This is the way I want to look. I do not care one tiny bit what this man thinks of me, because I will not marry him!"

"Ohhh?" Maria breathed as she placed her hand to her heart. "I think you will make your father very angry, little one. But, so be it. Come, he is waiting. Your father and the young man."

Instead of the parlor, where they usually greeted visitors, the meeting commenced in her father's masculine study, where business arrangements were conducted.

How appropriate, for I am nothing but chattel.

"Come in, honey." Her father greeted her with great heartiness and with his arms spread open wide. "Have a seat here." He stood behind a small wing chair that sat in front of his desk. The matching chair, slightly angled toward her, was for Harris.

Harris stood and watched her, grinning like a buffoon, with his chest puffed out and dressed in his finest suit. Before she sat, he held out his hand palm up, expecting her to place her fingers there, so that he might guide her to sit. When she ignored it and seated herself, he glared for a moment but quickly recovered, and the grin appeared once more on his pasty face.

"Now," began Mr. Harrington by slapping his hands together, "let's get started, shall we?"

"Yes, let's," said Harris.

"Cynthia, this young man here would like to ask for your hand in marriage. He and I have discussed the union, and if we can complete all the arrangements soon, we hope the wedding will take place on August fifteenth. That gives us a month to wrap up everything. Well," he said as he waved his hand at Harris, "go ahead. Ask." Then he sat back with his thick fingers linked together over his generous stomach.

Harris cleared his throat, pulled his snowy white handkerchief from his front jacket pocket, and mopped his brow. After properly folding and replacing it, he turned sideways to look in her eyes. Cynthia, however, would not turn toward him, so he scooted to the edge of the chair in an attempt to view her whole face.

Even though she was a well-bred young lady and knew better, she gave no response. Cynthia looked straight ahead, her back as straight as a rod, her hands clasped in her lap. What could she do? She had no recourse. None. If she did not say yes, her father would dig in his heels and all...well, all perdition would break loose.

"Father, is there anything I can say? Please, please don't make me do this. Can't you see I don't want to marry him? There's no one I want to marry right now. Why can't we wait and allow me to find someone *I* want?"

Harris interrupted by clearing his throat. "Miss Harrington? Will you look at me?"

With a heavy sigh and great reluctance, she did so.

"I know I am not the most handsome man in Nacogdoches, but Miss Harrington, I will become the best husband you could ever hope to have. I promise you, I'll work hard and do right by you at all times. I don't drink alcohol, or touch tobacco. I don't dance or go to parties. My passion is my work and my church. I am the assistant Head Elder at First Presbyterian, and I do not miss a meeting nor ever shirk my duties. And I tithe, Miss Harrington. My character is spotless, just as yours is, so we would make a good match. And I..."

Her shoulders slumped slightly, not so either man would notice. Goodness gracious. What a speech.

"All right, Mr. Newton, I'll marry you. Father, may I be excused? I have a headache."

****

Ricardo was in the tonsorial parlor paying for his haircut and shave, when he heard the barber and Mr. Newton discussing Cynthia. He paused to listen.

"Yes, that's exactly what I said." The short man was proud as a strutting peacock. "The lovely Miss Cynthia Harrington and I are betrothed as of today, and the wedding will take place on the fifteenth of August."

"You don't say, Harris," replied the barber, Mr. Oliver, as he cut the few wisps of hair the man had remaining on his head. "I only just heard your dear betrothed was on the road and out overnight; first alone, then joined by *Senor* Ricardo Romero. Yep, that's what happened, Harris." He nodded emphatically. "They spent the night together somewhere out there. Came in late the next day, as I

33

heard it, all rumpled and dirty."

Harris seemed to dismiss such a tale as the ramblings of a gossipy old man.

Ricardo didn't like the sound of that at all. He waited down the boardwalk until Harris Newton walked out of the shop. He decided to follow the pompous man for a while to see just what kind of man had asked for Cynthia's hand.

At the mercantile, Ricardo stayed toward the back and out of sight while Cynthia's intended bought a dainty lace handkerchief. Mrs. Ogletree chatted, as she wrapped the pretty gift in nice blue paper.

"Miss Harrington will love this and it will go nicely with the gift Mr. Romero purchased. His *was* a little more substantial; however, they did spend a night together."

Harris walked out of the mercantile clutching the wrapped gift in one hand, looking nauseous, and muttering. "Sordid gossip. For Heaven's sake, why can't people mind their own business?"

****

At First Bank and Trust the next morning, Mr. Harrington sat ensconced behind his massive mahogany desk, seated in his large leather chair. He spoke in earnest to Ricardo.

"So, Mr. Romero, we can finalize the transactions in a matter of days. I'll have the checks cut for your sellers right away, and then each man can come in and sign for his money. And hopefully deposit it in my bank." He winked. "It seems like you've done right fine in buying up the best blooded mares in these parts. Hate to see them all transported that far west, but that's what they were bred for. The horse owners around East Texas are mighty happy you made your way to our fair city."

Ricardo smiled. "I'm quite pleased, yes. The buying trip took much longer than I expected. Horse traders have earned their reputation for being shrewd and hard-nosed. Two of the bunch almost got the better of me in the bargaining process. Thought I was going to have to give up there..."

He paused in his speech because Miss Richardson had opened the office door without knocking. She slipped through the slightly opened door and leaned her back against it. "Oh, forgive me, Mr. Harrington," she hissed, "but we have a problem. Mr. Harris Newton insists on seeing you *now*, and he won't wait. He will not listen to me at all. He's...oomph!" She stumbled forward and almost fell as Newton shoved the door all the way open. The livid, ranting man burst in the room.

"You!" Harris pointed his forefinger at Ricardo. "You're the one who's ruined my marriage chances with Miss Cynthia. What were you thinking? You have sullied her reputation all over town!" The slightly built man approached Ricardo, spread his legs, and clenched his fists.

Ricardo stood up and turned toward Harris.

Mr. Harrington stood, as well. "What's gotten into you, Harris? What in tarnation are you talking about?"

Harris puffed up, his face turned red, and he could barely sputter. "Him! He spent the night with your daughter! Didn't you know that? An entire night! Out of town!" He slumped, reeled a few feet to a side chair, and sat heavily on the split leather upholstery. Propping his elbows on his knees, he lowered his head into his hands. He actually moaned. "It's all a disaster. In all good conscience, I cannot marry your daughter. She's...she's ruined."

"Ruined! Gawd a'mighty, man, what're you saying? You sure as hell better not say that about my daughter! I'll...I'll kill you, you..."

Ricardo stepped between them but faced Mr. Harrington. "Listen! Listen to me. She is not ruined.

35

You hear me? You know that! She's as pure as the day she was born!" He took one step back and took a deep breath. "Mr. Harrington, I thank you for your assistance. I believe this matter is between you and Mr. Newton. If you will excuse me, sir, I must go. Good day."

With that, Ricardo walked out of the room, sedate to all appearances, but to himself, impatient and with purpose.

Ricardo quickly mounted the stallion he'd tied to the post at the bank and took off at a full gallop to the Harrington household. He knocked three times on the massive door of the residence. The housekeeper answered, looked him up and down, and with one raised eyebrow, asked, "Yes?"

"I need to see Miss Cynthia. *Now*, please."

The woman obviously knew when to wield her power and when to yield. "Yes, sir, follow me."

While he waited in the parlor, Ricardo thought through his plan once more. Was this the right thing to do? His schedule was to leave for home in three days. Would that be enough time? He paced back and forth in front of the large front window, hoping Mr. Harrington would not come home. All he needed to do was convince Cynthia to marry him, and he believed he could.

He heard her approach and spun on his heels. There she was, pale but beautiful, sad but strong.

"Cynthia?"

"What are you doing here?" She cocked her head to one side. She looked like she'd been crying sometime during the previous hours.

"Will you sit here beside me?" He swept his arm toward the love seat.

She sat and he joined her. "Cynthia, I have news. And I have a proposition. Will you hear me out?"

Turning slightly toward him, she leaned forward

in curiosity. "What do you want, Ricardo?"

"I want to ask you to marry me. Three days from now, if you will."

She gasped and pulled back. "What?"

"I ask for your hand in marriage." He studied her light blue eyes, so wide with surprise. She had not turned from him yet. "The marriage proposal you received yesterday will be retracted soon, before the afternoon is over, I'm certain. So, I ask you to marry me instead, but not a month from now—in three days."

"Why three days?" she asked. "And how do you know Harris will retract his proposal?"

He almost laughed. She asked why so soon, not why on earth he would ask in the first place.

"Believe me; Harris Newton does not want to marry you."

"Why?"

"He will retract his proposal because you were out on the road with me all night."

"Well, then, why should I marry you in three days?"

This was a good sign, a good sign, indeed. "Because I'm going home, and I want you to go with me—as my bride. Will you, Cynthia? Will you marry me?"

She was speechless, but she did not reject him out of hand. After some moments of heavy silence, she asked. "Where exactly do you live?"

He breathed a sigh of relief. "West of San Antonio, on a very large ranch."

"Why were you here in Nacogdoches? I've often wondered."

"To buy blooded mares to add to our herd."

"Our. Who else?"

"My father. He and I ranch together on property that has been in his family for generations. He and my mother live there, but it's a very large house, and an enormous operation. It takes all of us and many *vaqueros* to keep things going. My father is aging, so I am mostly in charge."

"A ranch? I know nothing of ranching or the West. I would like to live in a city. But you live..."

"Not *far* from San Antonio," he hastened to say. "But it is far enough away that we only go twice a year for a holiday."

She lowered her head and looked at her hands. "I don't know. That seems far out of my realm of expertise. I'm not certain I could do that."

"Answer this, Cynthia. Would you rather live here until your father finds another husband for you, or would you rather make your own decision? I'm giving you a choice."

At that moment, they heard heavy, hurried footsteps on the porch. Both knew it was the master of the house. Ricardo gathered Cynthia into his arms. He turned her just so, placed his lips on her soft, feminine ones, and kissed her with all the passion he could muster. For good measure, he moved his hand to one breast. Instead of fighting, she responded as though she hadn't heard her father.

"Cynthia Louise Harrington! What the devil are you up to?"

Ricardo and Cynthia pulled back, but they did not jerk apart. Instead, they gazed into each other's eyes and parted slowly. Without caring if the man was in the room or not, Ricardo placed his palm on her cheek, and kissed her on the other, ever so sweetly and gently. Before he let her go, he whispered, "Will you marry me?"

She nodded and whispered in return, "Yes, I will marry you."

Chapter Four

When I first thought of running away, I never imagined I would go this far.

Cynthia Romero gazed with idle interest out the soot-covered window of the Pullman and wondered how many more days the trip would take. She was grateful to be on a train instead of the stage as they had been from Nacogdoches to Brenham. That one-hundred-mile journey took three days—interminable hours of dusty, jarring travel, and two nights in way stations, trying to sleep on hard, narrow beds provided in small rooms for the overnight guests.

The wedding preparations had passed by in a whirlwind. She had two days to purchase a wedding dress, traveling outfits, and clothing Ricardo said she would need "at home." The snow-white wedding gown of her dreams was not to be, because the two ceremonies—yes, two—were short and simple. Instead, she found a suitable white dress made of the finest Irish linen, with long sleeves of diaphanous cotton. Actually, it was a beautiful dress with a slender cut to show off her tiny waist and rounded hips. It had no train, of course, but the bottom of the skirt flared, so that it swirled and danced when she walked. Her ensemble perfectly fit Ricardo's dark gray, long-tailed coat, pants, and fine cotton shirt.

The one major assignment she gave her father was to locate and hire a photographer. The jaunty little man came to the house the morning of the ceremonies and took great care in finding the perfect location for the first shot. When he presented the photos before they left town, Cynthia almost wept, for she and Ricardo resembled royalty—he sitting in a Queen Anne armchair with his black bowler held on one knee and the other hand on the arm of the chair, and she standing close to his side with her bejeweled left hand positioned just so on his shoulder. The photographer also took another one of them sitting together on the love seat, turned facing each other. While the first was perfect and showed serene faces toward the eye of the camera, the second was her favorite because it displayed slight mirth as they held hands and gazed at each other.

Cynthia insisted on a Protestant wedding, while Ricardo also asked the Catholic Church to sanction their marriage. Fortunately, the pastor and the priest were accommodating. The first took place in the pastor's office of First Presbyterian with only her father and Maria present. The second was in the big, empty sanctuary of Our Lady of the Forest Church.

While she shopped, made preparations and packed, Ricardo worked with the men he'd hired to transport the horses to the ranch. A portion of the journey for the horses would be by cattle cars, but the last leg would be on horseback. Two of the men were new employees who wanted to move west, and the other two were longtime *vaqueros* from the Double R. The herd of twenty-one horses represented a small fortune, so Ricardo made certain his instructions were clear and preparations were exact.

Now, they were on their way, but Cynthia was already lonely and homesick. The thought of her father standing alone with his hand raised in farewell, almost brought her to tears. What would he do without her? Whom would he talk to and discuss the day's events? Who would have dinner with him?

Unshed tears were in her eyes when Ricardo

returned from the smoking car. He entered their compartment, sat on the opposite seat, and watched her dab at her eyes. "What's wrong, sweetheart?"

He had been so sweet, so solicitous from the minute they began the journey. Every way he could be of service, he had done so—carried her small bag, helped her onto the stage or train, gave her the desired seat away from the sun. He had not kissed her since the ceremonies, though, where at least she had received two quick, sweet kisses.

Cynthia took a deep breath and smiled at him. They would have a Pullman bed tonight in which they could at least sleep in the same compartment. Would he, this night, show her the ways of love between a man and a woman? Would he kiss her and say he loved her? Oh, he had looked so handsome in the wedding suit, so different from the tight pants with silver conchos down the sides. Now, he was equally as stunning in real western denims, white shirt, and a butter soft, brown leather vest. The boots more resembled the ones other Texans wore, and his hat was black felt, a wide-brimmed Western style. His dark skin and black hair were fascinating.

Her heart beat a little faster.

"Ricardo?"

"Hmmm?"

"May I ask a question?"

"Certainly." He studied her.

"Why have you refrained from kissing me?" She cocked her head slightly, searching his eyes for the answer, and what she saw unnerved her.

The black irises smoldered beneath half-lowered eyelids, and his firm mouth tightened noticeably. He bent one leg onto the other, his boot resting on the knee. One long-fingered hand rested on the raised thigh, while the other arm was propped on the armrest. He might have appeared relaxed if she had not seen his jaw clench before he spoke.

41

"The time is not right, sweetheart. I want you to be rested and in our own comfortable bed."

"For a simple kiss?"

This time he visibly swallowed before he answered. His voice had lowered but his gaze was riveted on her face. "You don't know what you're asking, do you?"

"I thought I did. A kiss? Such as the one you gave me after each ceremony?" Her eyebrows arched.

"You see, darling," he drawled in a low voice, "there would be much more this time. The next kiss will lead further, and you are not ready, I think."

Cynthia was silent, mulling the possibilities over in her mind. *More.* She wished again she'd been able to read past the first chapter of the novels. Instead of a fictional hero in a book, though, she had her own sitting right here in front of her. Well, she could be patient, but maybe not willingly.

After four days and three nights on the train, Cynthia was quite weary. Where in the world were they? How far was she from Nacogdoches? She peered through the soiled window and saw green, rolling hills dotted with wide-spreading trees that appeared much shorter than the tall pines of East Texas. Large sunflowers grew in clumps in depressions, and smaller red and yellow sunflowers were scattered in fields. Ricardo pointed out the Fireweels, which he said were also called Indian Blankets. She saw a valley in the distance, outlined with white rock ledges. She counted three rivers the train crossed—one crossing was on a high trestle. Each river appeared to be running with clear, sparkling water.

Ricardo spent little time with her, so she was disgruntled and impatient with him. She couldn't understand his changed behavior and demeanor as they drew closer to the ranch. He paced through the cars like a caged tiger, moving back and forth between their compartment and the smoking car. There he discussed cattle ranching, markets, and horses, he said. The last night of the trip, he had not returned to the compartment to his made-down bed. She slept alone and felt even more hurt.

The only quality time he spent with her was at supper in the dining car. There they faced each other over a small, cloth-covered table. At least, the meal they shared was not finger food from a box. She still found they had little to discuss, because he wouldn't answer all her questions. After a while, she felt as though she were begging him for information about his home.

She learned that the nearest town was Rico Springs, very small, but adequate for staples and ranch supplies. What they could not buy, they ordered. The shipment arrived on the train.

His mother was Felicitas and Cynthia was to call her Mother. Inwardly, Cynthia rebelled because she had never called any woman "mother" and she wasn't certain she could do it. His father was Rafaelo and she should call him Father. She pursed her lips in rejection of the command, but kept silent.

****

Ricardo paced back and forth on the platform of the Rico Springs Depot; his boots thudded hard on the planks. Every so often, Cynthia heard a curse mumbled under his breath but understandable anyway. "Where is that good-for-nothing Paulo? Damn his hide. He knew we were coming!"

After an hour or so, Ricardo asked the stationmaster to send his young assistant into town to hire a carriage. "And make it quick."

Soon, the young man drove up in a carriage drawn by a sturdy team. Ricardo gave him a generous tip and walked inside to talk to the stationmaster. "When Paulo shows up, make certain he picks up every one of Mrs. Romero's bags and trunks. And tell him I said he'd better make good time back to the Double R."

"Yes, sir. I will, sir."

Cynthia's mood lifted, now that they were on the way to the ranch. "How long will it take?"

"Most of the remainder of the day. If we don't dawdle, we'll make it well before dark. Let me know if you need to stop."

Dismayed, she asked, "Dark? It's only a little past noon now. It'll take that long?"

"Yes, it will, Cynthia. The ranch is big, but at least the headquarters is not all the way in."

She tried to envision the size of the ranch, but her imagination failed her. Instead, she settled back in the cushioned seat and was grateful the carriage had a covering. The sun was quite hot in the cloudless sky, but they were shaded from the harsh rays.

The hours dragged on, and she alternated between extreme fatigue and great interest in the surroundings. The countryside was much like she saw from her train window, but now she viewed it up close. The land was rolling hills, and occasionally the landscape turned quite rugged with rock ledges and deep canyons. Then, it would flatten and the trees would thin for some distance, until it once more turned hilly and rocky.

As the sun began to lower, Ricardo pointed out an entrance ahead on the right. White rocks and timbers formed a tall arch with a back-to-back double R in black iron at the top. He drove through and from then on, the land looked more like a ranch.

Cattle roamed about, usually in small groups, and invariably near a water hole or creek. Often they bedded down under trees. These trees were mesquite, he said, which had light green, lacy leaves, and others were live oak, which had dark green leaves and rough, spreading trunks and branches. Small deer scattered as they passed or remained passive until the carriage moved past.

Excitement rose in her breast, for she would soon see her new home. Maybe the last one she would ever have. Here, she would live as a wife to a large ranch owner, and here she would bear his children. Every day, she could walk out on her front porch, look about, and think, "This is my very own home."

The first glimpse of the ranch headquarters, as Ricardo called it, stunned her. Buildings covered a very large area, and from the carriage, she couldn't count how many or determine what each was. Together, they resembled a small town. The main dwelling was easy, for it was a sprawling, one-story frame house trimmed in red. It truly appeared to be a home. Green grass surrounded it, and colorful annuals bordered the walkways to the front porch and around the house. Live oaks shaded it on all sides, and a two-person porch swing hung from a large horizontal tree limb. She yearned to sit in the shade and swing and drink cool lemonade.

"The large house is, of course, our home. The smaller house down a ways is for the foreman and his wife. Back off to the right, you see a row of smaller houses. Those are for our *vaqueros*, or cowboys, who have families. Single wranglers live together in the bunkhouse." He pointed it out to her. "And you see a chapel that's also used as the school for all our children, and several barns. To the left and far back, clustered together, are a tool house, a smoke house, a blacksmith shop, and even a commissary."

Ricardo explained with animation, as he described the ranch layout to her. He even laughed when he noticed the awed expression on her face. His black eyes sparkled and he talked rapidly, trying to show her everything at once. Obviously, he was a proud rancher.

A couple of hundred yards away from the house, he drew back on the reins and stopped the horses. He sat silently for a moment, and Cynthia became uneasy. He pinched the area between his eyes, which were clenched shut. He cleared his throat.

When he opened his eyes and turned them on her, he whispered her name. "Cynthia." He took her left hand, placed it on his thigh, and fingered the Marquis diamond surrounded by small rubies. "Cynthia," he began again, "I have something to say. Please hear me out."

She nodded; she sat mute.

"I ask you to be patient with my parents. They...they are strong-willed and have their own set of ideas and plans. Just remember this—I chose you, sweetheart. You. I wanted to marry Cynthia Harrington, and I did. Will you remember that?"

She nodded; she said nothing.

He leaned toward her and gave her a chaste kiss, but no thrill ran through her this time. Instead, a cold chill crept down her spine.

****

To: Rafaelo Romero. Double R Ranch. Rico Springs, Texas

From: Ricardo Romero

Arriving home Stop Twenty mares Stop One stallion Stop One bride Stop

Felicitas crumpled the telegram and let it fall to the floor. She despised the message. She stood by her husband, Rafaelo, and watched out the window as the carriage made its way to the front walk. She clasped her hands at her waist, turned her lips inward, and pressed them against her teeth. Her husband stood with his legs spread in a mutinous stance with his hands clasped behind his back. The telegram that included an announcement about a bride made her quite angry with her one and only child. How dare he bring an outsider into their lives.

****

Cynthia saw the silhouettes through the window. She was grateful Ricardo used his best and most precise manners to hand her down from the carriage. As they walked up the limestone path, he kept her arm through his and her hand anchored to his forearm. Before they reached the door, it swung wide and his parents politely asked them to enter.

In the foyer, Ricardo made the introductions. "Mother, Father, I present my wife, Cynthia Harrington Romero of Nacogdoches, Texas. Cynthia, sweetheart, my mother, Felicitas, and my father, Rafaelo."

"I'm very happy to meet you both," Cynthia said, as she held her gloved hand toward them. She forced herself to lower it when no one reached out in kind.

All four of them stood in place, glancing back and forth, as though none of them knew what to do next. Cynthia certainly didn't, she felt frozen, as if she had walked into an icehouse and the door had slammed shut behind her. It was not her place to say a word until her hosts did.

At last, Felicitas guided them to the parlor and all sat stiffly. Still no one spoke, and Cynthia felt her stomach knot as nausea churned. Maybe it wouldn't have been so bad if she were not so tired and hungry. She honestly did not think she could sit still and wait for the axe to drop. All she wanted was a cool, quiet room where she could be alone, lie down, and close her eyes. Perhaps all this would disappear.

She swayed and her eyes half-closed. *Please, I cannot faint.* Her husband noticed and stood to say to his mother. "My wife is quite exhausted. May we be excused?"

"Certainly." His mother nodded. "Take her to the second room on the right. And will you return soon?"

Ricardo barely nodded as he kept his hand at her waist and walked with her to the bedroom. There, Cynthia noticed the bed was for one person, and while the room was very pretty and comfortable, she wondered why he brought her here.

"Will this be our room?"

"Don't worry about it now, Cynthia. Let's remove your shoes and gloves so you may lie down. I think you've gone as far as you can for now. You rest, close your eyes, and I'll be in the parlor."

She followed instructions as a puppet doll might, for she was quite weary. When her head lay on the pillow and a light quilt covered her feet, she commented, "They don't like me. I've been in their presence exactly five minutes, and I know for certain that you chose the wrong wife, Ricardo."

"I..."

"Don't even answer. I know what I saw and felt. They treated me as if I were a non-person, a stranger in their midst, out-of-place and unwanted." She closed her eyes and turned away from him. She barely heard the door close, because she fell fast asleep.

Cynthia awoke disoriented and couldn't remember exactly where she was. The room was dark, but a sliver of light under the door dispelled the gloom a fraction. Her body felt heavy and her mind was sluggish. So tired. She closed her eyes once more and dozed.

The second time she awoke was a little better, for she was able to sit up on the side of the bed. Maybe morning had arrived, even though the room was dim. She heard muted voices from somewhere in the house, and the wonderful aromas of food wafted on the air. Her stomach rumbled. How many hours had passed since she had last eaten?

Standing unsteadily, she walked to the window and pushed open the curtains. The sun was barely peeking over the horizon. Now she looked down at her clothing. All that was missing were her shoes. She had slept the entire night completely dressed.

The lamp next to her bed was primed, so she struck a match from the box and lit the wick. Now that the room was illuminated, she looked around. One large valise and her small travel bag were on the floor next to a dresser. Someone had emptied the hand luggage and placed her things on top. There were her brush and comb, her hand mirror, and powder, cream, and hairpins. On closer inspection, she found the contents of the large bag were stored away, as well, and her personal things were in the drawers. She opened the small armoire and saw her traveling clothes on wooden hangers and pegs.

A sense of violation came over her. No one ever touched her personal belongings except Maria. Who came into the room and did this? She was almost certain it had not been her husband. Men did not perform such chores, and her husband certainly wouldn't since he knew absolutely nothing about her.

Why did she marry him? Oh, she knew the reasons quite well. Number one was so she might avoid marrying Harris Newton or someone like him. The second reason? She bit her lip in chagrin. Because Ricardo was too alluring, too masculine, and so very handsome. She hadn't been able to resist when he touched and kissed her.

The pitcher on the commode was full of water, and washcloths lay folded neatly beside a cake of fine milled, lavender soap. First, she simply must relieve herself. Behind a dressing screen, she found a covered pot. At least she didn't need to go outside.

In record time, she made herself presentable. Carefully, she cracked open the door and peeked into the hallway. It was empty, so she tiptoed toward the smell of food. She heard people talking, and flatware clinking on plates.

She never knew people ate in the kitchen, but sitting around the table were Ricardo, his parents, and another stout middle-aged man who sported a graying, bushy mustache. When she appeared in the door, Ricardo jumped to his feet to go to her, his mother stopped eating and placed her hands in her lap, and his father sat and blandly stared at her. The only other person who stood was the strange man, and he quickly wiped his mouth and smiled.

Ricardo stood directly in front of her and clasped her arms. "Sweetheart. Good morning. This gentleman is Jake Oliver, our foreman." He smiled that wicked one-sided grin and kissed her warmly on her cheek. He took her hand and led her to the table to sit next to him. He pulled out her chair, and when she settled, he called over to a large Mexican woman. "Consuelo, bring tea and a plate for my wife."

"*Si, Senor,*" she said with a smile.

That made three people who welcomed her.

Cynthia barely had a sip of the aromatic sweetened tea and only two bites of eggs, when a loud commotion arose outside.

"The herd!" Ricardo almost shouted. "They're here. See you later, sweetheart. Make yourself at home." He and everyone else grabbed a hat and were out the back door.

Chapter Five

Alone except for Consuelo, Cynthia sat for a moment uncertain what to do. She rose from the table and walked out the back door. The ranch had come alive. Cowboys ran from the smaller houses and jumped on their horses. The wranglers poured out of the bunkhouse, snapping on suspenders as they hurried to mount their horses. Ricardo and his father trotted to the nearest corral to find their saddled stallions. Even children ran about the ranch.

She watched her husband grab the pommel with both hands, and in one fluid motion slide into the rolled cantle saddle. He rode to the house, while everyone else raced out of the ranch yard and corrals toward the road to meet the new herd.

"Want to ride?" He grinned from ear to ear, revealing his deep dimple. "Come on. Ride with me." He held out his hand toward her.

"But...but I don't ride. I don't know how." She placed her hand at her breast, where her heart beat in double-time, and her breath came fast and hard.

"Come on, darlin'. You've ridden with me before. You'll be safe."

So much for being perfectly groomed and ladylike. Cynthia caught up her skirts and ran to her husband. He hoisted her over his firm thighs and there she sat. *Oh, what a thrill!* She laughed aloud with pure joy.

As they rode from the yard, she looped her arms around his neck as he directed, and in doing so, looked over his shoulder. There in the swing under the big live oak was his stern, unbending mother, staring right at her. From this distance, Cynthia wasn't certain, but she thought she detected pure hatred from those sharp black eyes. The woman more resembled a Comanche warrior, than the matron of a huge ranch.

Riding on the back of the big stallion not only excited Cynthia, it put fear into her heart. She had ridden a horse before, but now they were racing like the wind. Ricardo seemed to pay no attention to her trembling or her audible intake of breath every few seconds. Instead, he rode on, and in a few minutes, he had passed all the others.

The noise was wild and raucous. Men yelled, slapped their hats on their thighs, yee-hawed, and whistled. She had no idea why the arrival of a small herd of horses was so exciting, but she didn't care in the least. Probably, it broke the monotony, because she could already imagine how mundane and boring life on a ranch far away from civilization might be. At this moment though, she was as happy as she had ever been in her entire life.

"Whatcha got there, boss?" One of the *vaqueros* who had ridden in with the herd yelled their way.

Ricardo laughed as he jerked on the reins to bring the stallion to a halt. "Hey, *mi amigo*. Any trouble?"

"No, sir, not a bit. These beauties here were a dream to transport and herd. Me and my men, well, we had us a fine ol' trip. Made good time, too. Didn't we? The stallion was a little hard to handle, but that's why you wanted him, ain't it?"

"You know it. Jig, this is my wife, Mrs. Cynthia Romero. She's a Nacogdoches lady."

"Howdy, ma'am." He tipped his dusty, sweat-stained hat to her. "Mighty glad to meet ya. And welcome to the Double R."

"Why, thank you...sir. I appreciate that."

Ricardo directed his attention to the wrangler. "When you get the herd in the corrals, feel free to bathe, eat, and rest for the remainder of the day. You've earned it. Be sure to separate the stallion. I don't want him to get too feisty just yet."

He tipped his hat. "Yes, sir. Will do." He nodded to Cynthia. "Ma'am." Then, he rode away, following his herd.

Ricardo and Cynthia brought up the rear. The stallion now walked. Ricardo sat easily in the saddle, even though she was weighing him down.

"So, how're you doing, Mrs. Romero?"

Cynthia hesitated, because she didn't want to break the spell by bringing up unpleasant topics. She knew it would be difficult to speak with him privately once they were back at headquarters. She drew a breath to speak her mind.

"Ricardo," she began as she leaned away from him while keeping her arms around his neck. "I want to know where I stand. Your parents are very upset that I'm here. I can easily see they have not accepted me, and I'm not certain it'll be easy for them to do so. Why? Tell me what's going on."

She thought he would not answer, but after a moment, he did.

"They're stunned, is all. Maybe they thought I would do something different, and they're surprised and trying to get used to the idea."

"You mean they thought you would marry someone else."

"Hmmm," he sounded surprised by her deduction. "Maybe. But they'll soon see that you're here to stay."

"Ricardo? When will you and I share a room? The one I'm in now is for one person. Do you have a larger one?"

"I do, but I was giving you time to get

acquainted with your new surroundings and your new family. All right?"

She saw him look away as he told her this, and knew without a doubt he was lying.

"Suppose I don't wish to be given more time?" She whispered into his ear. "Suppose I think I'm ready to be taught…whatever there is. Hmmm?"

His body stiffened when she pressed her breasts against him and his hold on her tightened. Cynthia felt his warm breath on her cheek and closed her eyes as he placed his lips just beside her ear. He kissed her sweetly and lightly, but then traced the shell of her ear with his tongue. She felt him tremble and the thought of exciting him made her ecstatic.

Ricardo brought the horse to a halt in the middle of the road. The herd and all the men disappeared over a hill, leaving them alone, except for a hawk floating on the warm air currents in the sky. She was, oh, so glad they were all by themselves out here, far from the house and his family. An uneasy thought came to her—maybe they would rarely be alone, because his parents were right there all the time.

Before she could think any further, her husband wrapped both arms around her and drew her as close as he could to his body. She sat sideways across his thighs, but somehow, he bent her left leg at the knee, leaned her back, and pivoted her toward him so that she straddled his lean hips. He did not hesitate in the pursuance of his goal, as he placed one warm hand low on her tiny waist and moved the other around to her buttock. He pressed her closer still. She felt a bulge close to her private parts and unwittingly looked down.

When she looked up, she saw a deep red flush move up his neck and onto his dark cheeks. His eyes were at half-mast, and his breathing came hard. One hand moved up to a breast, and he cupped it and gently massaged, never taking his eyes off hers. Something happened she knew nothing about, but the feeling was so extraordinary, it was difficult to define. Her stomach dropped and moisture seeped from her womanly parts. She had the urge to clench her thighs together.

Her eyelids, too, lowered, and she became weak and limp, dropping her head to his chest. Both of them breathed hard and became quite still.

Interspersed with their audible breaths were mockingbirds calling, cattle lowing in the distance, and bees buzzing. The sun was warm on their heads and backs, and a horsefly aggravated the stallion so that he stomped his foot and swished his tail. Cynthia felt as one with nature at this moment, something that had never occurred to her.

Ricardo relaxed a little and she ventured a question. "When? When can we be together? Please don't make me wait any longer. What's the point?"

Before Ricardo answered, he took a deep breath and released it on a sigh. "Sweetheart, Saturday. I promise, Saturday night. I'll have Consuelo move your things into the room that will be ours. Not the one I'm in now, but a different one, away, all alone. We'll have a bedroom, a sitting room, a dressing area, and a water closet, all connected and all ours. Will you like that?"

"If that's what you want, but I would really prefer our own house. Is that possible?"

"We'll see, but not for a while. That's the best I can offer now."

"And must we wait until Saturday? What's going on?"

He sighed. "We're having another wedding ceremony in our own chapel. The priest will be here to say mass for all the Catholics, so he'll say a wedding mass for us around one o'clock."

"What? Another wedding? My goodness

55

gracious, how many does it take to be married? This is ridiculous." She withdrew her arms and crossed them around her waist. She began to feel silly straddling him on top of a stallion out in the middle of nowhere. Not once in her life had she ever done anything improper or unladylike. Her father would positively kill her. Then the whole thing struck her funny and she laughed out loud. Her amusement grew, so that she threw her head back and laughed with a deep throaty sound, like a barroom tart.

Her new husband leaned back slightly and watched her, grinning like a fool.

Before they parted, he told her he would be at the big corral farther back from the house, working with the mares. They had to inspect every animal for injuries, brush them down, and assign stalls. He needed to pay particular attention to the stallion, and for that, he did the inspection himself with the assistance of his foreman.

"Why did you buy the new horses?" she asked. "It looks to me as though you have quite a few already." She noticed the large fenced areas that held at least a hundred. More were in a pasture even farther away.

"Each cowboy or *vaquero* has five horses to call his own. It takes a lot of animals to run cattle, because they have to be cared for even better than we care for ourselves. Not that we allow human injuries to go unchecked, but a man knows his limits—a horse doesn't. So, they're rotated to keep them healthy and free of injuries."

"So are you going to...mmm...you know..." she stammered and looked toward the small corral where the stallion stood.

"Breed them?" He grinned. "Sure are, but these new mares and the stallion are special. They won't be used on open range." He leaned toward her and said, "They're our new fortune. Worth a lot now, but their foals will be worth even more."

Now she was genuinely interested. "What will they be good for? How will they bring a fortune?"

"The stallion is of Arabian stock, and he'll mate with the mares. The mares are Quarter Horses and Morgans—both good riding animals, but the Quarter Horses are more muscular and fast, while Morgans are strong and light. When they've bred with the stallion, we should have two lines of fine horseflesh. We plan to register our herd and put out the word. Ranchers all over are always looking for superior horses for their own use, or to start their own line, or to race. Believe it or not, racing is becoming big business in some parts of the country."

"Could I go with you to look at the mares?"

"Why don't you go in for a while? Get acquainted with the house, maybe talk with Mother." He looked around, left and right, as if searching for her. "I don't know where she is, but you'll find her. I'm sure you have female things to do. I'll see you at supper tonight." With that dismissal, he leaned over and pecked her on the cheek.

He gathered the reins to his horse and walked away, leading the stallion to the corral, leaving Cynthia bereft and alone. So far, her arrival with her new husband had been far less than satisfying. At least she felt rested, but now she was very hungry.

No one was in the kitchen, but she heard Consuelo humming inside the large panty. A bowl filled with peaches sat on the table, so Cynthia chose one, rubbed it around in her hands to remove the fuzz, and took a juicy bite. As she nibbled, she walked down the long hallway where the bedrooms were. At least, her room was there.

First, she entered hers but only stood in the door, finishing off the peach. *Nothing to do here.* She walked to the next door, cracked it, and peeked inside the room. All her other trunks and valises were stored here. All she could do was look at them, for there was no need to unpack just yet. Surely, she would move in with Ricardo on Saturday.

The thought of another marriage ceremony began to annoy her even more. Why in the world should she need to go through another round of vows? Weren't the first ones enough, or were they invalid for some reason? It was too silly and useless. She was a little perturbed with Ricardo, as well. He had done nothing to stand up for her or defend their other two ceremonies.

The next door opened into a sunlit room that she knew belonged to Ricardo. His traveling suit lay across a chair, and his freshly polished high boots sat beside the bed. She wandered all the way in to inspect his belongings more closely. She paused to place the peach pit on the chest of drawers.

"*What* do you think you are *doing*?"

Cynthia jumped and whirled in fright. Felicitas had scared her speechless. "I...I," she stammered. "I was...nothing," she finished. Why should she explain why she was in her husband's room?

The tall, thin woman clasped her hands at her waist, her chin jutted forward, and her long nose was in the air. Her dark, narrowed eyes glared at Cynthia. The woman trembled with rage, causing her braided crown of silver-streaked hair to tremble.

"So," she spat, "since you're here, perhaps this is the time for a discussion. Sit."

Cynthia obeyed the command, sat on a wooden straight-backed chair, and properly tucked her toes beneath her skirt.

"I have something to say, and I do not wish to be interrupted." Felicitas raised an eyebrow and Cynthia nodded. "Have you consummated your marriage?"

Cynthia almost choked. "Wh...what? That is

none of your business."

"It is family business. You must know my son has acted in a foolish manner, and he is now thinking about how to correct his error. You should have not made this journey."

"But…"

"I asked you to not interrupt," she said as though she spoke to a recalcitrant child. "Now, I ask you to hear me out. Do not talk; it will do you no good. If you have not had relations yet, and by your reaction, I believe not, we will have the marriage annulled. The priest can do this for us when he arrives on Saturday."

Cynthia couldn't stay quiet. "I thought we were to go through another ceremony, not an annulment."

"I have told you what will happen, and I will inform Ricardo. He will be relieved to be free once again."

"Suppose I informed him of your plan. Perhaps he merely believes we should wait until after the family ceremony, which he says you want."

"And perhaps he has deceived *you*. Will you confront him? I should think it would be better if you wait and see what he does. If he truly wants you as his wife, he will say no to the annulment, and me. But if he does not want you, he will cooperate. You see?"

Cynthia did see. She was in a trap, and now she wasn't at all certain that Ricardo wanted her. Today on his horse, well, he acted as if he did. She saw it and felt it. *He does desire me. I think.*

Felicitas left the room and Cynthia sat rooted to the spot. She stared sightless into the corner of the room, her mind whirled, and her stomach churned. *What have I gotten myself into?* She thought as far as she could but her mind couldn't figure out this bombshell. She thought she might cry, or maybe be ill.

After perhaps twenty minutes of confusion and dismay, Cynthia straightened her back. She was a Harrington. Her father had reared her as a genteel woman. He'd taught her that she held an honored place in society. No one was to gain an advantage over her; and no one dared demean her.

So. What to do? She rose, paused to retrieve the peach pit, walked to her room, and found her bonnet. Then, with firmness and resolution, she walked through the kitchen and out the back door. In anger, she threw the peach pit as far as she could. Then she stood in the shade of the wide back porch and looked all around the large area, trying to discern just what course to take. She must get away from this house. What could she do?

To the right was the foreman's home. Ricardo said some of the wranglers were married and had children. The man she met at breakfast was in charge of the entire operation under Mr. Romero and his son. Perhaps she should pay a call to the lady of the house. She hoped the woman was more gracious than her so-called mother-in-law.

With a regal air, as if she were taking a morning stroll, Cynthia walked next door. Actually, the house was a good one-hundred yards away. In Nacogdoches, the houses were much closer together, but here there was room to spare.

The porch was full of potted flowers and greenery of all kinds. The back door was open, so she could look through the screen into the kitchen, if she wished. Manners, however, dictated she not do that—it was impolite. She stepped forward, rapped three times on the doorframe, and stepped back. Soon, a stout woman came to the door.

"Yes? Oh, are you the new Mrs. Romero?"

Cynthia's heart lightened right away. The woman's round face glowed with a smile, and she quickly opened the screen door. "Please, come in."

"Just call me Cynthia, if you please," she said in her best boarding school manner. She held out her properly gloved hand and asked, "Mrs.?"

"Oliver. Mrs. Oliver. My husband is Jake, but I'm just plain old Sarah." She looked behind Cynthia in curiosity. "Are you alone?"

"Yes, yes, I am. I came to call. Are you involved? I should not like to detain you from your household duties."

"Oh, well, my no. I'm not doing anything a'tall. Just a little embroidering, but lordy, that gets downright boring. Come in. Come in."

Sarah led her through the kitchen to the parlor, and they sat across from each other in a moment of silence. Sarah wiped her palms down her knees but caught herself and folded them in her lap. "Oh! Would you care for tea?"

"To be truthful, Sarah, I only wish to visit. May I come again and have tea? I do so love a cup of tea with a little milk and sugar. Don't you?"

"Oh, yes, I do. Nobody around here likes tea, though. Everybody wants coffee. Usually that's what I have because my Jake likes his coffee, hot and black. And do you like little cookies with your tea?"

"Oh, yes. I love tea cakes."

"Well, then, do you prefer lemon tea cakes or vanilla?"

"At home, our cook, Maria, made a wonderful, crisp little lemon cookie, which I adored."

"Those I can make. I'm sure of it. The next time you come visiting, I'll have something real nice."

"Oh, thank you. You've made me feel so welcome."

Silence. The topic of tea and cakes was exhausted. Cynthia now knew she had an ally and could ask the question.

"Sarah," she said as she leaned forward. "I need some information."

"Oh?"

"Yes. I need a place to live by myself. Now, Sarah, you may not understand, and you may be shocked, but well, I must move out of the house next door. Only for a short time, you see. Do you understand?"

Sarah looked baffled but she kept her eyes right on Cynthia, and she, too, leaned forward in a conspiratorial fashion. "I suppose," she whispered.

"Do you know of a place where I might live for a time? On the ranch, of course."

Sarah sat back, took a deep breath, and briefly closed her eyes. When she opened them, she studied Cynthia for several seconds.

Since the woman hesitated, Cynthia considered the woman and her husband's position and the trust the owners put in him. Maybe she shouldn't jeopardize the Oliver's lifestyle.

"Cynthia, I cannot possibly help you. You understand it's not my place to get mixed up in any of your business. My husband's job depends on our loyalty and honesty. Do you see?"

Cynthia nodded and waited until Sarah spoke again.

Sarah began in a sad tone, "Oh, we had such a misfortune only a couple of weeks ago. I don't suppose it would interest you, since you've just arrived and all, and especially since you don't know a soul on the place, but dear old Mr. Hellman just up and died. His dear Olga passed on a number of years ago, but Mr. Romero senior allowed Henri to continue to live in *the third house from the end*. Then, God rest his soul, he passed on. Oh, the service was so nice, and we had a big dinner and all to celebrate his life on earth and mourn his passing to be with his Lord." Sarah nodded with satisfaction.

"My," Cynthia said, as she fanned her face with a lace handkerchief. "I know you'll miss dear old Mr.

Hellman. Oh, look at the time. I have things to do today, Sarah. I do so thank you for your hospitality. I will look forward to visiting."

Chapter Six

The row of eight small houses was farther to the right of the main house. They angled down a slight incline, so the last one was barely visible. Thick clumps of live oaks surrounded the little homes, making them shady almost any time of day. Each one was white and trimmed in red, just as all the other buildings.

Cynthia walked counting to determine the third house from the end. However, to continue the charade she had construed, she stopped at the first to "go calling." She stepped up on the small covered porch and rapped three times.

A quite harried young woman answered the door. She carried one child on a hip and another held on to her skirts. "Yes?" she asked, as she looked out the screen and all around.

"Hello. I am Mrs. Cynthia Romero, and I am calling to make your acquaintance. I like to know my neighbors." She smiled sweetly and graciously but thought the gesture might be lost on the young mother.

"Mrs. Romero? The boss's wife? Oh, well, come on in."

Cynthia stepped into the small four-room house, making a quick assessment. Clean, neat, but sparse. No frills. "I know you're busy, so all I want to do is say hello and learn your name. Then, I must be on my way."

"My name? It's Irene. My man is Tom O'Dell. Can I help you with something?" She asked as she cocked her head to one side and a mild frown appeared on her thin face.

"No, nothing at all. May I call again? When you have a little free time? Then we could become better acquainted."

"Well, sure, I guess. You want to be acquainted with me?"

"Yes, of course. We'll find a time to have tea."

The next two houses brought similar results. The women were bemused, wary, but in the end, friendly. The fourth house was a little different. The woman was older and invited her in right away. She offered coffee, but Cynthia declined.

"Just call me Annie. My husband is John, and he's Mr. Oliver's right-hand man. We've been here, oh, about eighteen years, now."

"So *long*. Then you must know everyone quite well."

"Sure, I do. A few of the younger, single wranglers are hard to keep straight, because I don't see them much. All the families right here are real close, though, especially the women. Sometimes I feel I'm the mother to all of them." She laughed. "When you live like we do, you need to be close to your neighbors."

"What about Sarah? I met her first thing this morning."

"She's my best friend. Been here about the same number of years. When Jake became foreman, she moved outta one of these houses and over to the bigger one. Truthfully? She's lonely, because we sorta don't mingle with the high-ups."

"By that you certainly mean Mrs. Romero—Felicitas."

"Oh, well, now, I don't mean to say I dislike her or anything. We just don't visit." Her voice trailed. "I don't mean no offense."

"And I took none." She drew in a deep breath.

"Annie, I have a problem. Perhaps you will help me, perhaps not. Possibly we may go about this clandestinely."

"Clan...what?"

"Secretly. Privately, quietly."

"Oh, you mean sorta sneaky."

"Yes, exactly. I sincerely hope I do not jeopardize your husband's position or your important place in the social structure. If anyone questions you or me, I will disavow any relationship or any assistance from you or any of the other women in these houses. Do you follow?"

Annie narrowed her eyes in concentration. "I think I do, yes. What do you need?"

"Annie, I must move out of the main house. I have no right to burden you with my problem, so could you possibly take my word for it? I cannot live there. For whatever reason, it is very private."

The older woman nodded emphatically. "Honey, I am at your service. You tell me how I can help, and I'll do everything I can to do it. But I will say I need to be clan...secret about it, too. If my husband doesn't figure anything out, I'll be okay. If he does, I may have to let him in on it."

"I don't mind about that. I'm only trying to protect you and the others, because, Annie, I want to move into the third house from the end. Mr. Hellman's house."

"So, you've talked with Sarah. Fine. Now, let me see." She took a moment to search the ceiling for answers. "Here's what we can do. The door is unlocked. I'll go in the back door. Let's go. I'll meet you over there."

"Shall I go in the back door, as well?"

"Yes, do that."

Before the hour was up, Cynthia had moved everything she brought to the ranch into the small four-room house. That included two large trunks, one small trunk, three valises, three hatboxes, and one smaller carry bag. She borrowed a child's wagon she had seen in a yard, and with the help of six children, one of which was a strapping twelve-year-old boy, she had lugged all of it across the expansive yard and placed the items in the spare bedroom of the small house.

No one had stopped her, and few people had even seen her. All of the men were far in the back pasture at various corrals and barns. She knew Ricardo said all the hands would work until dark, seeing that every new horse received proper attention and housing.

The women in the other seven houses watched out a window or stood on their porch to watch the proceedings. Cynthia saw them, and she could imagine the talk. She didn't know whether to laugh or cry.

Only the children chattered to Cynthia, with excitement and curiosity. Cynthia had learned all kinds of personal information about the adults who lived there. Most of it was quite funny, some sad or terrible. She would never repeat any of the details. Children were a mystery to her, but she did know they could prattle on about nothing of significance.

Two other people had also watched her.

Consuelo fretted and scolded, but in the end, gathered all Cynthia's things in the room and repacked them. Then she helped her lift each trunk across the child's wagon when Cynthia returned with it empty. Consuelo instructed the children waiting in the yard to walk alongside the wagon and hold the trunk or valise steady.

Felicitas heard the commotion from her room and walked in to find Cynthia packing and moving. She didn't even inquire as to where she was going. After a minute of glancing back and forth between her housekeeper and her daughter-in-law, she turned on her toes and strolled back to her room, smiling all the way.

Cynthia gritted her teeth.

Late in the evening, Cynthia sat in an uncharacteristic pose, which she knew was contradictory to all her life's lessons. With her shoes and stockings off, she sat in one kitchen chair and propped her feet in another. She rolled the long sleeves on her shirtwaist to her elbows, and unbuttoned the high, lace-trimmed neckline halfway to her waist. A low lamp burned next to her, and she studied the unfamiliar room as she nibbled on the meat pie and peach cobbler Annie had brought to her. Between bites, she sipped tea from a heavy white ceramic cup. Tea, which she had made all by herself. Well, close enough for the first time, anyway, because Annie had given her a tin of English Blend and instructed her on the brewing.

Annie gave her a first lesson in making a fire in the small wood-burning stove. Then she had rustled about in the tiny kitchen and found a rather large teakettle. She told Cynthia she could heat water not only for tea, but also to warm the cold well water for a bath in the round galvanized tin tub. Annie led her out the back door, and there was the tub hanging on a nail on the outside wall.

She told Cynthia the children bathed outdoors much of the year. The parents filled the tub near the well and left it in the sun to warm. Then each child took a turn before dark, so she suggested Cynthia might want to avoid being out there. The statement that made Cynthia laugh was after dark, in the hot months, the adults would do the same.

"Oh, my," she had said between laughs, "I don't know if I can do that!"

Annie had laughed with her. "You might rethink it, when you have to carry buckets of water from the well to the lean-to on the back of your house."

Cynthia smiled to herself in self-satisfaction. She had accomplished things today that her mind could never have imagined. Her bedroom was finished. Clothes hung on pegs on the wall, and shoes and boots sat lined up on the floor under them. Two shelves were stacked with folded chemises, pantalets, nightgowns, and wraps. She made the narrow bed with the finest cotton, lace-trimmed sheets, and pillowcases that probably no one else owned on this ranch. The quilt, pieced out of vibrant silks and colorful Egyptian cotton, covered the sheets.

She hated to delve into her hope chest—her marriage trunk. The collections began when she turned fifteen, and Maria explained all girls had "hope chests." Through the years, Cynthia had embroidered pretty things and crocheted others. She even edged dishtowels in lace or a crocheted border. Often, her father contributed something special, such as a Belgian cut-lace tablecloth and beautiful Irish linen napkins. With each piece, she imagined where it would go in her new home she would share with her imaginary husband.

Now, all her hopes and dreams were shattered. Nothing was turning out as she thought it should. Well, that's what a foolish girl deserves, she thought, when she spins fairy tales in her head of a handsome, charming prince sweeping her away on his powerful steed.

Cynthia happened to glance out the window as the sun disappeared over the horizon. The subject of her musings, at this moment, stalked across the yards of the foreman and five small houses to reach the third one from the end. His hat rode low on his forehead, and his long strides angrily ate up the distance.

Her emotions circled three-hundred-and-sixty degrees, from self-satisfaction and peace to surprise and not a little fright. Her unhappy husband was on his way.

Ricardo did not knock on the screen door. Instead, he opened it, slammed it back against the outside wall, and stepped inside.

In a low voice laced with anger and with his hands low on his hips, he asked, "What the hell do you think you're doing?"

Cynthia stood barefoot in her disheveled state, raised her chin, folded her hands at her waist, and with as much haughtiness she could muster, replied, "Do not use that sort of language in my presence, you...you clout!"

Some of his bluster disappeared. He swept off his hat and bowed. "Well, excuse me, Queen Mary," he said in an exaggerated moderate voice. "What I should have said was 'what the Sam Hill do you think you're doing?' Is that better?"

"What do you want?" she asked, never batting an eyelash.

"You know damn well what I want. I want to know what's come over you to create such a stir and pull such a stunt. And I want you to pack and march your little fanny right back over there to my house."

"Your house? *Your house*? Sir, you are deluded if you think that is your house, because I know who's in charge over there. And it's not you!"

"I have no idea what you're referring to. But I do know that as my wife, you..."

"Stop!" She held her hand up, palm out. "Your wife? Since when am I your wife? I have no husband whom I can call my own. Our marriages were shams—*both* of them. Why? Because the man I thought I married will not *consummate* the union to make us as one. No, he must wait because his parents say so, to have a third wedding to cement the vows."

"I married you, Cynthia," he said reasonably

70

and now without a trace of annoyance, "and you are my wife. You wear that ring to prove it."

She glanced at the beautiful piece of jewelry, and more than anything, she wanted to continue wearing it, forever and ever more. Now, it was just a ring with no benefits. With great sadness, she removed it. "Here. Take it, Ricardo, it means nothing. I thought it did; oh, how I wanted it to." Tears formed in the corners of her eyes.

Ricardo's shoulders almost slumped, but he did not bend. She watched his face, as anger turned to bewilderment. Slowly and cautiously, he took two steps to gather her in his arms. She sniffled once, twice, and with her face pressed to his shirtfront, mumbled, "Let me go. Take the ring and leave."

He loosened his hold but did not release her. He tipped her chin up and looked down into her face. With the pad of his thumb, he wiped away one lone tear, and lowered his lips to hers. The kiss began sweet and gentle, but soon changed to sensuous and warm. Against her will, she kissed him back, the best she knew how, but still, a sob escaped. "Don't," she whispered.

When he raised his head, he took the ring but lifted her left hand and replaced it where it belonged. "Cynthia, listen to me. Can't you tell me what this is all about? Have I neglected you too much since the wedding? Whatever I've done, I did it unintentionally. Do you understand?"

She moved away from him to talk. "I think it best that I stay here for a while. I considered finding a way back home, but I'm not a little girl anymore, and I can't run home to Father. In a couple of days or so, you should be able to learn what's going on. I can't tell you. It's not my place to explain."

"You're not making any sense," he said gently. "You know that, don't you? Should I court you? What?" His exasperation increased as he talked.

71

"You need not do anything. Just leave me alone."

"No, sweetheart, I won't do that. You can't manage on your own. Don't you see? How are you going to eat? Who will do your laundry? You've been reared as a lady, and you don't know how to do anything."

She flashed her eyes at him. The tears were gone, and in their place, cold anger. "You may leave now."

Ricardo did not slam out the door or stomp out angrily. Probably his rearing was as ingrained as hers was, so he strolled out as if he had all the time in the world.

****

By ten o'clock the next morning, Cynthia had struggled with every aspect of her new life. First, she slept poorly, partly because it was a strange bed and place, but mainly because of her heartbreak. Once she was up and dressed, she felt better, but the wood stove almost caused her to surrender. She worked twenty minutes trying to light a fire. Annie had explained the process, but she hadn't listened carefully. With that feat at last accomplished, she had black soot on her forehead from wiping perspiration from her brow, and on the front of her yellow linen day dress.

She selected another dress—a simple one made of blue calico—and donned the new boots Ricardo instructed her to buy. They looked like cowboy boots to her, but once she had them on her feet, she felt supremely confident. Instead of piling her hair high on her crown, anchored with a dozen hairpins, she pulled it back to her nape and tied it with a ribbon. Now she felt as if she would fit in with her new friends.

One of the women showed her how to draw a bucket of water, which turned out to be quite simple.

Another brought a pan of biscuits and a jar of jam, and another donated eggs. All she had to do was boil water for tea, which had taken quite some time. The eggs presented the greatest problem, because when they were cooked, they in no way resembled the eggs Maria served. Now, she wondered if she should have some sort of grease or butter in the pan to keep them from sticking and burning.

She heard a knock on her door.

"Annie! Oh, Annie, come in. I'm so glad to see you."

"And how are you today?" She waved her hand in front of her face. "Is something burning?"

"My eggs." Cynthia laughed. "I need some butter, I guess. Come, sit down."

They sat at the small kitchen table across from each other. Cynthia leaned forward. "Will you be in trouble by coming here?"

"No, maybe not. I decided to take a chance. I reckoned you would need help. What can I do for you?"

"Where can I get food? And what should I look for?"

"Umm, well, the commissary has staples, you know, flour, sugar, salt, baking soda. It opens up around three in the afternoon. Do you have money? You might need some. I'm not sure you do, since you're a Mrs. Romero."

"I have a little money. I'll find out. How much does, say, sugar cost?"

"Tell you what. I'll come back and go over there with you. How about that?"

"Would you? Thank you."

"Have you seen the horses?"

"Just a glance. They're pretty, aren't they?"

"This is only a suggestion, mind you, but you might want to go out there to the big corral and watch. They're showing them this morning. Right

73

now. That means each one will be led around and then ridden to figure out a ranking."

"Why?"

"To place them in order to be bred. It doesn't matter that much why. It's just interesting. I think you should go. Now." The woman was very insistent.

"I'll get my bonnet."

Annie went home, and Cynthia wondered as she strode along why Annie was so anxious for her to watch the proceedings. She was happy to go, though, because the walk would do her good, and she had no other plans for the day.

As she approached, a crowd surrounded the corral. Men leaned their arms on the top rails, and most had one booted foot propped on the bottom rung. It seemed to be a uniform stance. Of course, she knew no one except her husband, his father, and the foreman, and a couple of the wives who were there. At least, she did not feel so out of place.

She walked the perimeter of the large corral, searching for an opening with an unobstructed view. What she did see brought her up short. There was Ricardo leaning on the railing in the same exact stance as the other men, except he turned to the side a little more. The reason was because a tall, slender woman with blue-black hair stood next to him, and he was laughing down at her. Laughing! With his hat pushed back off his forehead, his bright eyes sparkled, and they focused on the beautiful woman.

The strange woman was dressed as the men—cowboy boots, tight denim pants, and shirt. Cynthia saw her and Ricardo talking and as the discussion progressed, the woman became agitated. She actually stamped her foot, leaned closer to Ricardo, and talked rapidly. He shook his head, pulled down his hat, and removed his boot from the railing. Now, he was angry, she was certain, because he placed his hands low on his hips in the same manner as he had done last night. He was angry, all right, but they both turned back to the railing and seemed to resume normal talk. Then he took her arm and they walked away from the crowd and toward the barn.

Cynthia felt invisible. No one looked at her, no one paid attention if she were there or not. Maybe they didn't know who she was. Without thinking, she followed the pair and watched as they disappeared into the barn.

When she stood inside the cavernous building, the smells of horses and droppings and hay assaulted her. It was something she knew a little about, because she owned Little Dixie. This was almost overpowering, though, because the place could hold many horses.

When her eyes adjusted to the dimness, she saw her husband and the woman at the end near a stall. Ricardo had his back to Cynthia. He hooked an arm over the stall door, and the woman looked at him. Their conversation continued.

Cynthia walked closer.

"You're ruining everything," the woman said vehemently.

"Starr, I never agreed to any of this. I told Mother and Father I wanted nothing to do with the plan. You're going to have to let it go, because we'll never be married. I've told you five times today, I'm already married, and my wife is here."

"Where?" She spread her arms. "I haven't seen her yet."

"Well, she's here. Take my word for it."

"She wasn't in the house," she said accusingly.

"Never mind her. We're talking about us."

We're talking about us.

Starr's voice turned soft and whispery, so that Cynthia could barely hear. "Yes, us, Rick, us. If you're waiting to consummate your marriage to make it real, well, then think. *We've* already *consummated.* More than once. We're more married than you and that other woman. All you have to do is skip the ceremony Saturday, and she'll go home, and the church will annul your marriage."

"How do you know this?"

"Your mother told me, darling. You see, we can still be man and wife, and our families will combine the ranches to make the biggest and richest in the state. Think about it. Bigger than the Loma Linda Ranch."

He removed his hat and raked his fingers through his hair. "I don't want to be bigger than the Loma Linda. Don't you know that by now?"

"But have you told your parents? They're the ones pushing this. Your mother especially wants..."

Cynthia heard enough of the conversation. She turned and walked as quickly as she could from the barn. Once she was in open air, she stopped, placed her hand at her waist, and took a deep breath. *What on earth is going on? This is crazy.*

The remainder of the day was interminably long for Cynthia. Everything was in such a mess. She looked at the ring on her finger. Ricardo had bought it especially for her and placed it on her finger. Twice.

She now knew Felicitas was behind all this. Rafaelo too, according to the woman, Starr. The older man had not been unkind to her. How did he feel about his son marrying an outsider? Did he also wish to join the two properties?

By the time darkness fell, she had a headache, but her heart hurt more. Naively she had fallen for a stranger, a Spaniard, someone almost foreign; except he made it clear he was an American. Oh, well, what did it matter? Had he been honest with her? That was the main question. Why would he marry her and bring her here if he had not been sincere?

That woman. The black-haired, beautiful

woman. Cynthia had always felt superior, secure, and loved. She had a prominent place in Nacogdoches. How would it have turned out if she had stayed there and married some important man?

The thought, while at one time foremost in her mind, was now dust in the wind. Here she was with a magnificent man who was her husband, but not her husband. Surely he thought well of her, maybe even loved her. In contrast to the black-haired woman, however, Cynthia felt mousy and insignificant.

Chapter Seven

Ricardo entered his mother's office and saw her consulting the feminine gold watch on a chain around her neck. He knew he was late. She had summoned him hours ago. He didn't have time for a discussion with her, because the priest would arrive soon for the service at one o'clock.

"Mother, you wished to see me?"

"Yes, my son. Will you sit?"

He took a seat on the Queen Anne chair as his mother paced back and forth on the deep red rug in front of her elaborately carved oak desk. She was not yet fifty, tall, slender, and while not beautiful, one might call her handsome. Her role on the Double R was not only that of a wife, but as an equal partner with her husband. She kept the books and managed the financial portion of the business. Of course, his father was owner of all the physical holdings, and she rarely interfered with decisions he made concerning cattle, horses, his men, or the land. He knew what he was doing.

Conflicts were rare between the couple, but since Ricardo had brought a stranger into their midst, his parents had been at odds. He knew his mother's plan had been in place for many years. He would marry Starr Hidalgo, the daughter of a long-time friend who owned the adjoining ranch.

Starr and Ricardo had grown up together, and her parents wanted the two ranches to merge just as his mother wished. However, Rafaelo, his father, now balked in deference to his marriage. Starr's father had agreed long ago that one gigantic kingdom was better than two larger-than-average ones. Each ranch boasted one valuable asset or another, but together, they would rival, if not surpass, the Loma Linda Ranch in the Wild Horse Desert area of South Texas. With added tracts of grassland and rivers, plus the combined wealth of the two families, better strains of cattle could be produced, as well as superior horse lines. Horses might be even more valuable than cattle in the coming years.

He knew his mother had another, more personal goal. Spaniards introduced cattle and horses into this continent. They owned the first ranches—original Spanish land grants. Ranching in Texas had begun with them, but now, more than anything, she desired to oust the Anglo usurper, the mistress of the Loma Linda Ranch. She intended to become the "first lady" of ranching and cultural leader of ranchers herself.

"What's this all about? I really need to stay at the corral as long as I can today. Don't worry, I'll be here in time to clean up and dress for the ceremony."

"Oh, my dear," she said quietly, as she placed her hand at her breast. "You don't know, do you?"

Warily he asked, "Know what?"

"Your wife. Cynthia. She has spoken with me, and she quite clearly said she has made a mistake by marrying you. No forethought, you see. She had no idea where you were bringing her, and she told me she couldn't abide living here. That's why she moved out of this house and into Mr. Hellman's old residence. She's waiting until Paulo has time to drive her back to Rico Springs to catch the train home."

Ricardo stood abruptly. "The hell you say," he spat. With his eyes narrowed on his mother and his hands low on his hips, he added. "She told me nothing of the sort. I don't believe you. I know she's angry about something, but I'm working on it."

"Well, I should be very careful, if I were you. Please don't allow your emotions to heat when you're with her. You may end up with a consummated marriage, of which you cannot rid yourself, son. You know that, don't you? If you have relations with her, you'll be tied to her forever, whether she wants to stay here or not."

Ricardo swiped his hand down the back of his head in exasperation. "You shouldn't speak to me of such things, Mother. I'm not sixteen any more, and I'm well aware of the ways of...love. I'll take care of this myself, and I'll have to hear it from my wife before I believe it." He turned to go, but Felicitas stopped him.

"Wait! No, don't talk to her. I assure you, she has no intention of going to the wedding ceremony. But if you go, all dressed up for the ceremony, and she is absent, think how embarrassed you'll be. Now, we don't want that, do we?"

Ricardo had no reply. He walked away from her and slammed out the back door.

****

Cynthia wished she had a mirror. Early this morning, she made a decision. She found the trunk with her new "western" clothes and found the riding outfit—a suede split-skirt with no petticoats. Even though she felt this might not be acceptable in Nacogdoches or to her father, this was way out West, where one needed the proper attire to ride a horse.

When she had seen the beautiful black-haired woman wearing men's pants, or least they resembled men's, she decided to try the new clothing. Her cowboy boots looked good with the skirt, or so she thought when she looked down at herself. She also decided the white shirt was great. All she had to wear under it was a chemise. The mercantile personnel had also suggested a wide leather belt with a feminine silver buckle. It was grand, she thought, and quite liberating.

She braided her hair in one long, thick rope and let it fall down her back, as she had done yesterday. Her hair was very thick and heavy, so this was a very comfortable way to wear it. The hat resembled Ricardo's, the flat-brimmed, flat-topped sort with a ball on a cord to slide to her chin. She shook her head back and forth. Probably it would stay on just fine.

Now, all she must do was locate a wrangler who might be amenable to teaching her to ride. She wondered how long it would take. If she could ride, maybe Ricardo would see her in a better light as he apparently did the other woman—*the one he had consummated with more than once.* The thought made her furious, jealous even. So far, he had spent more time with the black-haired woman than he had with his own wife.

Well, I did push him out of this house.

Yes, but he refused to consummate with me.

I'll show him.

Cynthia felt uncharacteristically shy about walking out alone dressed in such an unfamiliar manner. So, she paced around her little house, fretting and thinking how she could work up courage.

She wondered what Ricardo would do about the ceremony at one. She'd seen the priest drive up a couple of hours ago in his little carriage and enter the main house. Ricardo had gone back to the house earlier from the corrals but had not stayed long. Probably, he was back out with the horses. He obviously had no intention of going to the chapel, and she was not about to go over there, either.

At last, she worked up enough courage to step out of her house. Once she was on her way to the barns and corrals, she felt much more confident. Every so often, she met up with a ranch hand, and he would touch the brim of his hat and say, "Hello, ma'am. Nice day, ain't it?" Or "Howdy do, Miz Romero. How're you today?"

Not one of them doffed his hat as most gentlemen might do in Nacogdoches. Each one just touched the brim of his hat with two fingers and nodded, as if removing his sweat-stained hat might be too much trouble. She remembered some men, such as Buck Cameron, touched the brim of his hat as these men did. Perhaps it was the Code of the West—the way real Western men greeted a lady.

Before she arrived at the first barn, Ricardo rode toward her on his big, black stallion. He made no sign of greeting, and she was aware, too, of a grim look on his face. She turned her head away with her chin in the air and attempted to walk on past him. But he would have none of it.

"Where're you going?" He reined in right in front of her so if she wished to continue walking, she must sidestep the animal. That was a little difficult, so she stood her ground.

"I'm looking for a wrangler to teach me to ride. Is that against the rules? I promise I won't take one away who might be very busy. Surely there's one gentleman who might take a little time to teach me." She sniffed and looked away

He waited a few seconds. "I'll teach you."

The comment surprised her a great deal, but she tried not to allow him to see her reaction.

"Oh? When?" she asked.

"Now," he answered as he swung down from the saddle. "Here's what you do. Come over here and place your left foot in the stirrup."

She approached his horse, hiked her leg up to follow his directions, and balance herself by holding on to the edge of the saddle.

The horse tried to dance away, and she had to hop a few steps on her right foot. "Could you make him stand still?" she asked with a slight amount of panic in her voice.

"Of course," he said amiably. "Now, I'll give you a boost, and you swing your right leg over the saddle."

Cynthia made every attempt to do as he said, but her leg wouldn't reach all the way over the big stallion, plus the cantle was too high and in her way. She found herself hanging across the saddle with both hands, with one foot in the stirrup.

She looked over her shoulder. Ricardo strained to keep a straight face. From the corner of her eye, she also saw two of his men leaning against the barn, about to burst with silent laughter. He gave them a stern look and motioned with his head to move on and his action warmed her heart. He did care.

He grasped her waist and pushed her up and over, so in an instant she sat upright on the back of the horse. "There you go," he said.

Cynthia held on to the pommel for dear life. She couldn't look down: she was up too high. Fear froze her muscles. Being alone was worse than when Ricardo was with her.

Ricardo removed her foot from the stirrup, and in a quick move mounted behind her. There was hardly room for two, but he settled her snugly up against him. He kicked the horse's belly, turned him to the right, and off they went. He held the reins with one hand and kept his other arm securely around her waist.

Cynthia lost her breath.

Ricardo leaned forward against her back, urging the horse on, faster, and faster. In the midst of their wild ride, she felt him reach up and jerk off her hat. "Hold this! It's hitting me in the face!"

After what seemed like a very long time, Ricardo slowed his stallion to a gentle lope, but they did not stop. She didn't question him as to where they were going or why. She could only think of how he kept her securely pressed to his body with one strong arm. Innately, she felt he would keep her safe. She kept one hand on the pommel and the other over his arm.

Finally, he slowed the horse to a walk, and they kept on, to who knew where. Cynthia began to enjoy the ride and the sensation of being so close to her husband. She made no attempt at conversation, however, nor did he.

They approached an area that was different from the wide-open spaces they had been through so far. She saw a few small hills grouped together, and he guided the horse through thickets of live oak and mesquite. Then, she began to see different trees, some she had never seen.

"What are these?"

"Bald cypress and a few pecans. They like water."

"Oh, I've seen pecan trees," she said in reply, not knowing anything else to say.

They came upon a rugged canyon, and she peered over the side to gaze at the beauty of the rocks and trees, but she said nothing. At the bottom, she saw a river or stream, and it ran with frothy, tumbling water over flat, white rocks.

"What is that?" she asked.

"The Sabinal River," he replied without expression.

"We've been riding a long time, haven't we?"

"An hour and a half, maybe."

Cynthia was tired, but she made no comment after that exchange, nor did she complain.

After another half hour or so, Ricardo finally brought the horse to a halt. Trees, grasses, and flowers, forming a cool bower of surprising beauty from this rugged land, surrounded the area. She heard gurgling water and looked all around to locate the source of the sound. While she searched, he dismounted and lifted her off the saddle. When her feet were on the ground, she looked into his dark face, so solemn and inscrutable.

"My horse picked up a rock, I think. I need to tend to him."

"Okay," she answered, still gazing up into his face. "What's his name?"

"Diablo."

"Devil? Does that mean devil?"

"I suppose," he said.

She folded her hands in front of her, stood very still and calm, and continued gazing at his face. No smile; no frown.

"Is he? A devil, I mean. Is he evil?"

This caused him to chuckle. "No, he's as gentle as a baby, except when his lady is near."

She cocked her head to one side, never taking her eyes off his dark ones. "What does that mean?"

"He gets all fired up when she's around, because he wants her," he answered with his eyes narrowed.

Cynthia remained calm, as she had from the beginning. She knew she could be all haughty and excitable one minute, but when she knew exactly how things were, she became calm and collected and just took it from there. Some other females she knew would handle this situation with the hysteria, and soon, would be in a full-blown snit, but not her. She always tried to act the lady.

"This is Rico Springs," he said to fill the silence, and he swept one arm toward the sound of the water.

"I thought the town had that name."

"It does, but it's named for these springs. Actually, there are numerous ones around. It just so happens that these are the biggest and the best. And they're on our land."

Cynthia noted the pride in his voice. She turned from him and walked a few steps to peer down at the springs. Water bubbled up from the earth and formed a clear pool, which looked deep and wide. Flat rocks and boulders protruded around the edges, forming a series of places where one might sit and gaze at the water.

"Is it deep?" Cynthia asked as she peered down cautiously.

"Not really. Maybe twenty feet or so. Around the edges, the water is shallow, and it's forever changing just as the deep part is."

"It looks a little frightening," she commented and turned to look at him.

"Not if you can swim."

She crossed her arms around her waist. "Well, I don't swim."

Ricardo smiled and raised one eyebrow. "You can't?"

"Uh-uh." She shook her head. "Where would I learn to swim in Nacogdoches? The bayou is thick with...stuff, and its slow moving. Too much in there. Too nasty. And it has water moccasins, big, very poisonous snakes."

"I see. What about the river?"

"Well, I've heard of people traveling over there and camping and swimming, but Father never did such a thing. So, of course, I didn't."

"You led a sheltered life, didn't you?"

"Does that make me less of a woman? Do I have some flaw because Father protected me?"

"No, I didn't mean it that way." He turned away, walked to the ledge, and looked down at the springs. "Just an observation."

"Ricardo?"

He turned slowly on his boot heels and looked at

her. "Yes?"

"Are you sorry you married me?"

Now, he turned back to gaze at the springs. "No."

"Liar," she whispered.

Ricardo was very confused. His mind was in turmoil. The weddings had taken place so fast when he made his decision, he really didn't take time to think about the ramifications. He hadn't expected his parents, especially his mother, to raise such a fuss. Then there was Starr Hidalgo. She made him feel shortsighted, when she pointed out to him how rash his decision had been.

But he felt something for this blue-eyed, dark-haired beauty. Ever since he had met her at Robert King's place over in Nacogdoches, she had been on his mind.

Instead of acknowledging her accusation, he turned around to face her. "Would you like to learn how to swim?"

"Now?" she asked incredulously.

"This is the best place to learn, and we have all the time in the world."

Before she could stop herself, she asked, "What about the ceremony at one o'clock? Aren't you going?"

"Are you?" he countered.

"No, I didn't intend to, to be honest. I see no reason. We've had two ceremonies, already, and if that's not enough, a third one will make no difference. I didn't expect you would go, either. Am I correct?"

He shrugged one shoulder. "Why would you think that?"

"May I speak honestly, Ricardo? I simply detest beating around the bush. I warn you though; you might not like what I have to say."

He removed his hat and threw it on a large rock.

Then, he ran his fingers through his hair in frustration. At the same time, he smoothed out the circle of matted hair made by the hat.

"Speak, Cynthia. Say whatever it is you have to say. I don't care for deception or lies, either. If you think you made a mistake by marrying me, then just spit it out. Get it over with."

She hesitated. "May I ask another question first?"

He nodded impatiently.

"Do you feel that you made a mistake? Would you prefer that I leave and go back home? Is that why you've made no attempt to consummate our wedding vows?"

Ricardo studied her open, honest face. Cynthia Harrington would have difficulty deceiving a person on purpose. Oh, she knew how to sidestep and play the games that people in society played, but she wouldn't deliberately deceive or cheat. If she did make a mistake, she would apologize in her ladylike way and move on from there.

"Cynthia, I wanted to marry you. I've told you that. I didn't want you to marry that mealy-mouthed little accountant, so I stepped in on purpose. I had already been thinking about how to gain your attention, but you didn't seem all that interested in me. When the opportunity to ask for you suddenly appeared, I took it. To be perfectly honest, I took advantage of our night on the road, and then again, when your father walked in on us in your parlor. I knew without a doubt that he would try to force me to marry you then, but remember I asked *you* to make the decision."

"And I did," she whispered. "I said yes."

"So, do we have that understood?"

She nodded.

"So, what were you going to say?"

Cynthia knew in her heart Ricardo loved his

mother. How could she, now after his declaration, tell him what his mother told her? She had no reason to trust the woman, but Felicitas loved her son—her only child—and probably honestly tried to protect his interests. Ricardo would not appreciate Cynthia relating just how deceptive his mother was.

"I was going to say, so you would know how I feel, that I wasn't certain if I would like it here. But I do like your ranch, and Ricardo, I especially like having you for a husband."

The one-sided grin lit his face. The one, deep dimple appeared. Her stomach fluttered.

Chapter Eight

"Consuelo! Come here! At once!"

Felicitas had flown into a full-blown rage. Her son was missing, along with his useless little wife. How dare he ignore his parents' wishes!

The cook bustled into the office where Felicitas paced back and forth, waved her arms, cursed and threatened no one in particular. "Yes, ma'am?"

"Find Mr. Romero immediately. Tell him to come to the house."

"But...I...you want me to walk out there to the corrals, ma'am?"

Felicitas briefly glanced at her maid. The large, slow-moving woman could barely make it around the kitchen, let alone walk three-hundred yards to the first barn. "Never mind. Just ring the bell."

"But...it is not noon yet. And excuse me, but is there an emergency?"

"Yes, yes! This is an emergency! Go, go!"

She walked out to the hallway to ensure Consuelo rang the big dinner bell on the back porch. Several wranglers dropped their work and ran to the house. Rafaelo jogged, lagging behind the younger men.

The Padre had arrived and now waited in the parlor until the air cleared, but Felicitas had not related exactly what his duty would be. A wedding blessing? Or an annulment? He obviously heard all the commotion—the bell ringing, men yelling, and doors slamming. However, the little Catholic priest remained seated in the doily-covered armchair, sipped his honey-sweetened tea, and nibbled on his iced lemon teacakes. She rolled her eyes heavenward as she passed.

"Felicitas! What is it? What's wrong?" Rafael breathlessly asked. He approached her and placed his hands around her upper arms to keep her still and steady. "My, dear, are you hurt? Here, sit down."

She slapped his hands away. "Let go of me." She stepped back, took a deep breath, folded her hands at her waist, and announced, "Ricardo and that Anglo woman have disappeared. Find them! At once!"

Rafaelo gaped. "Is that it? I think you'd better explain, Felicitas."

"Ricardo knew to stay away from the church, out of sight, and I was to watch Miss Harrington to determine if she went to the church or not. We didn't think she would go, but perhaps she would. Ricardo said he wanted no part of a wedding blessing, indicating he wanted the annulment instead."

"Whoa, my dear madam. Wait just a minute. Ricardo said that?"

"Yes, right here in my office."

"That doesn't sound like him, Felicitas. Not at all. I was under the distinct impression that he is quite taken with his pretty bride."

"Well, he's *not*. I'm certain he wants out of this marriage contract, so he must not consummate the vows. If he does, we're ruined!"

"Felicitas, sit down." When she did not respond, he raised his voice. "I said, sit down!" She grudgingly obeyed, and he sat in a chair next to her. "Now, let's discuss this calmly." Rafaelo paused when he noticed four wranglers poking their heads in the door. Consuelo was there, also, listening and watching. He stood and reached for the door. As he pulled it shut, he told the wranglers to return to their jobs, and asked Consuelo to make coffee for the two of them.

91

"Now, let's start all over, my dear," Rafaelo said in his usual calm, quiet way. "You seem a little too excited to me, and in fact, you nearly gave me a heart attack. It'll be best if you calmly tell me the story again, so I can understand your thoughts exactly."

"Don't you know we're wasting valuable time, Rafaelo? Jake told me that Ricardo saddled Diablo around mid-morning, picked up his wife, and rode off toward the west. She was dressed to go riding, so she planned all of it. I *know* it's a ploy to derail the annulment."

"Exactly who planned the *ploy*?"

"Miss Harrington, of course! She probably wants the marriage, so she enticed him away to only God knows where. But it's not too late to follow them. Send somebody!"

"Felicitas, my dear, in the first place, she's Mrs. Romero, the same as you, not Miss Harrington. They're married, and I suspect they'll stay that way. Ricardo made no mention of an annulment to me. On the contrary, he told me he liked his beautiful wife very much and must see to her comfort and make her happy."

"You think she's beautiful?" Felicitas glanced sideways at her husband.

"Oh, yes. Very."

"But she's Anglo, Rafaelo. She will produce half—something. Half-breeds! This will dilute the Spanish blood!"

"Dear Felicitas. *You* are a half-breed. Your father was a Comanche warrior. He was not Spanish."

Felicitas became enraged yet again. "It's not the same thing! She's very white, with very light blue eyes, and hair that is not black." She slumped back in her chair. "Ohhh, you don't understand."

Consuelo tapped on the door and entered with

two cups of coffee. "Here, you go, ma'am. Lots of cream and sugar, just as you like it." She carefully placed the tray on a side table and quickly quit the room.

"Felicitas, why don't you drink your coffee and rest? I need to get back to work. By the way, where is Father Thomas?"

"Still in the parlor I'm sure."

"Well, be sure to tell Consuelo to have his room ready for tonight. He'll say Mass in the morning, and then be on his way." He stood and leaned down to peck his wife on the cheek. "I'll see you at supper."

Now all alone, Felicitas went to her own room, changed into riding clothes, donned a sturdy felt hat, and pulled on her riding gloves. Next, she proceeded to the first barn and corral where she stabled her own mare. There, she instructed Hector to saddle her mount and fill a canteen with water.

She walked Princess out of the padlock, mounted, and kicked the horse's belly. Her destination—somewhere west of the ranch.

Felicitas kicked her mare again and again, urging her on, faster, and faster. She was experienced as a horsewoman. She had practically been born on a horse. Her Comanche father, a wild warrior at one time, became a domesticated rancher when he married an aristocratic Spaniard, but his love of horses never waned. All six of his children— four boys and two girls—had been placed on a horse at the age of eight months and grew up in the saddle.

As she rode, some of her anger dissipated, simply because she was on horseback, but enough remained to hurl her onward toward her goal. Her boy had grown up on the ranch, so he knew every square inch and every corner. She knew he had numerous favorite places to hide, to daydream, or to play, but one or two stood out. He especially loved the springs and pool, the larger ones that were actually the Rico Springs. And rich they were, as their Spanish name implied. The water was the purest on earth, the bower was an artist's dream, and the seclusion was complete if one knew the location.

Well, Felicitas knew the spot, but the distance was still far if she stayed on the open range and the often-used paths through the trees and ledges. However, if she cut through diagonally and rode more northwest through the flatter pasture area, she would arrive there much sooner. Every minute counted.

Felicitas rode hoping and praying she had guessed correctly. If not, she would waste the whole day, and might not be able to stop them. She knew very well Ricardo's plan, because he was her son, a quarter Comanche. Felicitas knew him better than she knew Rafaelo, because she and Ricardo shared Native blood, which bound them together in heart and mind and spirit. No white man nor woman, nor even a Spaniard, could understand the mystic connection.

Spanish blood could mix with Comanche, but Anglo blood never could. She would not allow the union.

Of course, Felicitas had another goal, just as pressing as was assuring the purest blood possible in any offspring. That was the size of the ranch. If Ricardo married Starr Hidalgo, she would solve both problems.

She kicked harder. She rode even faster. Blind rage filled her vision.

****

The blistering summer sun beat down on the rugged Texas landscape. With every drop of moisture sucked from the air, the temperature rose by the minute, but the cool, green bower around the springs and pool provided comfort and refuge.

Cynthia and Ricardo sat on a flat rock, which jutted out over the pool. Serious conversation had wound down, and in its stead, there remained a peaceful communion.

Idly, he picked up a small pebble now and then and threw it into the water. Occasionally, she saw him peek at her, his gaze moving over the curve of her jaw, her neck, hair, and hands. She knew he studied her breasts under her cotton shirt. Somehow, though, she didn't feel as embarrassed as she might have been only a short while ago.

She leaned back on her arms, closed her eyes, and turned her face to the sky. Once in a while, a little hum came from her throat, not quite a tune, but a singsong sound nonetheless. She swung her feet back and forth, as they dangled over the deep, blue water.

"Cynthia?"

"Hmmm?" she answered without opening her eyes.

"Want to go swimming?"

She cracked open one eye and turned her face toward him. With a tiny smile, she said, "Silly. I told you I couldn't swim."

"I'll teach you." He came to life and began to remove his boots and socks. Next the shirt was discarded, exposing his dark skin with its smattering of black hair on his chest. He stood.

Cynthia caught her breath when she perused his body, now only clad in cotton drawers. His appearance was almost wild, as if he were a savage who lived in the forest, but his smile was gentle, teasing, as he held out his hand to her.

"Up you go."

Instead of hesitating or thinking, she placed her hands in his and allowed him to lift her to her feet. "What should I do?" she asked, looking first at him, then down at the spring-fed pool, and back to him.

"Let's get this shirt off first," he suggested, very gently and softly. Slowly, he reached for the buttons, released each one, and sensing no resistance, pushed the shirt off her shoulders. There he trapped her arms to her sides by the shirt itself. Holding her thus so, he leaned down and sweetly kissed the side of neck.

Goose bumps rose on her arms, and she swayed a tiny bit and lowered her lids halfway. She waited—docile, curious, enraptured. Complying with his silent orders, she lifted each arm from its sleeve while he tugged it away from her body, pulled it all the way out of her skirt, and discarded it on the rock. Now she only wore the skimpy lawn chemise, trimmed in rows of lace.

In short order he sat her down, removed her boots and stockings, stood her up, and pulled down the skirt. When she stepped out of it, he moved back one step and stared with hooded eyes, up and down, at her near-naked body, clad only in soft, white cotton underclothes.

"Now what?" she whispered.

"Now, we jump in the water." He grinned, causing the deep dimple to appear.

That got her attention. "Oh, no, no. I can't do that. May I go in a little at a time?"

"Okay, sure. Follow me." He led her down to the water by choosing a path that wound around small boulders and plants.

Cynthia's bare feet were soft and tender. Every so often, she would utter a slight sound but did not allow the mild pain to stop her. In a couple of spots he stopped, turned around, and lifted her over some growth that might stick her feet or rocks that might cut into her skin.

At the edge of the water, she peered in but stayed on dry ground. Without warning, she saw a blur and heard a big splash. Ricardo had dived right in, leaving her there on the bank. He disappeared for a minute or two, and she began to worry, but his head suddenly popped up in front of her, a few feet from the edge. She laughed.

"Walk in. Slow like. It's shallow for only a few feet, and then it tapers off quickly. I'm right here. I'll always catch you."

Cynthia experienced a surge of happiness. She knew without a doubt that he would do as he said— keep her safe, hold her up if she needed support, and protect her at all costs. The revelation brought forth a new feeling. She fell in love with her husband.

"Come on, sweetheart. All you have to do is walk toward me. You don't need to jump or fall or anything. Come on, now." Ricardo grinned widely as she daintily dipped one toe into the water.

"It's very cold. How do you stand it?"

"It's not really. The temperature's pretty much the same year 'round. It feels warm on a cold day. Cold on a hot day. It's all relative."

"Do you come here in the winter?"

"Cy-y-ynthia? You're procrastinating," he teased in a singsong voice. "Come on. Look, I can stand up." He demonstrated, but he had to raise his chin to keep his mouth out of the water.

"You promise you won't let me go under? Please don't do anything scary. Will you promise?"

"Yes, I promise. Cross my heart and hope to die."

"Does every child in America know that saying?"

He laughed. "Man, I've never seen such a coward. How many excuses can you make up?"

Without warning, she gave a little jump and fell on him. He caught her all right, but off-balance, which caused him to falter and fall back. Both of them drifted downward through the cool, clear water.

During the ten or so seconds they were under water, Ricardo opened his eyes to watch Cynthia. She clenched her eyes shut and rolled her lips inward and kept them sealed. Otherwise, she did not panic nor fight him. He kept a firm hold around her waist and kicked them both upwards. When they broke the surface of the water, she sputtered and coughed, opened her eyes, and laughed. A thrill raced through his body.

"My land! I've never had such an experience! At first, I thought I would die! But then, I felt your hands on me, and I knew I was safe. The sensation was...so exhilarating. Oh, Ricardo! It was so fine..."

He cut off her exuberant tale with a gentle kiss. Slowly, he allowed them to drift downward, but this time, he controlled the descent by kicking his feet. She kept her mouth on his, open to him, and kissed him back. When they surfaced the second time, she was subdued and her eyes were riveted on his.

He wondered how she would react when she climaxed. He hoped and fervently prayed that she would exhibit the same, uninhibited rush of joy.

For the next several minutes, he kept them together, body to body, with her a little higher than his head. That way, he could keep a firm grip around her waist. Around and around they turned, as if they danced suspended, a floating twosome, joined in body and heart.

Cautiously, he tenderly nipped at the swell of one breast. Instead of pulling away, she pushed toward him. So, he moved enough to kiss her breast, first near the breastbone, and next on the nipple through the thin, wet fabric. He felt her body lose all elasticity. She became a rag doll, barely hanging on to him, rolling her head back with her eyes closed.

He saw a desirable woman. He saw her as his wife, his partner, his companion. Most of all, he felt the sensation of...falling under her spell.

Chapter Nine

The afternoon was changing to evening, but the sun still shone brightly. Felicitas became tired and thirsty, but she did not stop to drink nor rest.

The horse was exhausted, because Felicitas had relentlessly spurred the pretty mare toward the goal. She knew necessity would force her to bring Princess to a halt soon, before she harmed her loyal mount. However, she wanted to cover just a few more miles.

During the ride, she plotted and planned. Suppose she did not find them until after the consummation? Could she realistically announce the pair had only been preparing for the act, but she was able to stop them from having relations? She had to do something, anything, to stop her son from truly being married to Cynthia Harrington.

The girl was so wrong for Ricardo. Starr was the perfect match for him, and she thought they had always known someday they would form a union. But no, suddenly without prior notification, he brought the other woman into their lives. Why? Why, in heaven's name would he marry such a person? Cynthia Harrington was the perfect lady and model daughter, presumably, but too soft, too ignorant, and quite inappropriate.

The girl knew nothing of the western part of the state. She was clueless concerning ranching, horses, and cattle. What good would she be? She could never be a partner with her son, but Starr could. Starr...

Without warning, Princess stumbled a little.

Pulled from her musings, Felicitas became fully alert, her heart pounding with adrenalin. She wasn't certain what had happened. Maybe the mare stepped in a hole or hit a rock. Frightened, she drew back on the reins in order to bring the mount under control. The horse stumbled again, though, jerked sideways, righted itself, and reared with front hooves pawing the air.

Felicitas frantically struggled to hold her seat. She grasped futilely for the mane, but could not get a good hold. Princess brought her front legs down hard and stiff, which caused Felicitas to pitch forward with great force. She flew over the horse's head with arms flailing and heart beating completely out of control. Her head cracked on an embedded rock, one arm crumpled under her body, and one leg bent as she hit the hard packed earth.

She lay still as death on the baked soil. She struggled to remain conscious. The hot sun would blaze for a few more hours. Bees and flies buzzed around her prone form. A lizard scrambled over a nearby rock.

Princess trotted away a few feet. She stood still, panted, and huffed, catching her own breath, regaining her equilibrium. She stomped one foot twice, snorted, and shook her mane. The dumb animal sniffed out some sweet grass close by, lowered her head, and began to eat.

Sheer hatred kept Felicitas conscious. *I will survive. I will not meet death on this day.* But her eyes closed against her will.

****

"I'm starving. I don't suppose you have anything to eat, do you?" Cynthia said.

Ricardo looked to his wife. She lay beside him on the flat rock, drying their bodies and the scant clothing they wore. They had romped and played for two hours, becoming acquainted with each other's bodies, as well as learning the other's personality. They barely knew each other, but the revelations today had opened a completely new world for them.

Ricardo had purposefully refrained from making aggressive overtures to Cynthia. He wanted the time to be right, and he enjoyed playing with her. She actually learned to swim a little, and she was a good student, so serious and determined. And her laugh. He felt he would never tire of it, for she held nothing back when she was truly amused.

"I have a suggestion."

"You do?" she asked. "What? Does it include food?"

"Yep. What would you think if I told you we have a cabin nearby, clean and neat, outfitted with food, coffee, and a lantern?"

She sat up cross-legged and peered at him. "What are you talking about?" she asked seriously.

"Our wedding chateau, ready and waiting for the happy bride and groom to stay there for the night. Sleep together, sweetheart. Our first night together."

"Ohhh," she whispered. "Are you serious, Ricardo? Did you plan all this?"

He smiled, but it was with a little nervousness, fearful she would reject his idea of an idyllic night together. "Actually, I did. I was coming to kidnap you this morning, when I saw you walking away from your little house. Perfect timing, don't you think?"

"Meant to be." She smiled back.

"Okay, then. Let's get dressed and ride over. It's not far. We can even come back over here, if we want to bathe and cool off."

The contented couple meandered over to the cabin where it sat under a grove of live oaks. It was on a rise, so they could watch the sunset later. When they arrived at the door, Ricardo gallantly carried her over the threshold and set her on her feet just inside.

"How lovely. Flowers?" She spun on her toes to face him. "That is so sweet and thoughtful. And food! Now, that's exactly what I want. Shall we eat?"

"Sure. I'll open the packages. You just sit."

"Who did all this? The table is even set and with good napkins, too. Who lives here?"

Ricardo continued his work as he explained. "This is actually a line shack. We have several scattered around the range. They're used some during roundup, but mostly they're for lone wranglers who are herding or scouting. Believe me, all these pretties and this food are not here waiting for them. I had a couple of my men do this. Didn't set too well with them, though," he said. "Thought it was sissy stuff and wanted no part of picking flowers and setting a table."

There was that laugh. She clapped her pretty hands together once and clasped them prayer-like under her chin. "I can just see them. Going out and picking these little daises. So," she said coyly, "you were going to kidnap me. Really?"

"Really." He winked as he folded back brown paper to reveal sliced roast beef.

"How? What was your plan?"

"I didn't have a plan, because I wasn't certain how to go about it. Actually, you set the plan in motion yourself."

"By walking toward the barn?"

"Yep," he nodded, and paused to open a package of buttered bread. "I saw that you were dressed to ride, so I took advantage. Clever of me, huh?"

Cynthia and Ricardo sat at the decorated rustic table and without preamble, dug into the food. In addition to the sandwiches, tomatoes, and bread and butter pickles, there were also peaches. He found the small bottle of wine he asked for and poured it into old metal drinking cups that stayed at the cabin. Without apology for the crude dishware, he raised his to make a toast.

"To you, sweetheart. God blessed me the day I found you. *Mi querida. Mi esposa.*"

"Ohhh. *Si. Muchas gracias,*" she answered with a sweet smile.

Ricardo chuckled and raised one eyebrow, clinked his cup to hers, and drank. "So, you speak Spanish?"

"Me? Heavens no. I know only those words. Did I say them correctly?"

"Perfect, my girl."

"So, what did you say to me?"

Softly, he said, "My darling. My wife."

He watched as the bright blue of her eyes darkened, and her breath came quick and shallow. She raised her small hand and placed it on her chest. The diamond in the ring caught the lantern light and sparkled bright and clear.

Ricardo leaned across the table and curled his fingers around the hand at her breast. Carefully, he brought it to his lips and kissed her fingertips. He never looked away from her eyes. She appeared hypnotized.

Without moving from his chair, he tugged on her hand and motioned with his head for her to come to him. She did just as he asked. When she reached his side, he pulled her to his lap.

With one arm around her waist, he picked up his cup. "More wine?"

"Yes, please," she answered so quietly he could barely hear her.

With her help, they filled their cups once more. "Care for a peach?"

"Yes, please."

He selected the perfect ripe peach, rolled it around in his hand to remove the fuzz, and held it to her mouth. With dainty precision, she wrapped her luscious lips around the juicy fruit and sunk her pearl white teeth into the flesh. A few drops of nectar ran down her chin.

Cynthia raised her hand to catch the juice, but Ricardo stopped her.

"Allow me." And he proceeded to lick and suck her chin and mouth—of course, to remove the dribbles.

Next, he picked up one full cup of wine. "Drink?" She nodded. He held the cup to her mouth as she took two sips. Without taking his eyes off her, he took two, as well.

He melded their mouths together before either could completely swallow the wine. The taste was truly the nectar of the gods. The sweetness of her mouth rivaled the peach and the grape.

The ritual continued a few more times until both were drunk, not on wine, but on the essence of each other. His hands roamed over her round, firm breasts and into her blouse, caressing the soft globes the same way as he had the ripe peach.

Ricardo stood with her in his arms and carried her to their marriage bed. He gently lay her down and began to unbutton the shirt as he had by the spring. He raised her shoulders enough to remove the garment. All the while, she kept her eyes riveted on his, as if waiting to see what came next. With great care, Ricardo showed her all night. Carefully and slowly, he moved from one area of her body to another, and taught her to do the same to him.

At dawn, Cynthia awoke in Ricardo's arms. Her hands moved over his flesh, and once more, their bodies joined.

"Good morning, my darling," Cynthia purred.

"And good morning to you, sweetheart. Did you sleep well?"

"Mmmm," she murmured as she stretched and

yawned. "The little I slept was nice." She rolled toward him to gaze adoringly into his glittering black eyes, and at the same time raised one finger to place in the dimple beside his smiling mouth. "I wanted to do that the very first day I met you. Did you know that?"

"You did? That's a surprise. I thought you detested me, the way you flounced around and made demands."

She giggled. "I did not flounce. I don't even know what that is."

"Yes, you do, oh, yes, you do." He began to tickle her ribs until she was limp from laughing.

"Oh, stop! Ohhh, how fun. You know something. I've never been tickled in my life."

"What? That's hard to believe. Every child gets tickled by his parents or somebody."

"Not me. I had no mother, and Father isn't the sort of man to play. He just doesn't know how. I think I was grown up at age five. That's how he reared me, to be ladylike and proper at all times. The only time I could romp and run was at church picnics that lasted all day, where the children played for hours."

"The ranch must be quite a shock for you, Cynthia. I hope you can learn to like it."

"Oh, Ricardo, I plan on it. I must admit, the first two days were trying, and truthfully, these wide-open spaces are daunting. And to be so far away from a town or city, well, that will take some getting used to."

"Remember I told you we go twice a year to San Antonio. That doesn't seem like much, I guess, but the trips are really holidays—one in the spring and one in the winter. We stay one or two weeks, depending on the amount of work back home. We shop, attend plays and musicales, and eat in the finest restaurants we can find."

"You say 'we.' Whom do you mean?"

"Mother and Father."

"Just the three of you?"

At this, Ricardo looked away and hesitated to answer. "Sometimes, the Hidalgos would be with us, at least, some of them."

She asked no more, because she knew the answer already.

"Well, anyway," she said brightly, "I'll finally get to see San Antonio. To think I had to marry you to go."

Ricardo laughed lightly and gave her one more kiss before rising from the bed.

****

They rode at a slow pace for an hour before taking a rest stop. Ricardo knew every spot of running water on the enormous acreage.

"How do you know where every little thing is on the land?" she asked as they stood by the stream.

"The ranch was my playhouse. My friends were children of our hands, and we always had quite a few. We went to school together in the chapel, taught by Mother and some other woman who might be capable. Father always took me with him when he could, teaching and explaining everything. I learned more from him than I did from books."

"You seem quite educated."

"I know enough. I attended school in Boston for two years at ages sixteen and seventeen. It was a boys' school, Catholic, of course. There's where I learned to act the gentleman. Do I still have it?" he said with a grin.

"Oh, yes, when you want to show off. At times, you seem to be two separate people."

"What about you?"

"Of course, I went east to school, for three years. Like you, it was a church school, and for girls only. Father had already ingrained in me to be a lady.

When his expertise failed, he hired a tutor for home schooling, but Maria was the one who mothered me. Maria and I weren't necessarily close physically, no kisses, no hugs, but she taught me about being a woman and all that. She was a surrogate mother, I suppose."

"Well, we'd better ride. We should be back by noon."

Almost another hour passed, when Cynthia pointed to the right. "Ricardo. What is that?"

"What? Where?"

"Over there by those scrubby bushes. You see? It looks almost like a person."

Ricardo turned toward the form on the ground, and when they were closer, he moaned. "Oh, God, no. What the *devil*?"

Felicitas lay in a heap on the hot, dry ground. Her face was sunburned and her lips were dry and cracked. Ants crawled over her, and flies buzzed around. She did not move.

Ricardo jumped from Diablo before the horse stopped and left Cynthia to dismount on her own. Unsure how to do it by herself, she was slow. By the time she arrived at the woman's side, Ricardo knelt next to Felicitas, feeling for a pulse or heartbeat.

"Is she alive, Ricardo?"

"I think, but barely. See what you think. I need to get the canteen."

Cynthia knelt, felt for the pulse, and found a faint, thready beat. Clearly, his mother was in distress. Ricardo returned, and she sat back on her heels. "She's in trouble, Ricardo. She's barely breathing and her pulse is very weak. I'm not an expert, but she seems almost gone." Her sympathetic eyes looked into his.

Ricardo's mouth was grim, set in a hard line, as he stared at his mother. "Do you have a handkerchief?"

107

"Yes, here in my pocket. What should I do?"

"Take the canteen, wet it down, and wipe her face. Then, dampen her wrists."

Cynthia did as he instructed, as Ricardo checked his mother the best he could. At last, he made a decision.

"Sweetheart, listen carefully." He knelt, sat on his boot heels, and took both her hands in his. "I must go for help and bring a wagon. The ranch is maybe an hour-and-a-half away if I ride hard. You must stay here, Cynthia. Do you understand?"

"Wha...no! No, no! Don't leave me here! You can't, Ricardo. My lord, how can I?" she gripped his hands and brought them to her breast.

"Shhh, now listen to me. This is the only way. Look at her, sweetheart. She's hit her head—very hard. I think an arm is broken, and maybe a leg. I don't know. She's in a lot of trouble. This is the only solution."

Cynthia whispered, "Oh, please, don't leave me. I'm scared, Ricardo."

"Sweetheart, you can be strong. I know you can. If you live on the ranch with me, there'll be times when you have to travel the hard road. You've got to pull yourself together and do this. Understand?"

Her voice dropped low, as she pushed her face close to his. "If you leave me here alone, I'll never forgive you."

Ricardo wiped his hand down his face. His voice became stern. "Now, listen. You're alive and strong. Mother is very hurt and may die. My first duty is to save her. If you were in the same situation, what would you do?"

Cynthia covered her face with her hands. Soon, however, she swiped her hands down her eyes and mouth, took a deep breath, and calmly said, "All right, tell me what to do."

"Fine. Now, here's the canteen. It's full. Use it

sparingly. Dampen your handkerchief a very little and wipe it on her lips and forehead. Not much, though, because you need to sip a little once in a while, but go easy on it. All right?"

She nodded.

"Now, don't move her, not at all. I'm going to give you the extra shirt I carry in my saddlebag. Take off your hat and drape the shirt over your head to form a cover from the sun. Just stay as still as you can. Conserve your water and your strength. It'll be three hours at the least. Now, sit tight."

Ricardo walked around the area and picked up rocks big enough to hold in one hand. He made a pile beside his wife.

"What are those for?" she asked suspiciously.

"These are for varmints. Maybe coyotes, buzzards, or even snakes. Think before you use one, but usually if you throw a rock, the animal will scurry away. Remember, they're afraid of you."

"Well, of course." She snorted.

This caused Ricardo to chuckle. "You'll do just fine, sweetheart. I promise on my life that I will return for you. One more thing, here's the pistol I carry in my saddlebag. Take it."

After holding it and listening to his quick instructions, he explained that she had six bullets. "You most likely won't need to use any, but if you do, take aim as carefully as you can before you pull the trigger. Think if a rock would do as well."

"Oh, no, please, no," she moaned. "Don't leave me here."

"Look at me. Look at me! That's better. Hold on, sweetheart, and remember I'll be back. I promise." With that, he kissed her and ran to Diablo. In only a moment, he was gone.

Chapter Ten

The silence was deafening. She watched her new husband ride away until he was a mere speck on the horizon. Before he completely vanished from her sight, the sound of Diablo's thudding hooves were even too distant to hear. All that remained was a buzzing in her ears.

Ricardo had talked to Diablo before he mounted, and when he was astride, he leaned forward to pat and rub the horse's neck, urging the stallion to run his fastest. In a split second, he kicked the belly of the horse with great force and rode away in a full gallop.

First, she worried that his horse might stumble somewhere out there, Ricardo would fall to the earth, and no one would know. Then the thought came to her that perhaps Rafaelo and his *vaqueros* were out in full force to locate Felicitas. After all, she'd probably left the ranch close to twenty-four hours ago.

Three hours. How could she endure it? The heat was unbearable out here. She gazed longingly at nearby shade. Nearby? Well, probably the grove of trees was a mile or so away. Judging distance was difficult. All she knew was that she couldn't move from this spot.

Uncharacteristic anger welled up in her breast. Why would Felicitas do such a foolish thing? What was she thinking? Where was she going? In her heart, Cynthia knew it all had something to do with her marriage to Ricardo. She recalled the intense hatred that emanated from Felicitas, as the woman told her she did not belong here, and her son had already decided he'd made a mistake by marrying an outsider.

At the time, Cynthia whole-heartedly believed the woman, because her new husband had withheld himself from the marriage bed. Then later Ricardo acted otherwise, even kidnapped her to be alone, and had declared his feelings for her. So, whom to believe?

Today, Cynthia believed Ricardo. If he'd felt as his mother described, he would not have gone to the trouble of preparing a bridal bower for her. Oh, it had been so lovely. The cool, clean springs, the food and wine and the night together. Today she was truly a wife. She and Ricardo were as one.

She gazed up at the sky to determine the position of the sun. What she saw frightened her. Vultures circled overhead. Big, black vultures! Did the vile creatures think Felicitas was dead?

Hastily, she positioned herself on her knees, so she could check her mother-in-law. The heartbeat and pulse were still there, but so weak and slow that Cynthia began to shake. Suppose she died right here, and she had to sit beside the body until someone came. *Oh, no, no, no.*

She poured a tiny amount of water on her lace handkerchief and dabbed at Felicitas' still, dry lips. She squeezed a few drops of water into her mouth. Felicitas did not swallow. Again, she squeezed a few more drops. She swallowed.

Cynthia became quite encouraged and experienced a kind of triumph she'd never felt. This woman would not die; she would keep her alive.

Felicitas moaned and vainly tried to move. Before Cynthia could react, she had returned to her immobile state.

Cynthia removed the shirt she had draped over

her own head. How could she make an umbrella for Felicitas? She glanced around and saw dead twigs around each bush in the vicinity. They were spindly, but perhaps she could locate enough to stick upright in the ground.

The project took only a little while. She formed a half-circle of short twigs around the unconscious woman's head and draped the collar and shoulders of the shirt over them. The twigs held it up off her face a few inches, and provided wonderful, cooling shade. She pulled the body of the shirt over Felicitas' upper body as loosely as she could manage.

Cynthia replaced her own hat, pulled it low, and turned up her collar to cover her neck. She pulled out her shirt from the skirt and removed her hot, leather belt. That was better. Carefully, she searched for ants crawling on Felicitas and shooed flies away. Occasionally, a lizard came near, but when it realized its mistake, turned and quickly scurried away.

She felt so drowsy and lethargic. The night had been active, so she missed a few hours of sleep. She sat and bent up her knees, circled them with her arms, and lay her head down. Blissful sleep came quickly.

A horrid odor awoke her. She jerked up her head and there in a circle around her and Felicitas were a number of enormous vultures, not twenty feet away. Some spread their wings for ventilation, some stared at her with their tiny, black eyes, and others shifted back and forth on their big, ugly feet.

Bile rose to her throat, and cold fear settled in her lower intestine. These hideous creatures fed on dead bodies...didn't they? They smelled like rotting flesh, and the horrid, terrifying creatures surrounded her and Felicitas.

Before she took any action, she wondered if the giant birds attacked people or animals. If they were scavengers, wouldn't they wait until something was dead? Surely, they didn't attack and kill. Holding her breath, both from the smell and fear, she slowly and carefully stood. Each bird took some notice of her movement; a few moved back; others sidestepped, but none flew away.

She slowly leaned down and picked up two rocks. With all her might, she hurled one to the right and one to the left, as fast and hard as she could. The birds scattered in confusion, not knowing the location of the movement. Every one of them flew high and away.

Cynthia dropped to her knees and lowered her head. She shook and cried, and then began to laugh. If anyone heard her, he might think she had gone mad, but in reality, she was elated. She had fought a battle and won! Now, if only they stayed away.

Time passed, but Cynthia had no way of knowing how long. She thought the three hours should be up but maybe not. Worse, perhaps the ride there and back with a wagon would take longer than Ricardo's estimate.

Her stomach rumbled, her skin itched, and she was very hot and thirsty. She tried to ration the water very carefully, because she wanted enough to cool off Felicitas' face and dampen her lips. Felicitas hadn't swallowed anymore since those first few drops.

Her greatest fear, now that the vultures had flown away, was Felicitas would die. If she died, Cynthia would feel guilty, as if she were responsible because Ricardo stole her away. The woman would never have been out here, except to follow her son and his unsuitable wife.

A movement to her right caught her eye. She stood in order to determine exactly what it was. A horse! There was a saddled and bridled mare just over there, walking aimlessly, it seemed. Poor thing!

She was looking for her mistress—whom she threw, by the way.

Cynthia tried to whistle, but she never learned how. That was something boys did, not sweet little girls. She called with a kissing sound. That usually worked with Little Dixie, but it didn't seem to gain this horse's attention. However, she did look toward Cynthia.

Keeping her eyes on the mare, she walked slowly toward her with her hand outstretched. She had nothing in it, but perhaps the mare was used to eating sugar or an apple from Felicitas' hand. She continued the kissing sound. The mare shook her mane and snorted but did not turn away.

When she was no farther than a few yards away, the horse walked to Cynthia with her head down, as though she were ashamed of herself.

"There, there, girl. You're all right. You did nothing wrong, baby girl, so don't feel badly. I'm here to help you. Come to me, girl. Come on now." The mare walked right to her.

Cynthia took hold of the bridle and led her back to Felicitas. She tied the reins to the nearest bush and the horse stood still and docile, as if she were oh, so glad to be found. Cynthia was almost certain she would stay right there.

The grandest thing about this new triumph was the full canteen hanging off the saddle. Cynthia almost wept. There were no saddlebags, so the water was all she found. She opened the cap and drank her fill.

Again, Cynthia sat next to Felicitas and performed the same rituals, over and over, taking care of her patient. Search for ants. Wet her lips and bathe her face. Check her pulse and heartbeat. She still lived.

The woman must be made of steel. She's very strong, and I'm sure, iron-willed.

Finally, she heard a welcome sound. Horses' hooves hit the hard ground, and a wagon rumbled over the uneven terrain. She stood and waited quite impatiently.

She saw Ricardo break away from the group and ride hard toward her. She ran out to him, and he dismounted on the run to meet her. Oh, what joy! His strong arms surrounded her and lifted her off her feet. He kissed her hard and hugged her tightly. He was shaking.

"Sweetheart, sweetheart. How did you do? You don't know how worried I was about the both of you."

"I'm fine, darling, just fine. Only weary."

As they walked to Felicitas, he asked, "How's Mother?"

"Not well."

Before they arrived at the unconscious woman, he turned to her and smiled. "Well, well, look at you. A tent to shade Mother. You're very resourceful, and you captured Princess. That's good. You did a fine job, Mrs. Romero."

Flushing slightly, she said a modest, "Thank you," in order to hide her great pride.

"Any real problems?" he asked as they resumed walking.

"One or two. I'll tell you all about it later. Let's see to your mother."

In half an hour, they had Felicitas in the wagon. Sarah, the foreman's wife, suggested they nail a sturdy blanket over the sides of the wagon, leaving a dip in the middle to form a body-sized sling. Then, she said, they should work a sheet under her, and as much as possible, keep her in the same position, then lay her in the sling.

Ricardo told Cynthia to ride in back and rest on a folded blanket. Another man would be there to watch Felicitas.

Sarah had thought to send fresh water and a

bundle of food for Cynthia. Gratefully, she allowed Ricardo to tell her to sit there, do this, eat that, and rest here. She didn't mind at all that he took care of her.

The ranch house was a welcome sight, but still did not look or feel like home to Cynthia. A feeling of being a misplaced person almost overcame her when the entourage arrived back at the ranch. Everyone hovered around and over Felicitas, and no one paid her much attention.

Sarah and Annie took charge of the injured woman and shooed everyone else out of the room. Rafaelo was beside himself with fear, but the women thought she would live. He demanded to know what they would do, so they patiently explained that they would cut off her clothes and remove them gently, and bathe her body the best they could. They would make her as comfortable as possible. They would not move her from her original position. Ricardo tried his best to calm his father's anxieties.

Paulo rode to Rico Springs immediately after Ricardo arrived at the headquarters yard and demanded someone race to town to fetch the doctor. All anyone could do now was to wait for Doc Sawyers to arrive.

In the meantime, Cynthia stood about for several minutes, not knowing exactly what she could do, or if she should do anything at all. Others now seemed to be in charge, even though it was *she* who had saved her mother-in-law's life.

Ricardo found his bride in the kitchen with Consuelo. She sat alone at the table, dirty, sunburned, and still thirsty. The cook had made tea for her, and she sat with her hands wrapped around the comforting cup of sweet liquid.

"Sweetheart, why don't you go bathe and change into clean, more comfortable clothes? Maybe lie down for a while. Take a nap. I know you're exhausted."

"Yes. All right," she replied listlessly.

He nodded once and walked back to the study to wait with his father.

Sometime later, Ricardo went back to the kitchen, because he could not locate his wife.

"Consuelo, where is my Mrs. Romero? I told her to clean up, but I can't find her."

"Why, she is over to her little house, sir. You know, where her belongings are. She said she would go draw water from the well and bathe. Her clothes are there."

The situation finally dawned on him. "Damn!" he said, and stalked out the door and across the open expanse to the third little house from the end.

When he walked in, she was nowhere to be found. He looked in the lean-to on the back. The round galvanized tub there had about two inches of water in it. He saw her approaching the back door, carrying a bucket of well water with both hands. She was struggling.

"Hell, Cynthia. What do you think you're doing?"

She stared at him for only a moment; then she tossed the bucket as far as she could, which was only a very short distance, and water splashed out and onto her boots. She glared at him. Her blood obviously boiling as she yelled. "What do you think? I'm drawing water for my bath. And it's...da...darn hard! And look at what you made me do. You made me drop my bucket. You...you sorry excuse for a husband."

Before his very eyes, she dropped to the ground and bent double with her head in the dirt. She began to sob uncontrollably and pounded the ground with one fist. "I hate you!"

"Whoa, whoa," he said very gently, as he hunkered down in front of her. He reached for her and pulled her up as he stood. "Up you go, now." His arms encircled her and he pushed her head to his shoulder. "Shhh, now sweetheart. I'm sorry, so sorry. Shhh, don't cry now. I'll make it all better. Now come with me."

She looked so tired, so spent. How could he have allowed so much to go wrong in such a little time? She was right. He wasn't doing his part.

"I'm sorry, too, Ricardo," she whispered. "I just don't know what to do. I don't know where I belong anymore."

"I'll show you. First, you're coming home, to the house, your real home. Not this little cabin. You won't live here anymore. Come on now."

When they arrived back in the kitchen, Consuelo hovered over Cynthia, patting and hugging her. She sat her down at the table and placed a plate of roasted chicken, mashed potatoes and gravy, and green beans. "You sit right there, *chica,* and Consuelo will take care of you."

****

Cynthia was pleased with the suite of rooms, which belonged to her and Ricardo. Now that she was clean and comfortable and rested, she lay propped up on soft pillows and studied the bedroom. The bed obviously came from the east somewhere. It was a high, four-poster made of cherry wood; something one might see in Boston townhouses or Chicago mansions. A matching armoire took up half of one wall. It was grand in scale, with rich brass pulls and carved doors. It had a graceful bowed front, completing a work of art. The best part was the two halves—one for her and one for her husband.

On the opposite wall was a tall, footed chest that had six deep drawers. Each side of the bed had its own round cherry wood table on graceful legs, and a personal lamp. The colors were rich burgundy in various hues, coordinated with cream silk pillows and a tufted, fringed coverlet. Thick French rugs were on each side, too, so she could stand on warm wool when getting in and out of bed.

Attached to the bedroom was a study or sitting room. She had a small pretty desk and chair in front of the window, and there were two soft armchairs side by side in front of a small fireplace. A luxurious chaise lounge occupied one corner, and it had a backdrop of tall potted plants.

The most wonderful thing was a fully equipped water closet for them. Next to that was a dressing room, complete with dresser and standing mirror. All of it was heavenly.

Cynthia loved pretty things, and someone had gone to a great deal of work to make this suite special. She hadn't walked through the entire house yet, but what she had seen did not compare to the opulence of this room.

She tried in vain to ignore the thought that crept into her mind. This room had been prepared for Ricardo and Starr Hidalgo. Without a doubt, she knew Felicitas counted the days when they would marry, and she would have the daughter-in-law she wanted. Was that all there was to it? It seemed as if Felicitas had gone far beyond a wish for her son to marry well. Perhaps the real reasons were a mystery.

Sometime after midnight, Ricardo came to bed and even though she slept lightly, he rolled toward her and drew her into his arms. His naked body was hard, smooth, and enticing, so she had no defense against his warm wet kisses.

Without a word between them, he made love first to her mouth, then to her swollen breasts, and at last entered her slowly but firmly. In her half-awake state, the sensations magnified, as if she were in a sensuous, intense dream. In that heightened awareness, Cynthia experienced her first orgasm, and as the spasms began to abate, she sobbed onto his shoulder.

Ricardo silently thanked God for his wife, so beautiful and pure, and best of all, she was responsive to his lovemaking. She had truly experienced a climax. The first couplings at the cabin had not been satisfactory for her, but he thought probably that was normal for an untouched female. Her body needed to be attuned and awakened to sensuality, and now he knew he was a fortunate man.

It had been so different with Starr. He had not been her first lover, and he always wondered if he were not the only one during all those years. Now, he marveled she had not gotten with child, but she always told him not to worry.

The last thing she said to him the other day before she went home still rang in his ears. "Don't worry, Rick, your honeymoon won't last long, but I'll still be around. Either I'll find you, or you can find me." She fully expected to continue their trysts. When she finally realized he was finished with her, there would be hell to pay. Starr was too proud and sure of herself to allow another woman take that which she thought was hers.

A distant sound of hoof beats floated through the open window. Surely, it was Doc Sawyers and Paulo. He rolled from the bed, stood naked there, and leaned his hands on the windowsill. The summer breeze felt good to his heated body.

He glanced over at his wife, and through the faint light from early dawn, he saw her sprawled on her back, all the cover kicked back. She had one arm bent up near her head, and the other lay across her stomach. One leg was straight, and one bent, with the knee touching the other. She wore a beautiful embroidered summer shift of soft batiste, just modest enough to be sensual. And she slept so peacefully. He had definitely made the right choice.

Chapter Eleven

Some commotion woke Cynthia, but she had no intention of jumping from the bed and rushing around to find the source. Ricardo had leaned over the bed some while ago and kissed her good morning, but it did not look as though the sun were up to her. He had been fully dressed and shaved, so he slipped out the door leaving her to doze again.

The last two days had been very trying, but she understood the necessity of taking care of problems when they appeared and especially if someone were hurt. She arose at last, performed her morning ablutions, and dressed. She rather imagined her day would pass here in the house, possibly with some assigned duty, and perhaps just waiting. Being in the house all day required a simple dress and comfortable lace-up shoes.

She fully appreciated the small dressing area she had. The dresser had a mirror attached to the back, and a matching chair. On the dresser top were all her familiar personal items, carefully arranged on the polished surface. Someone had placed a crocheted doily there to protect the wood from her jars and boxes and porcelain figurines.

When she had her thick hair coiled on top of her head in a proper arrangement, she proceeded out the door and down a short hallway. Their rooms formed a back wing, so she had to walk past all the other bedrooms in the house.

From behind one closed door, she heard murmured voices, perhaps two, both male, she thought.

The kitchen was the hub of activity. Consuelo, of course, was cooking. Ricardo stood when she entered, led her to a chair next to him, and kissed her on the cheek before he resumed his seat. Sarah and Annie were there, as well. Rafaelo was missing.

"Where's your father?" she asked Ricardo.

"He's with Mother and Doc Sawyers. Did you hear the doc arrive around five this morning?"

She shook her head and looked askance at him, for she knew full well what he was implying. The devil. He grinned at her, displaying his white, even teeth and the deep, oh, so alluring dimple.

Instead of responding to his teasing, she turned to Sarah and Annie. "How are you two doing this morning? It's good to see you. Do I thank you for unpacking and arranging my things?"

"We worked on it, and your husband had some hand in it. It was our pleasure." Sarah leaned closer and almost whispered. "You have some very beautiful clothes, Mrs. Romero."

"Oh, thank you. I've already learned many of them are inappropriate for ranch living, but I'll get the gist of it soon. And didn't I ask both of you to call me Cynthia?"

Both women looked to Ricardo for the answer. Somehow, Cynthia knew Felicitas would never allow these wives of ranch hands to use her first name. When she saw Ricardo smile and nod, her heart felt glad.

"Actually, ladies, whatever my wife says or wants is her business. There are no strict rules around here." He heard Consuelo snort. "Or," he amended with another grin, "I didn't think there were."

At that, everyone laughed and felt at ease. Consuelo placed a plate of eggs and biscuits in front of Cynthia, along with a cup of tea.

When they all resumed eating breakfast, Cynthia asked her husband, "What's the news of Felicitas? Is she better this morning?"

"Not really, but we're not discouraged by it. Doc Sawyers and Father are at this moment discussing possible procedures."

"Like what? What does she need?"

Ricardo cleared his throat. "I'll tell you later."

"Certainly," she agreed, not really minding. She could wait to hear the details. "So, what can I do?" She buttered her biscuit and smeared jam on it.

"You, my darling wife, will be the lady of the house. That's what. You have to take over for Mother, as much as you can. Doc believes she'll have a very long convalescence."

Cynthia gulped, feeling the biscuit form a lump in her throat. What on earth does Felicitas do? "Well, I shall be happy to do everything I can, but I'll need guidance. I have no idea what your mother does, Ricardo."

"One of her duties is to keep the ranch books. She enters all transactions and keeps everything balanced. She also keeps a running list of supplies we need, either to order or buy in Rico Springs. We do that about once a month."

Cynthia swallowed hard. Books. Numbers and such. That was her weakest subject in school, and she knew she had no aptitude to do accounting work. She couldn't add two numbers twice and get the same answer. Make lists of supplies? Well, she might do that, but where to start? She inwardly cringed; frightened that Ricardo would expect her to do so much.

"Is that all of her duties?"

"No, she runs the household. She and Consuelo work quite well together, and between them, they keep the pantry stocked, plan meals, and oversee the laundry and housecleaning."

"Who does the laundry?" she asked warily.

"We have a laundry, manned by a couple who do only that. They live in the last house over there." He pointed in the general direction of the worker's houses.

"Oh."

"They both work all day. A ranch this size has a mountain of dirty clothing and bedding. The laundry is over behind the commissary."

"Who does the housecleaning?" she asked with trepidation, for fear that he would ask her to clean. She never did that in her entire life. Maria cleaned. She didn't.

"Consuelo keeps the kitchen. No one else touches her things, and that includes the floor. A Mexican couple who live in the next to last house does the remainder. Near the one you were in."

Cynthia wanted to release a sigh, but she kept it down. At least, the most dreaded chores were the responsibility of others. Okay, she could handle being mistress of the house, but she could never touch those books. She would tell him later.

"Cynthia, may I see you in our room?" Ricardo asked.

She rose from the table and followed him down the hall. When they entered the room, he quickly closed the door and gathered her in his arms. He immediately began ardent kissing and embracing. "Baby, I couldn't wait to get my hands on you. Mmm, you smell so good, so sweet, and nice."

Cynthia lost her breath with the kisses, and almost melted at his feet. He was so insistent; she stumbled from his weight pressing on her. Suddenly, she began to giggle. "Oh, stop, Ricardo, please, please!" Then she collapsed into hysterical laughter.

He stood back but held her arms and laughed with her. "I don't know what came over me. I sat there at the table and watched you butter that biscuit, and I thought of you spreading it on my chest. Then you sank your teeth into the bread, and I felt it clear to my...well, toes."

"Oh, I do adore you, Ricardo. I'm ever so glad I married you. I can't wait to really get settled and feel as if this were my home."

He kept his arms circled around her waist, molding them together from the waist down. She leaned back against his strong arms and swayed from side to side. "It's so nice here, much better than I first thought. And darling, I want to do my part to make this my home, too."

With a slight frown, Ricardo gazed down into her sweet, open face. "That's twice you said that. About this not really being your home. Is that how you feel?"

"Well, I must admit, it's all very strange, and so much has happened in only a few days. I've hardly been here, let alone become acquainted with everybody and everything. But don't worry, it'll come eventually."

The remainder of the day was tense for everyone. Ricardo decided to stay in the house, even though his men sorely needed him at the corrals. His men were quite adept, and as long as Jake Oliver reported to him, things would move along without him. He was very anxious to begin working with the mares. The sooner the breeding began the better.

At the end of a long discussion, Sarah was the one to assist Doc Sawyers. First Rafaelo wanted to be in the room, but the doctor wouldn't allow it. Ricardo held his hands up and shook his head. Not him. Cynthia was out, even though they considered her for a few moments. The logical choice all along had been Sarah.

Doc Sawyers closed the door and everyone else waited in the parlor, or the kitchen, or on the back porch. At times Ricardo left the house and walked outside, up and down the walkway, and around and around the house. The waiting was bad, because Felicitas moaned loudly and even screamed twice. Doc Sawyers had tried earlier to get laudanum down her, but she would hardly swallow anything. So, he relied on her unconscious state to do the difficult tasks.

In the end, he found that her right forearm was broken and he had to set it forcibly. After straightening it, he placed two small, narrow boards on either side and secured it to her arm. Next was the ankle. Her leg was not broken after all, but the ankle was shattered. He did the best he could in straightening it, and splinted it as he had the forearm.

Her head was a different matter. There was nothing visible to mend. A large knot was on one side of her skull, and that seemed to cause some sort of swelling which kept her unconscious. He tried his best to reassure everyone that she would wake up and show no real effects. His theory was she was unconscious and not in a coma, because in extreme pain, she had cried out, and that was a good sign. He and Sarah cleaned her whole body and tried to get her to drink something, but she barely swallowed a couple of times.

When she was at last clean and dressed in a loose, cotton gown, he allowed her husband and son to visit. Rafaelo was so distraught that all he could do was blame Ricardo.

"If you hadn't run off with your bride, and stayed where you belonged, this wouldn't have happened! What possessed you, anyway, to do such a foolish thing? Just look what you did! Your mother must have been frantic, worrying about where you were, and rode out to find you. Maybe she thought you were dead!"

"Father, that's not it," Ricardo replied in anger.

"That is utter nonsense and you know it. She never in her life rode out after me, fearing for my safety or anything else! That's not what she did!"

"Then tell me, young man, what was her intent? Tell me, if you're so damned smart!"

"Father, let's stop this right now. You're tired and upset. Come with me. Let's have some bourbon."

"No," he said petulantly, as if he were a little child. "I don't want any."

"Well, I do. Now, come on. Do it for me."

Rafaelo grudgingly obliged.

When they left the room, Doc Sawyers asked to speak with Cynthia. They went to the parlor. She had Consuelo to fetch a shot of whiskey for him.

"Thank you, child. You're very thoughtful. I want to say a few things. Ricardo told me how you cared for your mother-in-law out there in the open all those hours. I only found two ant bites. It's a wonder they didn't cover her, which might have caused a bad reaction. So, you did real well there. Also, you used your common sense when you made the covering for her head. You probably helped save her life. And he said you got her to swallow a few drops of water, and she licked her lips."

Cynthia nodded, so happy to hear praise; she could hardly maintain her serene, ladylike manner. "That's correct, sir, but she only did it once. So, I just kept wetting her lips every so often."

"Very good. Now, I understand you'll be the lady of the house, since Mrs. Romero will be out of commission. I also know you're the new bride. I offer my congratulations, by the way. Ricardo is a fine man, fair and honest. You two should get on just fine. I don't know your background or experience, but you'll be the one to see to Mrs. Romero's care. I suggest you get help, such as Sarah and Annie. They've been here many years and are good women. But they know their place, you understand, and won't overstep your authority. Ranches are like little communities with unspoken guidelines and rules. They see you as their superior."

Cynthia's stomach roiled around. She never expected to be in this sort of situation. She thought her days would be carefree and easy, just as her life at home had been. No one had ever expected anything of her. Her every need was always fulfilled. She took a deep breath.

"Doctor Sawyers, could you make a list for me? What needs to be done and when, that sort of thing? For Felicitas."

The doctor studied her face for a moment before he cleared his throat.

"Certainly, dear. Why don't we meet in an hour in the kitchen, and we'll make it together?"

****

Noontime was over, and everyone scattered to various chores and locations. Doc Sawyers returned to town. Cynthia was alone in the house with Consuelo and Felicitas.

She sat at the kitchen table with her lists. Somehow, she ended up with several. It seemed as if everyone had particular chores for her learn.

There was the one from the doctor. *Hand-bathe Mrs. R each morning. Change the cloth between her legs.* Cynthia shuddered. *Change sheets every other day or when soiled.* "Oh, Lord." *Do not leave her alone until she fully wakes.* "Well, I'm not doing all the checking by myself." *Keep the window and door open when possible. Dampen lips hourly. Try to get her to swallow.* "And on, and on, and on. I really wish they did not require this of me," she muttered.

"You talking to me, *chica?*"

She hadn't seen Consuelo enter the room. "Why do you call me that? What does it mean?"

"Oh, it's just a sweet name—for you only."

"Does it have a meaning?"

"*Si*. It means 'little girl.' That's all." She shrugged one shoulder.

Cynthia leaned back in her chair and placed her fingertips on the edge of the table cocking her head to the side. "So, you see me as a little girl? Helpless, you mean?"

"*No, por Dios*! Never! You are a well-bred young lady."

"Do you have a pet name for Felicitas?"

"No, no, never. *Perdon!*"

"Is that, 'forgive me'?"

"*Si, si.*" Consuelo twisted her hands in her apron.

Cynthia laughed, and Consuelo slowly smiled at her young mistress. "I'm teasing you, Consuelo, my friend. You know, I like *chica*. You may call me that, but not in the presence of the family. All right? Just you and me. They might not approve."

"Good, good. Now, you go over your lists, and you tell me anything I can do for you. I am very good help. I will work hard."

"I know you will."

The list Ricardo gave her was quite disturbing. He asked her to go to Felicitas' office and do the following: study the big ledger book to become acquainted with the ranch business, gather and stack any and all correspondence and invoices, and find the supply list.

"I'm going to check on Felicitas, Consuelo, and then head to her office."

"Yes, all right."

Cynthia entered the room with dread. Felicitas hadn't moved. She pulled a chair near the bed and leaned over to study her face and movements. Her breathing was slow, as if she slept deeply. Occasionally, her eyelids fluttered. Perhaps she was trying to open them.

"Felicitas? Can you hear me? This is Cynthia.

Would you take a drink of water?"

No response. The doctor instructed them to talk to her when they were in the room. Ask questions, talk about the weather, and touch her. Cynthia dampened the cloth and bathed her forehead and cheeks. She dabbed it on her lips several times, which caused the woman to move them a little. As Cynthia repeated the action and watched, Felicitas made the same movements. Cynthia dribbled water into her mouth, and Felicitas swallowed several times. She was pleased.

After sitting with Felicitas for half an hour, Cynthia walked down the hall to the office. She felt as if she were a trespasser or an eavesdropper. However, her husband had given her some responsibilities, and she intended to carry them out to the best of her ability.

She sat at the large, very feminine desk and glanced at the myriad of items there on the top. The big green ledger was right in front of her, but she wouldn't open it yet. No need to, anyway. She knew nothing about finances. She began to tidy the space. First, she placed opened envelopes of the same size in one place, then stacked loose papers together, regardless of what they were, and collected anything else odd in another stack. A handwritten note caught her eye.

February 10, 1880

Dear Felicitas,

I hope this finds you well. Mama is quite ill, and the doctor says she might die in a few months. I cannot explain how badly I feel for her, for she suffers so. He said she has a cancer and there is nothing to do. Father and I wait.

In the meantime, dear Felicitas, I dream of the day when I wed Ricardo. I admit that I will be as happy to have him as my husband, as I will be to have you as my mother-in-law. Will it not be wonderful to not only join our families but merge our ranches, as well? You will have the honor you are due, as mistress of perhaps the largest ranch in Texas. In addition, Spaniards will own and operate it instead of Anglos, such as our rival, the Loma Linda Ranch.

But dearest Felicitas, may I confess something to you? Ricardo seems reluctant for the marriage. I fail to understand him, for I'm certain he loves me, yet, he will not commit to a wedding date. In truth, he does not completely agree to a marriage at all. This is very curious, for he and I have grown up together and shared so very many things.

I can only assume he will soon relent, or rather, agree, to what seems to me to be inevitable. For in truth, what other woman is there? None and he knows it. I wait and hope for his proposal. Perhaps soon.

With love,
Starr

Cynthia sat with the letter in her hand, staring at the words, attempting to solve the puzzle. Starr wrote the letter six months ago. It was probably hand-delivered. Starr and Felicitas were in league with each other, and both had a problem with Ricardo. But why should she worry? He had come to Nacogdoches, they met, and he married her. So, why did she have a niggling feeling something was amiss?

Chapter Twelve

Ricardo held out his hand to his beautiful wife. "Come out to the corrals with me. You haven't been out of the house all week."

"Since your mother awakened it's been a bit hectic. She's sleeping soundly now and I so wanted to see the mares and hear all about what you're doing with them. Let me tell Consuelo."

They walked side-by-side across the yard to the barns and corrals. Ricardo circled her waist with an arm, bringing her close to his side. She placed her arm over his in order to touch him and hug him closer to her.

"What a week this has been," she told him. "I've done things I never knew about, and when one thing is done, there's always another waiting."

"And you've done a mighty fine job, sweetheart. I'm proud of you."

"But I've made mistakes. All I can say is that I'm trying, and I'm truly grateful for Sarah and Annie. And Consuelo, of course."

"It was wise of you to set up a rotating schedule to care for Mother, and even to get some of the younger women involved."

"They're all really nice, and even fun, when you get to know them. I have some plans where they're concerned, but nothing to explain just yet. I must talk to you soon about the accounting ledger, but I don't want to ruin my special outing with anything unpleasant."

"The ledger book is unpleasant?" he asked and

turned to look at her. "What's wrong?"

"Nothing. I just said I don't want to spoil our time together."

He chuckled. "All right." He leaned closer and whispered as they approached the first barn. "Speaking of time together, I would really like to take you right in there to a barn stall and make love to you on a nest of sweet hay. I would remove that blue dress, and..."

"Shhh." She laughed. "Too many cowboys nearby. They're going to hear you."

"It's nothing they've never heard before. Hey, there, Luis! Is corral number four working?"

"Yes, sir. Five are in there. Joe and Mario are out there with them."

A small group of men lounged around the corral. As before, each had the same stance—one foot on the bottom rail and crossed forearms on the top one. To Cynthia, it seemed that there was not only a dress code, but also a behavior one. Every man had a stalk of hay or grass between his teeth and talked with it protruding from his mouth. Most had a wad of something in one cheek or in the bottom lip, and said person spit ever so often into the dirt. When a man talked, he jerked with his chin or nodded his head this way or that to indicate some object he was discussing.

She was inordinately relieved Ricardo did not place that disgusting yellow substance in his mouth and spit. She was also as pleased as could be he didn't chew on a stalk of hay.

Men began to call out to Ricardo as they approached.

"Hey, Mr. Romero! Glad you're here. These are fine mares you got here."

"Glad to see you. Look at the bay. Is she not *muy bonito*?"

"Ain't that'un a purty lil' thang, Mr. Romero?"

"I sure am pleased with them, that's for sure. You boys have done a good job cleaning them up. I think these are about ready, don't you?"

"Maybe. That there stallion is, ain't he, boss?"

Ricardo laughed heartily along with all the other men. One or two glanced at Cynthia and flushed a little as the laughter died.

"Men, I know you've seen my wife, Mrs. Romero, but I'd like to formally introduce you. You can call her that for now, but when Mother is well and out and about, we'll find some way to distinguish the two. Sweetheart, this is…"

Cynthia whispered to him, "They could just call me by my first name. I wouldn't mind."

He turned his head close to hers and said quietly, "Uh-uh. They'll address all owners with respect and use proper titles."

"Oh, certainly. Sorry."

All heads turned toward the road when they heard the sound of a galloping horse. Cynthia almost wanted to stomp her foot and pout. Starr Hidalgo had come to visit, so all the attention moved in that direction, everyone forgetting all about the new Mrs. Romero.

Starr rode hard, reining in her horse so forcefully the gelding sidestepped. She easily held her seat and with only one hand on the reins. She laughed gaily and waved to everyone.

"Good morning, all! Men. Ricardo." She nodded. "Oh, and Mrs. Romero."

She swept from her saddle and one of the men ran to grab the bridle and lead the horse to water. "So, what's going on?" she asked, standing with her feet spread and her hands on her hips.

Ricardo abandoned Cynthia to her spot, while he walked to Starr and began talking. "We're looking over these five for the first ones to be bred. They're all two-year-olds and I think they'll come into heat

134

real soon."

"Mind if I take a look?" she asked.

"Not at all. Let's go in."

Starr and Ricardo climbed over the fence. He stepped up on the second railing, placed his hands on the top one, and swung up and over to the ground as if he mounted a horse. She climbed up to the top, boosted herself to sit up there, swung her legs around, and Ricardo held out his arms for her. She placed her hands on his shoulders; he placed his around her waist and lowered her to the ground in front of him. He released her, but she kept her hands where they were. Coyly, she held his gaze and murmured, "Thank you, dear heart."

Now, all attention was on the two inside the corral. The men resumed their positions at the fence and left Cynthia alone outside the circle and the action. She had no place, no role, and her hurt and anger built.

She began to turn away, but thought she might be more conspicuous if she did, so she moved down the fence and found a place of her own. The trouble was, she couldn't quite see over the fence, and to see between the top and second rail, she had to lean down. Not so ladylike and quite uncomfortable. She ended up standing on tiptoes as long as she could, but soon had to place her feet flat down. So, she alternated, back and forth.

"This sorrel is nicely built, good muscles, good back." Starr circled the mare but was careful not to get too close to her rear hooves. She stood directly in front of the horse's head and placed a hand on either side. "Clear eyes and intelligent, I think. She's no dumb girl." She pulled the upper lip up and studied the teeth. "Very healthy."

Starr continued her inspection. She turned her back to the mare's front, reached down for a back foot, and lifted it. "The hoof rim is solid, no wear. No gouges in the hoof walls, no bruises." She stood straight, brushed her hands, and smiled prettily to Ricardo. "And she's beautiful."

He placed his hands on his hips, threw back his head, and laughed. "Yep, you read her right. Look at the little Morgan over there in the corner. She is something. Really coy and flirty. I fell in love with her right away. I like her light weight—makes a good riding horse, but too good for the range."

"So, how are you separating them?"

The pair came over the fence just as they had gone in it. Ricardo led Starr to Cynthia, but continued talking to Starr.

"We want to have two lines, but we're not finished thinking it out. Maybe one group would be strong racers, or another, quarter horses. There's a real market building in the country for racetracks. I heard over around Kentucky, they're using thoroughbreds, English breeds, but we think their legs are too fragile for anything rough out here. The other line would be special riding horses, prized for their beauty and strength."

"Good thinking. I agree."

"Fine. I'll keep you posted."

Finally, he turned to his wife. "Sweetheart, why don't you go in and get out of the sun? You might get that nose burned. You really should wear a wider-brimmed hat out here."

Cynthia seethed. "Yes, darling. Miss Hidalgo, would you care to come in for tea?"

"Well, I don't really like tea. I'm a coffee drinker. Anyway, I don't want to bother Consuelo with any more work. She has enough as it is. I'll be in after while, though. Rafaelo sent a rider over to say Felicitas woke up. I'm very anxious to see her and talk with her."

"Come anytime you're ready, but I might warn you. She's awake, yes, but not quite aware. She's groggy and lethargic and talks very little. She says her eyes won't focus, so she keeps them shut much of the time," Cynthia said.

Ignored and feeling completely shut out, Cynthia left the group and walked alone toward the house. Ricardo had asked *her* to go to the corrals with him, so he could show her around, introduce her, and explain the plans he and his father had made. However, as soon as Starr arrived, she was the one who heard all the explanations about their plans, and she was ushered about to actually view the mares. It was rude of Ricardo to exclude his own wife.

At one of the barns, she heard a loud noise that sounded like banging or thudding. She turned into the open door and looked down the long aisle. A number of roomy stalls lined the center walkway, and a few held horses. The noise came from a stall at the far end, toward the other open door. A breeze blew through, but the building still held the fecund smell of horses.

A man stood outside the stall of the offending horse. Rafaelo. He had his arms crossed over the door and silently watched.

"Rafaelo? How are you? I don't see you much during the day."

"Hmm?" He appeared sad when he turned his vacant gaze on her.

"Are you all right, sir?"

He lowered his arms, tugged on his waistcoat, and cleared his throat. "Let me get my jacket." He had thrown it over the door of an adjacent stall and had his white shirt sleeves rolled up, exposing brown, sinewy arms.

She placed her hand there, on an arm. "No, don't. You needn't. I don't mind."

"Felicitas always likes me to wear my jacket."

"But it's a little hot today, don't you think?"

"Sure is." He studied her face, as if he saw her for the first time. "What are you doing out here?"

"Ricardo asked me to walk out to the corrals with him. But, I have duties to attend, so I left."

"I saw Starr ride in." He turned sideways to peer at the horse. "Meddling female."

"Sir?" She wasn't certain she had heard him correctly.

"Never mind. Have you seen this stallion?"

"Actually, no. Is he the one making the noise?"

Rafaelo chuckled. "Yeah. He's quite a guy, isn't he? Look at him. So strong and proud. Raring to go, but we keep him penned in for now. He ought to be free, roaming the range, finding his own way."

"Does he have a name?"

"We don't name our stock, except the one special one we ride."

"What did you name yours? Where is he? Or is it a stallion?"

"Which question do you want me to answer first? Mine is a stallion. His name is Captain, and he's getting old, just as I am. He's a fine Appaloosa, but most ranchers around here don't want such a plain horse."

"I know an Appaloosa when I see one, and I think they're very pretty."

"Sure, they are, but they're common stock. Just a sturdy saddle pony."

"What is this one? I mean, what kind?"

"Breed? Ricardo thinks he has some Arabian in him, but he's no particular breed. Just a bay. Look at that red coat. Isn't it gorgeous?"

"I like it, and his lighter tail and mane really make him unique."

"He is that. My son chose well. He's a work of art, don't you think?"

"Yes, I do."

Suddenly, the stallion became agitated and

kicked the side of the stall. The powerful hooves rocked the whole side of the building, but he settled down quickly.

"Likes to show off for the ladies." He grinned, stretching his thin black mustache across his upper lip. "He knows his harem is out there, waiting for him. His sap's running. Won't be long, now."

Cynthia's stomach fluttered and jumped at the thought. She knew what he talked about, and it made her uncomfortable and excited at the same time. A flush rose on her breastbone and continued up her neck.

"Well, I should be getting back to the house. I have things to do."

"Would you like to see Princess? Felicitas' horse? You captured her, I heard."

She laughed. "Oh, I really didn't. She was lonely out there, so she walked right to me. But yes, I would like to see her."

"She's in the little barn next to the house. Let's go."

Rafaelo gallantly took her arm and tucked it through his. He walked proudly, as though he escorted a fine lady.

When Cynthia arrived at the back door of the house, she changed her mind and walked out to the porch swing hanging from a tree limb. She sat in the middle and gave herself a little push. There was so much to think about, she didn't even know where to begin.

First, she knew without a doubt Felicitas resented her and maybe even hated her. The letter she read from Starr disturbed her a great deal. Starr and Felicitas, at least, had a well-developed plan, but Ricardo obviously ruined it when he married another. So, now what? The two ranches would not merge, at least not by the original plan. Did they have another one concocted to accomplish the goal?

Another curious statement in the letter concerned her. Starr wrote Ricardo was reluctant to marry her for some reason. That was back in February, six months ago. His sudden marriage must have changed the landscape a great deal.

So, that's why Felicitas tried to make her believe Ricardo wanted out of the marriage, for her own plans and goals. Wasn't it?

Starr Hidalgo was very familiar with Ricardo, so much so, they looked and acted as a team. The woman felt right at home and even appeared to have some authority around the place. All the men had almost bowed to her, while ignoring Cynthia.

Cynthia was a reasonable young woman, even though she might be green and untried. She would give Starr the benefit of the doubt for the time being. After all, Starr had been around her entire life. Cynthia had been on the ranch a little over a week.

With a heavy sigh, Cynthia stood and walked to the house. This was not how she envisioned her married life. All the married friends she had at home kept their houses, minded children if they had any, and socialized on a regular basis. Cynthia was included in afternoon teas, the churchwomen's group, lunches, and shopping trips. If she had married Harris Newton, that's how her life would be right at this minute. No wonder she jumped at the chance to marry handsome, charming Ricardo Romero.

Who was, by the way, at this moment totally engrossed in another woman.

Consuelo turned from the stove when Cynthia opened and closed the screen door. "*Chica*, you want tea? I will make some for you."

"Thank you, no, Consuelo. I don't want to put you out."

"No, no, no. It is no trouble. You know that. I can make tea in my sleep."

Cynthia laughed. "I'll wait until Starr comes to the house. She may want something by then, and I'll visit with her."

Consuelo shrugged one shoulder, said nothing, and turned back to her pie dough.

"I'll go check on Felicitas."

Felicitas seemed to be sleeping, so Cynthia walked to her own room. She sat at her little dresser and peered into the mirror on the wall. Perhaps she should make herself prettier, so Ricardo could see her in a better light. She rearranged her hair so that it was in a more attractive coil on top of her head. She tied a blue ribbon around her neck so it would show above the high cut of the dress. Lastly, she pinched her cheeks and pressed her lips together to bring up some color. That was better.

Voices from the kitchen caused her to hurry back down the hall. Probably the newcomer was Starr. When she arrived, she was surprised to find not only Starr, but also her husband and Rafaelo, and they were all talking and laughing. Consuelo was setting out cups and saucers and pouring coffee for all three.

"I have also sugar cookies." She piled a plate high with the large, sweet treats, and all three of them sat with coffee and cookies. Right at home. No one even noticed her in the doorway.

At last, Ricardo looked up and saw her there. "Come sit down, sweetheart. Would you like to try coffee?"

"Certainly."

So, Starr didn't want to bother Consuelo. Humph!

After twenty minutes of talking and drinking coffee, Ricardo excused himself to return to the corrals, and Rafaelo followed suit. Starr informed Cynthia she wanted to visit Felicitas.

"Don't expect too much, Miss Hidalgo," Cynthia

said as they walked down the hall to Felicitas' room. "She's awake, but she's talked very little. Most of the time she keeps her eyes closed because of a persistent headache and blurry vision. Give me a minute to check."

"No need. You may leave. I'll see to her."

"Oh, well, as you wish. If you need anything, I'll be around."

Around? Where should she go? No one needed or wanted her in the kitchen. The house was clean and orderly. All the laundry was finished, folded, and put away. Every list she knew how to make, she had done so. Felicitas didn't need her—she had Starr. Her husband didn't seem to need her either. He had much better conversations with...Starr.

She entered the study—the one that belonged to Felicitas. Everything was in neat stacks, but that didn't mean much, because she had no idea what to do with anything. Maybe this was the time to open the dreaded ledger.

The ledger was large and heavy. She positioned it in front of her and opened it to the first page. *Continued from Black Journal. Begin—1860.* This was 1880.

The second page was the beginning of the transactions and entries. The page looked like a huge jumble, a complicated puzzle of words, numbers, squares, and colored lines. Numbers in vertical rows, but what was a debit? What was a credit?

This was impossible. She studied the page as if the answer would magically come to her. In the end, she looked toward the bottom at the total. That, she could understand, except the number was in red. What did that mean? *$2,469.34.* In red.

She decided to turn to the latest page, which turned out to be toward the very back. Felicitas would need to buy a new ledger very soon.

This page resembled the first, but she looked first to the total. *$1,612,996.45.* In black.

Goodness, gracious! Even she knew that was an enormous amount of money. Now that she thought on it, she had heard her father say such things as, "He's in debt up to his ears. In the red." So, maybe if one were 'in the black,' that would be good.

In twenty-two years, the family had gone from practically nothing to well over a million dollars. She sat back and thought about the ranch. The Romeros had spent a great deal of money on buildings alone. Cattle were the same as wealth, she knew, and they had to buy some of them. The Romero family was quite well to do. Were the Hidalgos as rich? She wondered.

Laughter came from Felicitas' room. The woman was actually laughing, and no doubt, the reason was Starr. She closed the ledger. It was giving her a headache, anyway.

She walked into the bedroom where Starr was visiting.

"I'm glad to see you feeling so well, Felicitas. May I get something for you?"

Both women turned to her with annoyance written all over their faces. Felicitas said, "Get out. Nobody invited you in."

"Felicitas," Starr purred, "don't be so surly. It's not becoming."

Cynthia whirled about and quickly left them alone.

****

In late afternoon, Starr finally went home. Consuelo was setting the table to eat in the kitchen again. Did they ever have a meal in the dining room? She sent the woman to look in on Felicitas before the men came in, and when she returned, she told Cynthia her mother-in-law had summoned her.

"Sit down." Felicitas ordered when Cynthia

entered the room.

Obediently, she sat in the small, straight-backed chair near the bed. She waited until Felicitas gathered her strength.

"Now, listen to me well," she began in a low voice. "You have ruined everything by marrying my son. Surely you know by now, that a marriage between Starr and Ricardo would have joined our ranches, and we would be the biggest in Texas." She stopped, closed her eyes, and took deep breaths. When she opened them again, she continued.

"But that is not what I have to say to you. I want you to know this, in particular. Ricardo never wanted the ranches joined. I had to convince him, and still, he was reluctant. So, how did he avoid my commands? How did he succeed in winning the battle against me? He found someone else to marry. Anyone would do, you see."

Cynthia bit back a gasp. The statement almost knocked her off the chair, but the woman in the bed would never see her true reaction. Her schooling taught too well always to act the lady, so she brought all her teaching to the fore. She kept her eyes directly on Felicitas and merely waited. Felicitas continued.

"So, what will you do, Miss Harrington? You have married a man who really did not choose you. You were convenient and willing. You…"

Cynthia stood with her hands folded down in front of her. Coolly she asked, "Will that be all? I have duties to attend to."

Felicitas yelled in a raspy voice. "I said…what will…you do?"

Cynthia walked from the room and found Consuelo.

"Consuelo, I'm going outside."

As she walked off the porch and out to the swing, she heard Felicitas yelling at Consuelo. The crazy woman would make herself sick with rage. Cynthia knew without a doubt that Felicitas tried to make her so angry or so hurt, she would leave. She could not, of course. The wedding had taken place in not only a Catholic church, but a Protestant one, as well. Neither Heaven nor Hell could break those bonds of matrimony, no matter how hard Felicitas might try. God had sanctioned the marriage, and a marriage it would be.

What sort of marriage was the question. At this moment, she was so enraged at Ricardo she could hardly breathe. She was mad at her father, as well. He had gone right along with the marriage, but he should have questioned where she was going and what the situation might be. However, he hadn't done either.

Now, she knew exactly why Ricardo had married her. Felicitas had made her point. He needed a way out of joining the ranches, and he had conveniently found one. Well, so be it. She was the lady of the house, the wife of the owner, and those facts would not change. Cynthia vowed to herself that one way or another, she would make the marriage work, and find her own place on this ranch.

But could she cope with the fact Ricardo did not care for her after all?

Chapter Thirteen

Ricardo stomped into the house, dislodging loose dirt and hay from his boots. Rafaelo did pretty much the same thing. Cynthia had watched them do this every evening when they came into the house for supper. Consuelo never said a word, but later she always found her broom and swept the bits of straw and dirt out the door and off the porch into the yard. It seemed an acceptable thing.

"Hi, there, pretty lady," he said to Cynthia where he stood at the table. "Come here." He held out his arms to her, and she went as she had every day, but this time with sorrow and anger in her heart.

He kissed her soundly on the mouth, pulled out a chair, seated her, and then he sat beside her. "So, how was your day?"

"Fine," she answered blandly. "How was yours?"

"Well, we separated five mares into a separate corral. Father, will you pass the gravy? Thanks. But you were there, weren't you?"

He glanced at her and looked as though he truly did not remember if she had been there or not.

"I was there. I saw them." She selected a small piece of beef and placed it on her plate.

"Well, you know those are the first we'll breed. First, though, we have to make certain they're healthy, free of diseases, and such. Maybe by next week, we'll be ready to pair them up."

All through the meal, the men spoke of the ranch business, the mares, the stallion, and their plans. Occasionally, they remembered she was at the table and asked a question, but every time, it concerned Felicitas.

"Perhaps you should go in and spend time with her tonight, Ricardo. You've hardly seen her, and she's wide-awake now. You, too, Rafaelo. She needs stimulation, conversation, and you two can provide those things far more than I can. We have little to talk about."

"Well, sure, sweetheart. We'll do that. But don't you two need to discuss matters concerning the house?"

"Not really. Actually, she's more interested in hearing about the horses than the list for the mercantile."

"Well, okay," Ricardo mumbled with a shrug.

When supper was finished, Cynthia stood and made a request. "Ricardo, Rafaelo. I have some things to discuss. Since I am mistress of the household, we shall have a few different rules. Beginning tomorrow night, please clean off your boots outside before you get to the porch. Also, clean up and change into nicer clothing—it needn't be dress suits—just something besides work clothes. We'll have supper in the dining room, thirty minutes later than usual. This will be our new routine."

The two men glared at Cynthia with surprise and obstinacy, but she knew both would do exactly as she asked.

****

Early the next morning before the sun had risen, she felt Ricardo turn to her. It was too hot for covers, so she lay spread out and relaxed. "Sweetheart." He began to kiss her on the side of her face, her ear, and around to her mouth. Unable to resist him, she rolled to him. He moved atop her, and pulled up her short nightgown.

Cynthia willingly opened her legs and allowed

him entry. She wrapped her limbs around him as he moved in and out with hard thrusts, kissing her and calling her name all the while. Both climaxed in a great spasm.

What a mess. She loved him with all her heart, while at the same time, hated him for how he had fooled her. All she could do was allow him to make love to her. That one thing was all hers.

At least, it had better be.

"Cynthia, you're wonderful. You know that, don't you?" He was on his side with his face nuzzling her neck. "You are so sweet and good. I've never known anyone like you."

She had no response. What could she say? She would never say, "I love you" to him again. Never. "And I've never known anyone like you either, Ricardo."

"So," he said as he yawned and rolled to his back, "day has arrived, and I have a mountain of work to do. What will you do?"

"Oh, my usual housekeeping chores. That sort of thing."

Felicitas had to be cared for, even though she berated Cynthia's ministrations every step of the way. Cynthia had to ask Consuelo to help her bathe and dress the bedridden woman.

The doctor should arrive soon to check Felicitas. Surely, she would be able to sit in a chair and perhaps walk with the help of a crutch of some kind. That decision was not Cynthia's, but she hoped to distance herself from Felicitas when that meeting took place.

Half the morning was gone when Cynthia finally escaped the house. Finally, her time was her own. Since she was so good at making lists now, she had one of her own. No more would she sit around waiting for others to pay her attention. Every person on the ranch had a job and was far too busy to include her.

Since she had no expertise or even much knowledge of horses, she studied the ranch community to find weak areas. To her, there certainly seemed to be room for improvement in more than one place. Maybe she should take charge of certain things and see if she could make a difference.

Annie had told her the first day they met, Sarah was lonely and far too idle. Annie, herself, was the same way, but at least, she lived near the other families. The two women were best friends, about the same age, and missed working together and visiting as they had before Sarah's Jake became foreman. Their grown children lived elsewhere, so they had no small ones to care for, as did the other women.

That was another thing. The younger women rarely left their small houses. Their lives seemed stifling and boring to Cynthia. She had seen them gather at twilight under a tree and talk and laugh, but then separate to return to their tiny world. They should be included, if she could work out everything on her list.

First, she must meet with Annie and Sarah. She walked to Sarah's house next door and explained her vague plan. Together, they walked over to Annie's house.

"Why, come on in! I was just doing some mending. Let me get you a chair. Here, Cynthia, sit at this end of the table. Sarah, you sit right there. Now, I made some oatmeal cookies yesterday. I have some left, after I shared with the others. When you fire up this old wood stove, you want to use it all you can at once. Oh, listen to me ramble. Would you like some coffee?"

"I would love some, Annie," replied Cynthia. "I never would have believed I would learn to like coffee."

"So what brings you over?" Annie asked as she pulled three mugs from the cupboard.

"I would like to ask for your help. I believe there are a few things around here to alter or rearrange. Will you help?"

Both eagerly agreed.

"Now, first are the children who live on the ranch. I've watched them every day. All they do is run wild and play. I know the mothers have a few chores for the older ones, and that's well and good, but their lives should have more structure with learning activities. First question: why is the school inoperative?"

Annie spoke. "Mrs. Romero taught all the children when her own son was growing up, but when he went away to school, she pretty much let it lag. Don't know why, but I guess it could get a mite tiring. No one else is available."

"So, do they have any schooling?"

"A couple of the mothers do a little teaching. Like, Irene O'Dell. Well, she can read pretty good, and she has those little primers and slates, and even tries to get paper and pencils when she can. Her four do more than the others do. But, you know they have to do the work at night, and that's not too good."

"Hmm, well, what I would like to do is restart the school."

"Will Mrs. Romero let you do that?"

"I am the mistress of the house, at least for a time. Even when Felicitas is back on her feet, she'll continue her usual work, which does not include anything that I wish to do. Whether she cares or not is beside the point."

Cynthia didn't miss the look that Sarah and Annie sent one another.

"So, I need to know if you'll work with me or not? If, my dear friends, you are fearful of Felicitas, I ask you to go no further. You must make the choice."

Cynthia sat with her back straight and her hands folded on the table. Her chin was up, and her voice and purpose were clear. Sarah and Annie looked at each other and back at Cynthia.

"We don't want our husbands to lose their jobs."

"They won't. I assure you. I will do battle with her, if I must, but in the long run, I will have my way."

"I'm in."

"Me, too."

"Great. The second thing on my list is the infirmary. Maybe should I say, about the lack thereof? I asked a few questions and learned when any body part is hurt, say a cut, or a bone is broken, the man either cares for it himself in the bunkhouse, or must wait for Doc Sawyers to arrive—which may take two days. Now, I'm no nurse, and certainly no physician, but I believe if we outfit a clean, stocked space and designate it as an infirmary, the men will go there instead of using their own dirty knives and handkerchiefs. I heard many infections have occurred, and we can stop most of that."

"Now, that I can do," said Annie. "I know I'm no good in the classroom, not a'tall, but I can clean wounds and sew up men better'n the doc. And I've set a few bones, if they're not sticking out of the skin. Can I be the infirmary keeper?"

Cynthia reached over to take Annie's hand. "Annie, dear, you are a lifesaver. Thank you. We'll work on a list of supplies and find a place."

"Oh, I know where to have it, and thank you so much. I'll work hard for you."

"And Cynthia, I hope you're going to be the schoolmarm. I can't do it all, but I would really like to help teach. I'm good with numbers, sums, and such, so could I do that?"

"Sarah, I was so hoping you would be my

assistant. We'll sit down, make out lessons, and plan our day. Do you know if there is anything usable over in the chapel?"

"A few things. Benches, a few tables, a chalkboard, but we'll have to clear a space. Pews take up most of it, but we don't use more than two or three of them."

"We can use those, as well, for some lessons. Oh, you two are grand! I never imagined I would have two such wonderful friends! Thank you so much. Now, let's get to work."

By the end of the day, the three women had made great progress. The younger women with children were thrilled, not only because their offspring would have an education, but also because they would be under someone else's care for a few hours each day. The school hours would free them up to take care of their own chores much better, and perhaps have time for projects, such as, quilting, sewing, and more satisfying meals.

The only reluctant woman was Irene O'Dell who had four children. She thought her husband might not want her to turn the two school-age girls over to other people, but she was enthusiastic, all the same.

Annie knew of a small lone building close to the commissary that would be perfect for the infirmary. She went directly over there and began to clean it out—sweeping, mopping, washing the two small windows, and looking for needed repairs. She should have a long table, a chair, and a cabinet, so she began to scour the ranch for the furniture. Then she made a list of supplies to stock the medicine cabinet.

Sarah and Cynthia worked in the small chapel the remainder of the day, and when they finished, felt a great sense of satisfaction. They made out their list of supplies, including primers, math books, slates, pencils and paper.

At suppertime, Cynthia cleaned up and donned

a pretty dress with a deep ruffle around a scooped neck. The fabric was plain cotton, but it was a spring green, one of her best colors. She was bursting with pride and news of the day. She attuned her ears to the back porch, and she waited to see what the men would do tonight.

Exactly on time, Ricardo and Rafaelo approached the porch, paused and stomped their feet on the steps—not even on the porch itself. She couldn't keep from smiling to herself.

"Cynthia?"

"In here, Ricardo. In the dining room."

When Ricardo stepped in he had an expression of pleasure on his face that he had not shown for a long time, not even when the horses had arrived. Cynthia smiled when she looked up from her task of placing the English silver next to the china plates.

"Looks great, sweetheart," he murmured. He stepped close to her, turned her toward him by holding her shoulders, and kissed her warmly on her mouth. When the kiss ended, he looked into her eyes. Without warning he drew her flush with his body to kiss her with forceful passion. The forks she held against his breastbone pressed into both their chests. He drew back, a little short of breath, looked down at the forks, and laughed.

"Well, this is a most welcome change indeed," Rafaelo said. He stood at the doorway and surveyed the table with obvious appreciation, then looked to his son. "I do believe you chose a bride with greater care than you chose the horses. You did a superb job."

Ricardo laughed, as Cynthia blushed and looked away.

The three who dined that night would remember the supper as one of the most pleasant evenings any of them could remember. Cynthia had planned smothered chicken with onions and celery, buttered squash, green beans from Consuelo's garden, and thick slices of vine-ripened tomatoes. Large, fluffy yeast biscuits completed the main meal, and the dessert was pecan pie with thick cream.

With the dishes cleared, the three had a glass of sweet wine, and their amiable conversation continued for another hour.

Cynthia was extremely happy, and if she weren't careful, she would not be able to keep her confession of love for her husband to herself. Somehow, she thought if she allowed him to view her whole self—body, soul, and heart—she would be somehow diminished.

Nothing on this ranch belonged to her, except her own being and personal possessions. Until Ricardo fully accepted her as a partner in their life together, she would remain on the outside. Patience would be required to obtain her goal, and she vowed to herself to make the best of each day. She would find her own place, and perhaps her hopes and dreams would come true.

I must have my own home. Ricardo must completely give up Starr. And Felicitas will not have one iota of power over my husband or me.

Chapter Fourteen

The evening had been so enjoyable, Cynthia decided to wait until morning to speak with Ricardo about her plans and ideas. They ate breakfast together, along with Rafaelo, so when her father-in-law went to visit Felicitas, she took the opportunity for the discussion.

"Can you give me fifteen minutes, Ricardo?"

"Why sure, sweetheart. Here at the table?" He walked to the stove for more coffee. She shook her head no when he offered to pour some for her. "Okay, so what do you need?" he asked with a gentle, indulgent smile.

Feeling emboldened, she jumped right into the request, or rather, the pronouncement. "I've taken stock of several things around the ranch, and I have plans to make some changes. First, the children here should be in school, even though it's summertime. They run wild all day, and their mothers stay quite harried. For these hot months, we'll only work three hours in the mornings. Sarah and I will teach, and we're in the process of rearranging the chapel so it will be suitable for classes."

"Whoa," he said and held up a hand. "When did you do all this? And what makes you think the parents will allow you to school them?"

"I've talked with the mothers, and they're all in agreement and quite excited, I might add. Only Irene O'Dell is reluctant because of her husband. Anyway, even if they balked, I think you, as the head of operations around here, might have some say about the educational requirements of the children. It's similar to living in a community, where the town council passes regulations that all children will attend school for a certain number of years. It's for the good of the society."

"Well, even so, it's too much for you to take on. You have too many other duties."

"No, I do not, Ricardo. Someone else does everything, which is well and good, because I certainly don't wish to scrub floors or do laundry. Annie and Sarah are in the same situation. They're lonely and bored, and believe me; any woman of worth needs a responsibility to feel she contributes. So, to my mind, all arguments are moot."

Ricardo kept his face expressionless, but she knew his brain worked overtime. She couldn't tell if he was suspicious of her motives for some reason, or only processing the information. Finally, he said, "Well, I suppose you could try it, at least."

Taking the statement as acquiescence, she moved on. "Fine. Now, the next item..."

"There's more?"

"Yes, and it concerns an infirmary."

"An infirmary? What for? We've always taken care of injuries well enough, unless we need to call in the doc. I don't know why you're even suggesting this."

His mild objection did not deter her. She continued in the same tone as before. "Many of your men have infections as of this minute, caused from using dirty knives which have been used on God knows what. Surely, you don't want your men to work with infected cuts, or boils, or...anything else. "

"They pour whiskey on wounds. That seems to work pretty well."

"And an expensive treatment it is, since they probably pour half a bottle over a wound. We can use whiskey, but only small amounts to clean a wound.

Our methods will be cleaner, too. We'll use lye soap and boil utensils and cotton dressings."

"How did you learn all that?"

"At school in Chicago. One of our required courses at the girls' school included home nursing. Just simple but effective methods."

"You know, come to think of it, one of our men died a year ago from a gash in the calf of his leg. From barbed wire. He became real sick and died in about three days. Wasn't that blood poisoning?"

"Yes, of course, an infection in the blood. Same thing."

"Well, what do you know," he said thoughtfully, with a partial smile on his dark face.

"So, Annie will man the infirmary," she continued, very businesslike with her hands clasped together and resting on the edge of the table, her spine straight and away from the back of the chair. "She's in the process now of making the place presentable. It's the small building next to the commissary. She needs all sorts of supplies, too. Now, it won't be open all the time, but perhaps only one day a week—something like that. But if anyone needs immediate attention, then she's willing to go over there and assess the situation."

"Well," he said as he nodded slowly, "that sounds logical. Yes, okay.

"Well, fine. I've also made a list of foodstuffs for our own larder. Consuelo and I worked together on it. The commissary? I assume someone takes care of that?"

"You've met Juan and Elena, haven't you? Our housekeepers. Well, since they don't work for us all day, every day, they run the commissary. Usually Juan rides into town one day every other month and brings back a wagonload of supplies."

"Oh, yes, Annie told me. Well, I believe the little store could use a good cleaning, and I'll see they do

157

that. To my knowledge, we don't need some of the items at all, while we may need to add others. I'll work with them and revise their list."

Ricardo leaned back on two legs of his chair, rocked back and forth, and studied her. Cynthia smiled to herself when he observed her that way, as though there were more to her than he first thought.

"Okay, so now what? Should I ask Juan to pick up your things?"

"He's welcome to work on his own supply list, but I want to go into Rico Springs myself," she firmly announced.

Now, Ricardo brought all four legs of his chair to the floor with a thud. "No, I don't think so." He shook his head. "I'll find someone to ride in for you. All you need to do is tell him what you want."

"Well, that is not acceptable, Ricardo," she said. "I wish to go myself. There are too many things to select, and not just read from a list. I should go and see for myself just what is available in town, and what I should order from...where? Where do you order supplies?"

Ricardo unknowingly stepped right into her trap. "We order from San Antonio. George at the mercantile has catalogs, and you order from those. Orders take about three to four weeks, since the mail goes by train, and the goods arrive back by train. Not your speedy delivery. But it's always worked pretty well."

Cynthia smiled to herself and stood. "Well, Ricardo, I shall not take any more of your time. I have much work to do today, as I'm certain you do. Who'll drive me to town? And we need a rather roomy buckboard for all the supplies."

He stood as well, looking slightly bewildered. "No, wait." He held up a hand. "I didn't agree that you could go, in fact, you can't. The trip takes five hours, you know that, and five hours back. It's too exhausting for a lady, especially you. I told you I'll send Juan for everything."

"Absolutely not. I intend to stay the night in Rico Springs. There is a hotel, I presume?"

"Yes, and it's good, but you can't drive there with Juan...no." He shook his head, "This is not a good idea. I'll worry too much about you. You'll have to think of some other way."

"I could take Sarah, also. She could help me, and we could share a room. Maybe we could go to the hat shop, too, since I need a hat with a wider brim to shade my nose. You remember. You're the one who told me I need a new hat."

"I did?"

"Yes, darling, you did." She smiled into his face.

"Nevertheless, there must be another solution."

Cynthia walked close to him and pressed her body to his. She raised her slender white arms and circled his dark neck with them, and linked her fingers there. "Well, why don't you take me? Hmmm? We could eat out and spend a night, completely alone. Will you please say yes?"

Ricardo pulled her closer still and buried his face in her hair He took a deep breath and said, "Yes. Well, oh, all right. I'll take you."

****

By the end of the day, Felicitas knew of the planned changes. The wranglers never had an opinion one way or the other, unless the changes directly affected their schedules or lives. She heard the young wives were excited because something different was in the air, but why did it matter what they thought? How dare this faux daughter-in-law go about issuing orders and creating new activities in her midst? The impudent woman was practically rearranging the ranch. And how dare Ricardo put her in charge of the ledger?

"Felicitas, *querida*, please calm down. You will

make yourself have a setback, and you're doing so well right now," Rafaelo pleaded.

"Don't tell me what to do! How dare you allow that little nobody to take over while I'm here flat on my back! She will not, I repeat, she will not start the school without my knowledge and approval, and the infirmary can just shut its doors right now! Things are working just fine the way they are. And know this—" She took a deep breath before she spoke, "*I* will be the one to make changes, if and when I so desire. So, you find her, Rafaelo, and tell her I said to stop all of this nonsense as of this minute!"

"Well, now, you see, Ricardo is the boss around here. Remember? We placed the responsibility on his shoulders last year, when we thought we might like to travel to Spain. Yes, I know, you're still in charge of the finances, but Ricardo and Cynthia will do most of the work. That's the way it will be, you see?"

"Oh, go away," she snapped and turned her head away from her husband. "I don't know why I'm wasting my breath on you. You act as if you approve of that pasty-faced little tart."

"Felicitas! That is quite enough!"

When he walked from the room, she glared at his back. She hated being confined to this bed. What could she do to stop the intrusive young woman? How could she induce her to leave the ranch and return to Nacogdoches? Little Miss Cynthia was out of place here, unwanted, and unwelcome. Since all she had to do was lie here hour upon hour, surely she could think of something.

****

Long before dawn, Cynthia and Ricardo were up and dressed, ready to make the trip into Rico Springs. Now that he had agreed to go, he was happy about the plan, for he would have her all to himself for two days and one night. He was also anxious to show her off in the small town, and he wanted her to learn all about the area where he'd spent much time.

Most of the boys he played with as a child had moved on to other places. Rico Springs was at the far western edge of civilization in Texas, so some of the young men had continued on farther west to find their fortune. One who had stayed now owned the bank, because his father owned it before him, and upon his death, had bequeathed it to his only son. The friendly relationship with the banker had worked well for the Romero family for many years. Ricardo planned on stopping by the bank for a short visit, just to let Leonard Sterling know he was around.

Another one was Jimmy Clark, a friendly, outgoing man, just as he had been as a child. He and his wife ran the only café in town, so Cynthia would meet them. He thought of several others who were around, but they lived on smaller ranches or farms, far out in the wide-open spaces.

As they approached the town, Cynthia exclaimed over every little thing, which made Ricardo enormously proud.

"It's in such a pretty setting, Ricardo. The way the road dips down toward the river, and curves around the rock ledges, and with so much vegetation. It's like you drop down into an oasis."

"It's different from other towns way out here. Most sit out in the open. This whole area used to be a haven for the Comanche during the Indian Wars many years ago. The Comanche fought the Cherokee, the settlers, the Spanish ranchers, and the Rangers. They fought everybody and lost in the end."

"That's sad, don't you think? Strangers coming in and taking your land? It's not right."

"It might not be right, but that's the way civilizations are formed. One group fighting another and the stronger always wins. Just like the North fighting the South. The South might have been bigger, but it was weaker than the North. Remember my grandfather on my mother's side was Comanche? A few decided to blend in and stay, and that always happens, too."

"Oh, I'm so excited, Ricardo. When we arrived on the train, I didn't even see the town."

"And you were very tired, weren't you?"

"Yes, I was." She turned in the seat to look at his profile. "This is a whole new world for me, one I never imagined, let alone have as my home. Well, actually, I never knew it existed."

Ricardo chuckled. "You're a wonderful woman, sweetheart. How lucky I am."

As they entered the town, the first building was an open-ended barn. The sign read "Livery and Blacksmith."

"Hey, Ricardo! Glad to see you! You want me to come on over to the mercantile and fetch your team and wagon?"

"Hi, there, Walter. I'll bring 'em over sometime later. You going to be here?"

"Sure, sure. I'll be here 'til 'bout nine o'clock."

"Okay, see you later."

Ricardo pulled the team up in front of the mercantile and turned to Cynthia. "It's a little past noon. Let's eat, then I'll show you around. You'll still have hours to shop and place your orders. I'll go over to the hotel after we eat to pay for our room."

"Yes, that's fine," she said.

They entered the small café, and Jimmy Clark stood by a square table, talking to three men. He had a dishtowel tucked in his belt. He looked up when Cynthia and Ricardo entered.

"Well, well, if'n it ain't ol' Rick. And who do we have here?" He wiped his hands on the already soiled towel and waited until Ricardo spoke.

"Jimmy, I would like to present my bride, Cynthia Harrington Romero of Nacogdoches, in East Texas. We've come to town to shop, but right now, we're starved. Sweetheart, this is my good friend, Jimmy Clark."

She held out her dainty hand, and he held it with both of his big ones, very gently and lightly, as if he held a delicate robin's egg. "I'm pleased to make your acquaintance, Mr. Clark." She smiled her best social smile at him, and he stood still and blinked a few times before he moved.

"Well. Well," he said, but seemingly couldn't make any other sound.

"Jimmy, do you have a table for us?"

"Uh," he said as he came out of his trance, "well, sure. Come right over here by the window. It's the best seat in the house. Rick, let me tell Lurene you're here."

When they sat across from each other, Ricardo laughed. "I've never seen that guy at a loss for words. I think you won him over."

"Oh, stop." She smiled. "I didn't know what to think."

"It only meant that you impressed him by your beauty and graciousness."

"*Rick?* He called you Rick. Is that a nickname? Do others call you that?"

"Just friends." He knew she was making a reference to Starr but merely shrugged.

"I like it, but I like Ricardo better. That's the only way I know you."

After the meal, Ricardo took her to the mercantile and introduced her to the proprietors. They were all smiles and treated Cynthia as royalty. She shopped and purchased everything she could, while the man and his wife piled all the goods together on the long counter. Her purchases filled the entire length, and he had to make more stacks on the floor. Cynthia then sat down at a table with four catalogs and began to locate all the other items on the list. When she was finished, she asked about a milliner's shop in town. He escorted her down the boardwalk to the small store.

"You take all the time you need, but wait for me here. I'll come back in an hour or so.

The selection in the shop disappointed her. Most of the hats were suitable for women who worked on a farm or a ranch. None seemed fashionable or appropriate. She did not want one that was fashioned after a slat bonnet, and most of them were in one way or another.

"May I help you?" asked a well-dressed middle-aged woman.

"Hello," Cynthia said as she held out her hand. "I am Mrs. Cynthia Romero, the *new* Mrs. Romero. I wish to find a bonnet of a certain kind, but..." She turned in a circle and looked about for the sort she wanted. "I don't seem to see one."

"So, you're Ricardo's wife?" The woman asked, as she pushed wire-framed spectacles further up on her nose, and smoothed her gray hair along one side.

Cynthia turned back to the woman and looked her in the eye. She was uncertain what she saw, maybe wariness, or maybe only curiosity. "Yes." She smiled. "I am. And you are?"

"Mrs. Covington, proprietor. I know Felicitas Romero pretty well. We've worked together a few times on town hall meetings. Things like that. I hadn't realized that Ricardo got married."

"Yes, well, we married over in Nacogdoches, which was my home." Unwilling to impart any further information to the woman, she moved back to the subject of hats. She wasn't certain how close this person was to Felicitas, and she didn't wish to know.

"I'm looking for a bonnet or hat which will be

serviceable, one that will keep the sun off my face, in particular. The hats I brought with me are more decorative or social in nature—not very well suited to the harsh rays of the sun. However, I don't wish to wear one that resembles a slat bonnet."

"I understand." She nodded. "I really do. These bonnets are for the farm and ranch women who work out of doors, Mrs. Romero. I don't like to make them think they're buying a hat that might be out of fashion or unsuitable for the society person. So, my displays are geared toward them. Do you see what I'm saying?"

The statement endeared Mrs. Covington to her, for her words showed she was a sensitive, knowing woman. She admired that very much.

"Yes, I do understand."

"Now, over here," Mrs. Covington said as she swept her arm toward some side shelves, "are bonnets for many of the women around here. While they're not out of Godey's or Peterson's, they're festive enough for most. These are made of straw, mostly, and designed to shade the face fairly well. However, you can see that the brims are generally small, so the side of the face may be exposed."

"These are very pretty, actually, but I'm still looking for a wide-brimmed one. Am I out of luck, Mrs. Covington?"

"Not at all. Follow me." She walked to the back of the store and pushed back curtains, allowing Cynthia to enter the workroom. "Excuse the mess, but this is where the work takes place. I keep a few boxed up for special requests. Let's have a look."

In a matter of minutes, Cynthia had found not one, but two perfect wide-brimmed hats with ribbons to tie under the chin.

"I love these. They're perfect. I'll take both. Perhaps I'll have another look at those with the smaller brims, too. I saw one that caught my eye."

When she rang up the sale, Mrs. Covington smiled at Cynthia. "I couldn't be happier you chose to come shopping today. You know, at first," she confided, "I thought you would be like Felicitas. Oh," she said on an inhaled breath, "what have I done? I really shouldn't have said anything." Straightening her spine and clasping her fingers at her waist, she asked, "Will that be all, Mrs. Romero?"

"Yes, and I enjoyed this very much. Could you write up an invoice, please? And my husband will pay you."

"Yes, ma'am. I'd be happy to."

Ricardo paid practically every merchant in town, and truthfully, he was pleased to do so. Each person he encountered who had served his wife was full of praise and compliments. How proud he was, and he became more and more enamored with her. She was a dream come true, and he'd become one lucky man when he had impulsively married her.

She spent a large amount of money, but the entire experience was worth it. Not only was he fully able to pay for the many purchases, his confidence in her grew enormously. While he'd thought he'd married a green girl who would do his bidding, he learned she most certainly did have a mind of her own and could express exactly what she wished.

Early the next morning, he drove them back to the Double R in peace and contentment.

Chapter Fifteen

Shortly after noon, Cynthia and Ricardo arrived home. The buckboard contained piles of goods, covered with canvas and tied down with ropes. The sight created much excitement and speculation concerning the contents.

Children appeared from everywhere. They ran barefoot toward the wagon, laughing, and shouting, and danced around and around the wagon. Their lives were as carefree as a bird's. Soon though, Cynthia would have them in school for a few hours each day, and they would need to adjust to a new routine. Just as everyone else around here.

"What'cha got? Is it for us?" asked one little boy with long brown hair hanging over his eyes.

"I wanna see! I wanna see!" A small girl jumped straight up and down in sheer excitement, causing her skirt to balloon out, and then deflate.

"Let me help! I'm the biggest! I'm twelve years old!" called out the bigger boy who'd helped her with her trunks the day she moved into the little house.

Cynthia laughed, as Ricardo helped her to the ground. "Children," she said above the din, "it's so good to see you. Just wait until you see what we brought." She waved toward the wagon. "Why, we have books, and paper, and pencils. And even some maps."

"Why? What's it for?" asked a Mexican girl who had large inquisitive eyes but was solemn and spoke softly.

"For our new school. For you, and you, and you,"

167

she said with a laugh as she touched a nose for each 'you.'

Two little girls looked at each other, placed their fingers over their mouths, and said, "Ohhhh."

Just then, the back door opened and Starr Hidalgo stepped onto the porch. Cynthia immediately became somber and glanced at Ricardo. She couldn't imagine why the woman was here, but she would act the lady. Truthfully, it infuriated her to see the neighbor intrude on their family business.

Ricardo looked directly at Starr, and the tall beautiful woman walked right to him and placed her hand on his chest. "Rick, it's your mother. I'm afraid she's taken a turn for the worse."

He quickly stepped around her and with long strides took the porch steps two at a time. The screen door slammed behind him as he disappeared into the house, completely forgetting his wife standing beside the wagon.

Starr turned her cold eyes on Cynthia who could do nothing except helplessly watch the unfolding scene. "You really shouldn't have left the ranch, you know, and especially with Ricardo. It's caused all sorts of problems for Felicitas."

Cynthia instantly became furious, but she kept her feelings in check. She could hardly speak from the anger that threatened to bubble over, but she regained her voice and calmly asked, "What on earth do you mean? What's happened?"

Starr crossed her arms over her waist and stood almost as a man might, hip cocked, head thrust forward in anger. "When you left, no one was in charge of looking after her. She was literally alone in that bedroom, unable to get up when she needed to and couldn't call loudly enough for anyone to hear."

Cynthia didn't believe her for one minute. "Where was Rafaelo? He knew we were gone."

"That I can't answer. All I know is that she said

even he didn't come in to see her enough to help. She needed to relieve herself, but there was no one, so she soiled herself and the bed. She needed a glass of water but went thirsty because she couldn't call out."

"And where was Consuelo?"

Starr unfolded her arms and waved one dramatically toward the house. "Apparently since you and Ricardo were not here, she went to her own room, and napped, and read, and embroidered! She even forgot to take dinner to Felicitas." Her voice rose on each word.

"I won't stand here and defend myself to you, Miss Hidalgo, but I don't believe any of this. Not one word. Sarah and Annie had assigned duties at specific times, and Consuelo was certain of her responsibilities. *None* of them would disobey my orders. Rafaelo? I simply don't believe he shirked any duty he had toward his wife. Now, if you will excuse me." She tried to sweep away from Starr.

But Starr caught her arm before she could move away. Cynthia looked down with disgust at the hand holding her, and then into the icy eyes staring her down.

Starr kept her hand on Cynthia's arm and leaned forward to speak into her face. "We'll see who is believed here, Miss Harrington. We'll see."

"It's *Mrs. Romero* to you, *Miss Hidalgo*," Cynthia said, as she jerked her arm free from Starr's grasp. "*Don't* make that mistake again."

In the house, Felicitas poured out her story to her son. He sat on the edge of the bed and held his mother's hand. Cynthia walked into the room, and both her husband and mother-in-law looked up and glared at her.

Ricardo turned his attention back to Felicitas. "Mother, don't worry. I'll straighten all this out. It won't happen again. Now, close your eyes and rest. I'll send Consuelo in to tend to you." He leaned over and kissed her forehead, and she whimpered in response.

Cynthia narrowed her eyes. Ricardo said to her, "Please follow me to the dining room. We need to talk."

Ricardo pulled out a chair for Cynthia and he sat adjacent to her. He wasted no time in attacking his wife. "Did you or did you not leave specific instructions for Mother's care?" he asked in a cold, quiet voice.

She sat with her back straight and hands clasped in her lap. With her chin up, she answered, "Of course, I did."

"What exactly did you do?"

"First I talked with Consuelo and reviewed our established procedures in caring for her. We've worked as a team every day, in perfect accordance. She understood perfectly well."

"Well, tell me, so I'll know, too."

"First thing of a morning, we help her relieve herself. Next, we move her to a sitting position and work until she says she is comfortable. Then, Consuelo gives her a warm, wet cloth and she uses one hand to wash her own face, before we serve breakfast on a tray. After she has eaten and rested for about thirty minutes, we hand bathe her whole body and dress her in a clean gown. One of us brushes out her hair and braids it once more. We help her as many as six times a day. However, Sarah and Annie alternate with us, and Ruth and Nancy work as a team to take a turn. In between, we come and go, and Rafaelo visits three or four times a day."

"Then, we need to talk with the women. I'll begin with Consuelo."

For the next hour and a half, Cynthia sat with Ricardo as he questioned each woman. In the end, every one of them repeated Cynthia's version. All were in perfect agreement, and claimed they had carried out their assignment the best they could. Only Ruth Milford dared to add her two cents' worth.

"Mr. Romero, I must say my piece. You won't like it, but I ask that you not take it out on my husband Job in any way. May I speak?"

He nodded with a curt jerk of his head.

She cleared her throat. She scooted forward on her chair. "Your mother rejected almost everything any of us tried to do. She yelled at us, told us to get out of her room and not touch her, and don't come back, but of course, we did. We managed most of our duties, because they were quite necessary, but she became so angry, we feared touching her or forcing her. She wouldn't eat and dumped a tray that Consuelo brought on the floor. Consuelo cried, she was so hurt, but she cleaned it all up and tried again later. However, Mrs. Romero did the same thing all over again. It was quite an impossible situation."

Ricardo sat silently for a few moments. He tapped his fingers on the arm of the chair. He in turn studied Cynthia, then Ruth. Both women kept their eyes on him—Ruth in fear, Cynthia in seething anger.

At last, he spoke, "When did Miss Hidalgo arrive?"

"About two hours before you did."

"Mother looked clean and fed to me just now."

"Miss Hidalgo talked with your mother for a few minutes, then ordered Consuelo and Sarah to help care for her. Mrs. Romero and Miss Hidalgo were real angry, and Consuelo cried again. I didn't see her in the kitchen just now. Is she okay?"

Cynthia spoke, "She's in her room lying down. She says she has an upset stomach."

Ricardo announced he should unload the wagon. "I'll get a hand or two to help me. Where do you want the school things?" He asked tersely and impatiently.

As coolly as she could, she told him where to place each item.

"I'll carry my own purchases to the house."

"That's certainly what you should do," he answered as he spun on his heel away from her.

Cynthia whirled back to face him. "Just a minute, here. You don't believe anything I said. Do you? Neither do you believe all the other women. Well, their hands are tied, Ricardo, but mine are not. I have dutifully carried out all my responsibilities, distasteful though they may be, and so have the other women. Don't speak to me again in that tone of voice. You have no right."

"I have no right? Just who do you think you are? I'll make the decisions where Mother is concerned, and you'll follow my instructions. You may think you have a free rein around here, but that's only so because I have allowed it. That's the way the ranch works."

"What? You're being unreasonable. Of course, you're the man of the house. You're the boss. But I thought we had a working relationship. I respect your work, and you respect mine. I will never shirk my duty, and I don't need you to remind me just what it is. I know what I'm supposed to do. The problem is that you think I'm lying. You think my friends are, too. Did it ever occur to you that your mother might be lying?"

"Now, that's going a little too far, don't you think?" he said, with his mouth in a hard line and lips that barely moved. "Why would she? Why would she lie there in her own waste and go hungry and thirsty to prove some point? No person in her right mind would do that."

Cynthia became very still. "You're so right," she said softly.

****

Starr stayed until mid-afternoon, babying Felicitas and acting quite solicitous. Before she went home, she walked out to the corrals to find Ricardo. Cynthia watched from the back door as they came together. He gathered her up, hugged her, and patted her back. Right there in the wide open, she rose on her tiptoes and kissed him on the mouth. He released her and placed his hands in his back pockets. After they talked for a few minutes, she rode away.

Cynthia dreaded the evening meal, but she went about preparations as she had in the days before. She consoled Consuelo and encouraged her to stay positive and they would work together. She took a few minutes to walk out and visit with Sarah, Annie, Ruth, and Nancy. Nancy had taken Felicitas' accusations quite hard, and while she did not appear happy, she took Cynthia's warm words to heart. From Ruth, Cynthia heard that Felicitas in particular berated Nancy. Apparently, the woman called Nancy every derogatory name in the English language that described a Negro and she forbade her from ever entering her home again.

By the time supper was ready and Cynthia saw that the dining room was set with the better china and crystal, her stomach was in knots. When Ricardo and Rafaelo came to the house, she was at least pleased that they followed her new routine. The mealtime, however, was uncomfortable. Everyone seemed on edge, and the three had little to say to each other.

Cynthia was brokenhearted. She wondered how they had gone from such joy to abject misery in the space of a heartbeat. The situation made her ponder how she and her new husband could ever build a solid, happy marriage.

****

The morning dawned bright and hot on the July

day. Cynthia dragged herself from the bed, exhausted even before the day began. She and Ricardo had spoken little to each other since supper the night before, even though she attempted to let go of her anger. His demeanor was very stern and somber, and he had nothing to say to her. The previous evening when she went to bed, he told her he would be in the study, looking over the books, but he did not join her until the early morning hours.

He never turned toward her during the few remaining hours of sleep.

When she was dressed and walked into the kitchen, Ricardo and Rafaelo had already eaten breakfast. Consuelo was trying to care for Felicitas by herself, but the task created so much tension, that the poor housekeeper was angry and near tears.

Cynthia decided to take charge. "Go back to the kitchen, Consuelo. I'll finish here in the bedroom."

"But you haven't eaten. Can I bring something?"

"No, thank you, but when I finish here, I would like coffee and toast and one egg."

"*Si,* it will be waiting."

She pulled the straight-backed chair close to the bed and watched the mutinous woman there propped up on a pile of pillows. "Did Ricardo tell you we talked with the doctor while we were in Rico Springs?"

That got her attention. "No, he said nothing," she said sharply without looking at Cynthia.

"Well, we did, and I'll explain to you what he said."

"No!" She jerked her head around to face Cynthia. Her eyes snapped with anger. "I will wait until my son tells me. You will lie. I know you will. Now, go away and leave me alone."

"No, I won't go. It'll give you more ammunition to use against me, and I won't stand for it."

"You are a spoiled girl, used to everything

174

handed to you. You have worked for nothing in your life, have you?" Felicitas spoke in a voice laced with disgust and contempt.

"I've earned my place in this world as I was reared. Now, I am your daughter-in-law, and I will do that which is necessary, and you won't stop me. Now, about the doctor." She watched Felicitas close herself off and turn her face away.

"He'll bring a wheeled chair when he comes to visit. Have you seen one?"

No answer.

"It's a high-backed chair with wheels attached. Someone may push you about, or you may become strong enough to do it yourself. Soon, he wants you out of this bed and outside. Possibly, he'll have you walk a little, but that remains to be seen. Your anklebones may not have healed yet. Nevertheless, you'll not be confined to the bedroom. Even now, he said, we could carry you to the porch and you could sit in a chair out there to watch the goings-on of the ranch. Wouldn't you like that? To see what others are doing?"

"No."

"Fine. As you wish. Well, good day."

She walked from the room and did not look back. If she had, she was certain to have seen a look of pure unadulterated hatred in the older woman's eyes.

Cynthia was anxious to go to the school and open all the boxes of supplies she had bought. She walked next door to find Sarah, and together, they walked to the chapel. During the morning, they opened packages, made stacks of supplies, and rearranged the furniture in the building.

The children would sit on long wooden benches in front of tables to make a desk for them. They could seat ten children. When they counted the school-age children, that's the number they calculated. Sarah and Cynthia smiled at each other in satisfaction.

Their next chore was to talk with the mothers and inform them that school would begin the very next day for those who were eligible. She told them a child must be six years old now, or would be before Christmas.

Chapter Sixteen

School would open today. Anticipation woke Cynthia before the sun rose. Very little had gone well since she and Ricardo had returned from Rico Springs. She was not accustomed to strife in a household. She and her father usually agreed with one other and cooperated on a daily basis, because she knew her place and he knew his. While he could be domineering and overbearing at times, she knew without a doubt he loved and adored her. She always knew she was the center of her father's world, and he was hers. Whom else did they have?

Here at this remote ranch, though, circumstances were quite different. Ricardo had parents, and they were ever-present. At least Felicitas was, and she ruled the house, if not the entire ranch. Rafaelo seemed to be a bystander, always on the fringe, never involved, really, and vaguely aloof.

Ricardo now treated her as a hired hand. He couldn't seem to let go of his anger and suspicion of her and the other women on the ranch. Clearly, he believed every lying word his mother told him. Not once since they had returned from town had he touched her, let alone made love to her.

Cynthia was very tempted to pack it in, ride into town, and take a train home. Where was it now? In reality, this ranch was her home. She had married a stranger, and now she worried every night when she lay awake in their bed that he had married her simply to avoid the merging of the ranches as

177

Felicitas had said. If she allowed her imagination to run away with itself, she could even believe Ricardo and Starr were still involved in an illicit liaison.

****

The chapel had a bell in the small tower, and at eight o'clock Cynthia rang it five times. A few wranglers walked forward and looked but saw there was no emergency, and certainly, no mass, and walked away. Only women remained in the houses, and those with school age children dutifully fed and dressed them for the first day of school. The first two arrivals, a boy and a girl, belonged to Jim and Nancy Smith.

"Good morning, children. I'm so happy to see you. You may stay outside, here by the steps until everyone has arrived."

"Yes, ma'am," they said in unison, their little faces glowing with happiness, and their button eyes, like pieces of coal, sparked with excitement.

The next boy and two girls were the Garcia children. They, like the Smiths, were clean and neat. The three Milford girls came next, holding hands, acting shy and reticent, and equally spotless. The two missing belonged to the O'Dells. She decided to wait five minutes, and if they had not arrived, she would begin without them. But the two girls slammed out their front door and raced toward the other waiting children and their new teacher. Ten. All present.

"Children," said Cynthia, "I want you to line up single file and follow me into the building. When we get inside, take a seat anywhere on a bench behind a table. And please, be quiet."

Every child followed the directions, and Cynthia's stomach settled somewhat. She was not a real teacher, and only drew on her experience as a student herself. She remembered the instructions her own teachers had given their students the best she could. She attempted to speak authoritatively, but kindly, as hers had.

She walked to the front of the tables, which she and Sarah had arranged near the chapel entrance on the right side. That portion was shaded by large trees, so she could leave the windows open for a breeze. She had turned the tables toward the center aisle of the church, so the windows were at their backs. No daydreaming and gazing out the window. A framed six-by-four foot blackboard sat bracketed to the top of a two-foot high narrow bench. Someone had attached four small wheels to the bottom corners, to move the apparatus about. Cynthia had placed it in front of the tables to form a partition, effectively forming a room in a corner for the class. She did not have a desk, but she turned a wooden box on end until she could locate one.

Each child sat obediently and waited expectantly for anything their teacher might say. This was a room full of inexperienced people—ten children and one teacher, Cynthia thought.

"My name is Mrs. Romero. How many of you know that?"

Every child raised a hand.

Mary O'Dell spoke aloud. "But now we have two Mrs. Romeros. Which one are you?"

Her older sister nudged her knee under the table and said, "Shhh, Mary. That's not nice."

Mary's bottom lip began to quiver as she looked down at her yellow-flowered dress and flattened her palms on her knees. "Sorry."

"No, that's all right, Mary and Hortense. It's confusing, isn't it? It needn't be, though. When you see me, you know to say 'Mrs. Romero,' but at home if it confuses you or your parents, just call me 'teacher.' Will that work?"

"Yes, ma'am," Hortense and Mary said in unison.

179

"Now! Let's see what we shall do next. I should group you by grades, so you may work with your own level. How many of you went to school last year?" No hands. "Two years ago?"

Rhesus raised his hand. "I went over in Uvalde. See, we just came here last year, 'cause we lived over to there. So, I learnt some readin' and spellin' and addin', but I don't remember none. Or much."

"I see. Fine. Well, let's do this. I'll begin here at my left. When I stand in front of you, you state your full name and age. Okay?"

"Hortense O'Dell and I'm twelve."

"Mary O'Dell and I'm ten."

"Katy Milford and I'm thixth."

And on through all ten children, until Cynthia had a good idea of the groups.

"Group One will sit on this second bench on the left. You are the oldest children. Hortense, Rhesus, Maria, and Lizzie." The girls made Rhesus sit on the end because as girls, they wanted to be together.

"Group Two will sit over here. You are the second oldest. Mary, Deigo, and Julie."

Again, the girls made Deigo sit on the end so they might stay together.

"Now, I'll give each of you a slate and a piece of chalk for now, but later we'll use paper and pencils. I even have paints to use another day. On your slate, write your full name the best you can."

Katy Milford raised her hand. "I can thay my name, but I can't write it. Ith Katy."

"I'll teach you later, okay?"

The morning sped along, and Cynthia was encouraged by the children's responses. She felt a satisfaction she had never before experienced. Her life had been completely self-absorbed at home, just as her father reared her; he expected her to do nothing except to play the lady and perform the dutiful social functions expected of all girls in her circle.

At noon, Cynthia dismissed class for the day, because she had promised the parents they would only work in the mornings during the summertime. She planned the serious teaching for the fall.

As she straightened the benches and tables, her husband appeared at the door. He looked somber, but lately that was not unusual. Ever since they had returned from the trip to town, their relationship had been in turmoil. At night, they slept with a wide gap between them, perhaps an even wider expanse than they felt during the daylight hours. For some reason, Ricardo could not move past the episode of his mother's discomfort while they had been gone. Cynthia knew with certainty both Felicitas and Starr lied, but Ricardo would not stand by his own wife. She slightly understood his supporting his mother's tale, but the fact that he believed Starr instead of her made Cynthia both sad and angry. At the present, she could see no way around the roadblock.

Ricardo was taking a chance by going to the schoolroom. He wanted to see Cynthia so badly, but there was that niggling idea that something was not right. Until he figured it all out, he couldn't let go and return to their newfound easy relationship.

"So, how did it go today?" He leaned one shoulder on the wall and crossed his arms on his chest.

She halted her work, folded her hands down in front of her, and looked directly into his eyes. "Fine."

"Good."

"Did you want something, Ricardo?"

"Just asking a simple question. What's that?" He pointed to a rectangular piece of paper with red and white stripes and white stars on a blue background. It was hanging from the top of the blackboard.

Cynthia laughed lightly as she looked at her

own artwork. Ricardo almost smiled when her face lit up and her eyes sparkled for a moment, but he kept himself in check as he looked at the good-natured young woman he had married. Lately, she displayed a mask of blandness, which did not suit her, or haughtiness, which he knew by now as her "airs." She used both to disguise unhappiness, boredom, or displeasure. Any one of the three hurt him, because he knew he was the cause. For some reason, he could not break himself out of the deep thoughts he harbored about the real state of their marriage and the course their lives was taking.

"That," she pointed, "is Old Glory. Our United States flag, symbol of freedom for all and love of our country. There. Is that a good explanation?" She still smiled.

He shrugged. "I count thirty-nine stars. Those are for the states, aren't they? Are there that many? Guess I lost track somewhere along the way."

"Yes, thirty-nine states, now that Colorado has voted for statehood. Did you know women have had the right to vote in the Wyoming Territory since 1869? And they don't even have statehood yet."

"No," he said. "I didn't know that."

"Yes, well, it may be a long time yet before women get the right to vote across the nation. But one day, mark my word, it will happen."

He nodded once, just enough to acknowledge her bold statement.

"All I'm trying to do with the children is teach them the Pledge of Allegiance. None of them know what I'm talking about, so I certainly can't expect them to know or understand about states."

"So, when did Texas become a state?"

"Ummm, 1845, I think. About ten years after the Texas Revolution when we won our independence from Mexico. The United States won their independence from Britain in 1776, and we won ours in 1845."

Ricardo moved away from the wall and approached her. "How do you know so much?"

She stepped to the side only a few inches, but Ricardo noticed the pulling away and felt it low in his gut. He did not proceed any farther but removed his hat, because he suddenly remembered he was really in a church.

"Many years and endless hours of school and tutoring. Since I was an only child, and had no mother, Father, I suppose, tried to teach me as much as two people would learn. I think he always wanted a son, but he got me instead."

"He loves you, Cynthia. I've seen evidence of it."

"I know he does," she said softly. "And I love him. I always tried to please him, too."

"But you defied him to marry me, didn't you? Do you regret it, Cynthia?"

A little nervously, she turned away slightly to gaze out the small window toward the house. "No, of course not."

"It's difficult here for you, isn't it?"

Without moving a muscle, she answered, "I suppose I'm still assessing the situation, Ricardo. Everything is so new, so different."

"You're not used to teaching or doing any kind of work, are you?"

"No, I must honestly admit."

"Then, why are you? Don't you have enough to do in the house? What else do you need?" he asked kindly.

Cynthia kept her boarding school demeanor as much as she could.

"What do I need? That's a difficult question to answer. I suppose I don't *need* anything. What do I want? The same thing every young woman dreams of, Ricardo. A home of my own, a family."

"You're leaving out something, aren't you?"

"I can't answer specific questions, nor can you, probably. Or can you? How do you feel about me? Am I really all you ever wanted?"

Ricardo shifted his weight from one foot to the other, and placed his free hand in his back pocket and gently slapped his hat on his thigh. Instead of answering, he asked, "Would you like to walk out to the corrals with me tonight after supper? I thought you might enjoy seeing the mares."

What she wanted to reply was, "I've already tried that, and it didn't work." Instead, she replied, "Well, yes, that would be nice," and oh, so politely, "Thank you for asking."

Ricardo chuckled a little and asked if she was ready to go in and eat dinner. "Consuelo has the noon meal ready, I'm sure."

****

Just as Cynthia, Ricardo, and Rafaelo sat down at the kitchen table, the sound of a horse and buggy brought them alert. Consuelo looked out the door and announced the visitor was Doc Sawyers, and he had something tied to the back of the little one-seater.

"Come on in, Doc." Ricardo walked out to greet the man. "We just sat down for our meal, but haven't started eating yet."

The two men came in and Consuelo placed a plate for Doctor Sawyers on the table.

"Fried steak, cream gravy, green beans, tomatoes, and biscuits," the doctor said. Well, well, I timed this just right. Let me wash up first, if I can."

Once again, they all sat and began to eat.

"How's the missus?" the doctor asked taking a long sip of water. "Has she sat up out of her bed, yet?"

"Not yet," Rafaelo answered. "She's pretty shaky and real thin, too. She won't eat much, and seems to want to pine away instead of trying to get stronger.

We've all tried to help her and encourage her to move around, but she's adamant about staying in bed."

"Hmm, well, that's not too unusual for patients who have severe injuries and traumas. Seems like the hardest part of convalescence is the patient's attitude and outlook. Knowing Felicitas as I do, I would have thought she would have more determination. Something must be holding her back."

"She's not been very cooperative, that's for sure," said Rafaelo. "Gives the women a hard time when they try to help her."

Cynthia raised her eyebrows at this statement. It sounded as if Rafaelo might believe her explanation about Felicitas' tirades.

"Doctor Sawyers, you will examine her physically, won't you?" Cynthia asked. "Maybe she's hurting more than we think, or more than she'll express. She doesn't complain about how she feels, but certainly she doesn't feel well."

"So, what does she complain about?" the doctor asked as he looked around the table.

Cynthia knew the question was directed to her, but she chose to keep quiet She was very interested in what the other two might say.

Ricardo spoke. "To be truthful, Mother believes she's being neglected. When I talk to her, she says no one feeds her, or cleans her up in the mornings. She complains that no one visits her, and she lies there all day by herself, with nothing to do and no one to speak with."

"Well," the doctor said, as he laid his knife and fork down to look at each person, "Is any of that true?"

Ricardo answered slowly, "No, I don't really think so. Actually, this began when my wife and I returned from a trip into Rico Springs. That's when it started."

"The accusations?"

"That's right."

"Well, I can hardly believe any of that, and I don't even live here."

"My wife left instructions for five different women on how to care for her. But when we got home, she started in on this sort of behavior."

"So, she hadn't done it before?"

Ricardo shook his head.

"Umm, did something happen while you were away?"

"Nothing that we know of. Starr Hidalgo had only just arrived before we did, and she heard Mother's explanation and told us."

"Ahhh, I see. How did *you* find your mother?"

"Clean, dressed, fed. Starr said she had seen to Mother, and Mother said so, as well."

"Okay, listen, I think I should go in now and visit and examine her. May I?"

"Come with me, Doctor Sawyers. I'll go with you," Cynthia said.

"Thank you, my dear, but I'll just walk in unannounced. If I need any of you, I'll call."

After examining Felicitas and talking to her for an hour or so, the doctor asked for a conference with Rafaelo, Ricardo, and Cynthia. The four of them retired to the parlor.

"Well, here's what I found," he began. "Felicitas is healing nicely; in fact, she could sit up a good portion of the day, perhaps out on the back porch so she could see the activities. Her ankle is weak, but I want one of you to rotate it for her twice a day, if she'll allow it and if there's no pain. The right forearm is another matter. It was broken in several places, shattered, really, and I'm not certain how much use she'll have there, but it may heal just fine. Time will tell."

"That sounds pretty good, Doc," said Rafaelo hopefully.

"I'm sorry to say, that's all I can tell you that you'll be happy about."

Ricardo leaned forward and propped his forearms on his thighs. "Go ahead, Doc. I think we're all worried that something else is going on here, but we can't figure it out."

"Well, see, we don't know much about the mind and how it works. If a bone is broken, we can fix that, and so on, but medicine is not that advanced. Maybe someday we'll be better equipped."

"And?"

"Your mother is in the doldrums, I think, most likely from the crack on the head. One thing's for certain, she can't see very well, and she says her head hurts all the time. This could account for her irrational behavior."

"Irrational behavior?" asked Ricardo.

"Well, didn't you tell me she claimed she'd been neglected, especially when you and your wife went into town? Isn't that irrational?"

"Tell you the truth, Doc, we don't know for certain. All we can go by is her word and Starr's. They say the women sorely neglected her. The other women say they tried to do their job, but she wouldn't allow it much of the time. Maybe though, they only wanted some free time while we were away."

Cynthia had heard enough. Suddenly, she stood and addressed the men. "If you will excuse me, I have duties to attend. I think I have learned all I need." With that, she walked from the room as sedately as she could, when in fact, her blood was boiling, and her stomach churned.

How dare he believe that nonsense.

Chapter Seventeen

Cynthia walked out the back door into the bright sunlight. Where to go and what to do? Her husband completely disappointed her, and she had no idea how to move forward. He thought his own wife lied, and believed the other women had, as well.

Aimlessly, she meandered away from the house and toward the corrals. Ricardo said they would walk out here tonight, but she didn't intend to take an evening stroll with him now.

The ranch was an interesting place. So many people and each one seemed to have a specific job. From her right, she heard the sounds of children running about and playing chase. Little girls squealed, boys yelled, and they all laughed. A mother called to her child "to stop that" or "come in this house this instant" or "do you want me to come out there?" Cooking odors wafted over the hot air—fried chicken, corn-on-the-cob, and peach pie.

Toward the barns, men came and went, some carried harnesses, a few performed some chore, while others led a horse in or out of the barn. On she walked toward the corrals—there were five of them, some fairly small, some large.

At the third one, she halted because a pretty mare caught her eye. She was all black, probably a Morgan, lightweight, agile, graceful. The horse was all alone, but she pranced around anyway, as if she showed off for someone. She looked young, as she danced around the enclosure to her own silent tune. Such a beauty. She whinnied, tossed her head until her mane flew, and every so often, danced sideways.

Cynthia climbed to the first railing and held on to the top one. She made the kissing sound. "Come over here, girl. Please? Come to me."

The mare obeyed and pranced close but stayed a short distance from the fence. She snorted and dipped her head, and pawed the ground once, twice.

"Well, hello to you, too, pretty lady. Are you lonely? Hmm? You're too beautiful to be alone. Do you have a gentleman friend? A nice, well-behaved stallion who would like you for his own? Well, shall I advise you, dear? Be careful, little one. Be very careful. Guard your heart at all costs. Don't succumb to the wiles of a handsome devil. He'll steal your heart away and..."

"Who are you talking to, Cynthia?"

The deep voice of her husband made her jump. She was unaware anyone else was there. She stepped down and turned as slowly and casually as she could, unwilling to allow him to see her nervousness, not only from being startled, but simply because he came near. He stood with that one hip cocked negligently, with his thumbs hooked in his front pockets. No smile on his classic Spanish face, no dimple winking at her from one sculptured cheek.

"Where's your bonnet? Didn't I tell you to wear one out here in the harsh sunlight? Your skin is too fair to expose it during the day."

Choosing to ignore his mild command, she turned back to the fence to continue gazing at the graceful, black mare. The Morgan stood still, swishing her tail, snorting a little ever so often, as if she wanted, once again, to be the center of attention.

In a soft murmur, he asked, "Cynthia? Why are you turning away from me?"

Again, unwilling to answer his question, she asked one of her own. "Why is she here alone? The others aren't isolated as she is. She's lonely, I think. Is there something wrong with her?"

Now, she did turn back to Ricardo for an answer, and he walked the few steps it took to be next to her. Once he had his foot propped on the bottom rail and leaned against the fence with one arm, he said, "She's in heat. We're keeping her here until she's bred; then she'll be back with the others."

"In...in heat?" Cynthia thought she could figure out exactly the meaning of that term, and she wished she hadn't asked. "Oh, I suppose I know what that is."

She heard him chuckle very quietly and low.

"Yeah, well, I guess it'll happen tomorrow, if both she and the stallion are cooperative. I know he's ready. That's for sure." He stole a sidelong glance at his wife.

"Oh." She knew nothing else to say, and in fact, the topic made her very uncomfortable. She had seen stallions out in fields, with their...members out, but she always looked away and rode on past, because the sight was not particularly pleasant. Once, she remembered glancing at a pair of horses as she rode by in her buggy, and the stallion was trying to...climb on the mare's...back...but she did not know what happened in the end. After all, she couldn't watch something so base and disgusting. Well, *probably*, it was. She really didn't know. Now, however, since she knew how relations were between a man and a woman, she might imagine.

"So," she ventured, without looking at him, "when will this take place?"

"Tomorrow evening, probably. The wranglers, those who work directly with the horses, want to be out here. The men who work cattle could come out, too, but to most of them, it's old hat. Plus, tomorrow is town day for about twenty of them."

"Town day?"

190

"Yeah. A two-day break. A couple of them have sweethearts in town, and one is engaged to a girl who lives on the Hidalgo ranch. The others like to go to bars and play cards, stuff like that."

Cynthia turned to look at him. "Are there any houses of ill-repute in Rico Springs?" She asked the question matter-of-factly, with a guileless expression.

He laughed. "Houses of ill-repute? I guess that's one name for them. To answer your question, not that I think you should know about such things, but no. Not in town, thanks to the good city council we have and the dominant presence of churches. But there are a couple out in the hills, run by madams too old to work anymore, but still want or need a business."

"So, do you approve or disapprove?"

"Of my men seeking out the company of women? I don't care. I do care, however, if someone wanted to set up business in town again."

She turned back to the mare. "Well, that's good to know."

"So, do you approve or disapprove?"

"Me?" She looked at him sideways without turning to him. "I don't think such practices are right, in a moral point of view, but then, Father always told me I should mind my own business concerning other people's affairs—literally."

"Well, whadda you know?" he asked softly.

"Well, I should return to the house."

"Wait," he said, and placed his warm hand on her shoulder. "I came out here to talk to you. Can you stay a few minutes more?"

"I suppose," she shrugged.

"What's bothering you, Cynthia? Something's wrong. Tell me what it is."

Now, she turned directly to him. She could feel the hot sun on her face, and knew her nose was beginning to burn. While she intended to explain to him how she felt, now she was hesitant, because certainly harsh words and bad feelings would result—on both sides. So, instead, she said, "You know, Ricardo, I really don't have the time right now. Anyway, my nose is burning. You were right. I should have worn my bonnet. I'll see you at supper, the usual time."

****

The wheeled chair sat before Felicitas, ugly and forbidding. How could she ever submit to sitting in the loathsome thing, let alone ride about in it? Doc Sawyers explained she could probably move herself around, even with the arm still bound in splints. She could use her fingers, and he told her the exercise would be helpful. How could she move herself into it without anyone's help? She was certain she could not. Probably Consuelo or her insipid little daughter-in-law would need to assist her. Well, over her dead body, neither of them would touch her again, if she had any choice.

The alternative was to stay in bed, just as she was now, and that, too, was unthinkable. What she wanted to do was rise from her bed, dress, go to the stables and saddle Princess. Then she could ride anywhere she wanted and carry out her own business.

Now, what was it again she had planned? For some reason, things seemed odd, for she often felt disconnected even to herself. Occasionally, such as waking from a nap, she felt so disoriented she thought perhaps she was still dreaming, or she had entered another realm of awareness. There was a plan somewhere in her consciousness, if only she could bring it forth. She closed her eyes and tried to concentrate on the conversation she had with Starr, but to no avail. Nothing came to her.

There *was* something she had discussed with

the Hidalgo girl, something very important, but what? Starr had suggested something, maybe more than one thing, to do what? It had something to do with her son, Ricardo.

Aha! Money. Something about the ledger and the Romero fortune. Somehow, she, Felicitas, could bring her son and his Anglo wife to their knees, but she must think a little harder. If she closed her eyes for a little while, then maybe she would remember the plan later. She was very tired, now. So very tired.

****

Early the next morning, Juan and Elena walked over from their cabin to clean the main house. They were small in stature and wiry, but very strong and quite cheerful. Cynthia met them in the kitchen to discuss the day's duties, along with Consuelo.

"Other than the usual chores, I would like Mrs. Romero's room to be given an extra freshening. Mr. Romero will return to the house in a few moments, and he and I want to encourage his wife to sit in the wheeled chair. Consuelo and I will give her the usual bath and dress her, and then the three of us intend to move her into the chair. If we accomplish that, we will push her either to the back porch or to the parlor. Or wherever she wishes to go. But one way or another today is the day."

"*Si*, Mrs. Romero. We will turn the mattress over, or perhaps take it outside to air?"

"Now, that's a good idea. Yes, let's do both. Otherwise, you do your usual work, and I won't interfere. Any questions?"

"No, ma'am."

In an hour, Rafaelo entered the back door and hung his hat on one of the pegs by the door. "So, are we ready?"

"Yes," Cynthia said, "We're ready. At least Consuelo and I are. Felicitas is in a dress today instead of a gown, and I might say she fought us every inch of the way. She has no intention of sitting in the chair. I'll work another fifteen minutes, but then I must go to school. The children arrive at eight."

"Well," Rafaelo sighed as he ran his hand over his head, smoothing the hair that was still thick and black, but showed silver strands around the temples. "Let's get to it. She's been more cantankerous than any wild mustang I have ever tried to tame."

Cynthia almost wanted to giggle at the uncharacteristic frustration Rafaelo displayed. She'd almost had it with the woman. She'd never had to care for anyone as she had her mother-in-law, and she hoped she was nearing the end. Her own life was in enough of a mess, without adding an irritable, hateful woman to the mix.

They walked in as a group—Rafaelo, Cynthia, and Consuelo—and Rafaelo announced, "Now, *mi querida* let's get you into the chair."

"Go away, all of you! I do not intend to move from this bed. Now, get out!"

"No, we won't. Today is an important day for you. You have mended quite well, but the next step is to get you out of this room. Consuelo, help me here."

As soon as Consuelo touched her arm, the woman shrieked. She cried that she was in pain and demanded they leave her alone.

In the end, the three of them bodily lifted her, and Felicitas displayed unusual strength in resisting and fighting. When they had her seated, she screamed at them, called them names, and wished them to perdition. Rafaelo calmly moved to the back of the chair and pushed her out the door and down the hall.

Cynthia quickly excused herself.

The woman is driving me crazy. This entire

*situation is annoying, and I am sorely tired of it.
She's not my mother, nor will she ever be, yet I must
cater to her and endure her insults and ingratitude.
She's impossible.*

I wish I could go home.

As soon as the errant thought popped into her
head, she regretted it. The decision to marry a
stranger and move west was her own, so she had no
one to blame but herself. One way or another, she
would make the most of her new life. The only
reason that would make her leave might be a
request from Ricardo.

****

The Milford children, Lizzie, Julie, and little
Katy, ran across the yard toward Cynthia before she
reached the front door of the chapel.

"Mith Romero! Mith Romero! We came to help
you!"

"Why, thank you, Katy. And hello, Lizzie and
Julie. Let's make the room ready, shall we?"

Inside, Cynthia asked the sisters to place a slate
and a piece of chalk on the table in front of every
place. "We're going to begin letters today. The
alphabet. How's that?"

"That's very good," agreed Lizzie, the oldest.
"But I already know my letters. I can say all of them,
and I can write them, too. Want me to show you?"

"When class has begun, yes, we'll see. Can you
read?"

"A little bit. We haven't been to a real school,
except when I was six. Katy was just four so she
didn't go. But Julie went with me." She turned to the
middle sister. "Didn't you, Julie?"

"Uh-huh."

"Can you say 'yes, ma'am,' Julie?" asked
Cynthia.

"Yes, ma'am."

"Me, too. I can thay yeth ma'am, too,"

announced Katy.

"Well, fine."

All the children arrived, excited and ready for the morning's work, except Hortense and Mary O'Dell. She asked about them, but none of the children knew where they were. Forty-five minutes into the lesson, the girls ran in breathlessly and scooted into their seats.

"We're sorry we're late."

"Is there a problem?" Cynthia asked.

Both girls only shook their heads but did not open their mouths.

There was a problem, however, and it appeared around eleven o'clock.

Tom O'Dell opened the heavy door to the chapel with great force and slammed it back against the plastered wall. He stomped in, his dirty feedlot boots tracking manure and straw into the aisle, ruining the fresh air of the building, and soiling and staining the wooden plank floors. The man wasn't large, but he was strong and fierce. With his head jutted forward and his jaw thrust out, he pointed his finger into Cynthia's startled face and with menace in his tight voice, said, "Don't you never, *never* come up to my house again, you hear me, lady? Stay away from my family, and that especially means my kids! They ain't going to no school, not now, not ever! You can stay away from my wife, too, while you're at it. Don't go be putting no fancy ideas in her head about schooling or nothing else! You got it?"

"*Mr. O'Dell*! I'll thank you to stop bellowing this instant! You have no right to berate me, no cause to upbraid, excoriate, or even objurgate! Why you are so intolerant and jaundiced is beyond me! Now, I demand an apology to me and the children, and I expect you to exhibit a little remorse and penitence."

The long statement with many foreign-sounding words brought Tom up short, and he stared at her for a moment, until he regained his own composure. Once more, he pointed his finger in her face. "That there. You see? That's what I'm talking about. That high-handedness and...and smarty-pants acting."

He walked to Hortense and Mary who sat close to each other holding hands, with eyes wide and full of fear. The little girls actually cringed as he approached. He took each by her little thin arm and jerked her from the bench. As quickly as he had entered, he was gone, dragging his small daughters along, for he walked with long strides they could not match. Hortense tried to make little running steps, but Mary had no such luck, as her feet often did not touch the ground.

Cynthia was infuriated, but she was more afraid for the girls and perhaps, even Irene. Most likely, his wife had disobeyed him in allowing the girls to go to school. With all the aplomb she could manage, she turned to her class and resumed teaching with calmness and authority. Amazingly, every child responded to her, and the group worked in accord until noon.

****

"I will not sit on the porch, nor will I sit in the parlor! Take me to my office."

"As you wish, dear, but are you up to any sort of work? I'm fearful you'll place a strain on your eyes if you try to read mail or work in the ledger."

"Stop telling me what I can or cannot do, Rafaelo. Just push me there."

Now that Felicitas was alone and behind her desk where she felt more in control, she studied the neat stacks of correspondence and the position of the ledger. Someone had been in here, doing who knows what. Probably that meddling little snip of a daughter-in-law. Lord, if she only didn't have to put up with her. Cynthia was the reason she was in this wheeled chair right now, but no one else could see that. Everyone only wanted to praise the girl for saving her life! Save my life, indeed, she thought. She tried to kill me. That's what she tried to do. She couldn't remember exactly how, but she knew somewhere in her mind Cynthia Harrington had tried to kill her out there on the range. Yes, that's exactly what the girl had tried to do.

Felicitas sat immobile with confusing thoughts swirling in her head. The envelopes and ledger swam before her eyes. She blinked and blinked, closed her eyes, then opened them slowly, but nothing would quite come into focus. The more she tried, the more infuriated she became.

Something was coming through the gray haze of her memory, but what? Money. That's it. Something about their fortune. Felicitas thought harder and then she remembered what Starr told her to do. Well, she only suggested it, but Felicitas had agreed this would be the best way to rid themselves of Cynthia—the sooner the better.

She needed Juan but had no way to call anyone. So, she picked up a brass candlestick and banged it on the side of the blasted wheeled chair.

Consuelo appeared. "Yes, ma'am? Do you need help?"

"I need to speak with Juan. Now. This minute. Fetch him."

"But Mrs. Romero, he and Elena have already gone home."

With narrowed eyes and ice in her voice, she said very slowly, "You walk over there, right now, and tell Juan to come to me."

"Me? You want me to walk all the way down there?" Consuelo moved very well around her kitchen, but her bad feet and cumbersome body prevented her from walking very far. "Why don't I wait until one of the men comes to dinner, and I'll send him?"

Felicitas slammed the candlestick down on the edge of her beautiful carved desk, knocking a chip out of the edge. "Now! Do you hear me? Go now!"

Consuelo did as she instructed, but not quickly. By the time Juan appeared, Felicitas was dizzy and nauseated and could barely give Juan instructions.

"Juan. Go find Paulo. Now. Tell him this—ride to town and tell Leonard at the bank to come out here. I need his...*say advice.* Tell him I need him right away."

Chapter Eighteen

Late that afternoon, a few hours before dark
descended on the long, hot summer day, the
wranglers gathered around the corral that held the
little black Morgan. Ricardo and Rafaelo stood at the
best viewing spot, waiting until the stable hand
brought the stallion to the corral. All the men were
calm outwardly, but there was always an
undercurrent of excitement and sexual tension.
Some of the men were very young, and women and
sex were constantly on their minds. Even Ricardo
felt tense and his Spanish blood coursed hotly
through his veins.

In a way, he wanted his wife out here, but then
again, she was a lady through and through. She
knew what would happen this evening, but she
apparently chose to remain in the house. It was best,
really, because not many women would be interested
in the act. On one hand, it was gripping, but it was
crude and savage, as well. Now if Starr were here,
she would understand, because she was very much a
horsewoman.

****

Cynthia was too curious to stay away. It was
unacceptable to stay locked up in the over-warm
house with a woman who clearly hated her very
presence. So, she decided to, at least, sit out in the
swing.

From her vantage point, the third corral was too
far away to see anything very well, plus men ringed
the fence, all with their arms crossed on the top rail,

and one foot propped on the bottom. As she gazed in that direction, she noticed Sarah was out there with one other female, probably Annie.

Cynthia stood from the swing and used her hand to shade her eyes from the lowering sun. A chill ran down her spine from the tension and agitation she had felt for the past hour. Mesmerized, she walked steadily toward the corral. Every man was far too involved in his own thoughts and feelings to notice she approached. Sarah, too, was intent on the action. Now she saw Annie was with Sarah, but neither woman turned her way.

As one body, every man turned his head toward the nearest barn, the large one where the lusty stallion stayed housed much of the time. An experienced wrangler had entered the building, and on the signal opened the stall door. He was careful to stand back as the stimulated horse trotted out and loped down the aisle toward the open door.

The scent of the mare in heat caused his nostrils to flare, and his ears stood straight with intense alertness. His engorged organ hung thick and long, and it bounced as he trotted toward the open gate of the corral. Every man who was close to the opening fell back, because a stallion, especially one as large as this one, was more dangerous than a raging bull. His hooves could slice a man open, and he could easily stomp a man to death in seconds.

Choosing a spot along the fence was not easy, because the men occupied almost all the rail space. She decided to stand next to her husband and Rafaelo. Without a word, the two men glanced at her and parted, so she might stand between them. Ricardo placed his warm palm along the small of her back, urging her forward. When she was in position, he removed his hand.

Quiet descended on the crowd, for the show had begun. No one wished to talk about the mating, but only to observe. To many, especially the owners, this was a momentous occasion, because if the mare caught, her foal would be the first of the new line for the Double R.

The stallion trotted around the inside perimeter of the corral, head held high and tail arched. He showed off for the pretty mare. She fell in behind him, and the pair moved in unison around and around.

Cynthia remembered seeing a carousel once when she was in school in Chicago. On a rare trip downtown, she and her classmates saw one on display as a new attraction. The painted, wooden horses were beautiful, each one unique, and they followed one after the other, up and down, as the merry-go-round circled a brightly colored pole covered in mirrors. Oh, how she yearned to ride the carousel, but the chaperones from the school would not allow the girls to experience such a tawdry, garish bit of frippery.

The pretty Morgan and the handsome stallion were as carousel horses come to life. However, the mare now ignored the highly superior male by holding her head even higher and swishing her tail as she trotted to one side and turned her back on him. He stopped and snorted, and she whinnied in response, tossed her head, and pranced away.

The stallion approached her once more, and she stopped and turned to him, but he remained a good distance from the mare. Once again, she circled away.

Now he seemed enraged at her refutation, so he blew and stomped. Then he raised his head, trumpeted loudly, and held it a few seconds, to call her and demand her attention. He shook his head, causing his mane to fly around his head, and he pawed the ground a few times. Almost as though she laughed, she once again tossed her head and pranced away. Then she turned on a dime and lunged at him to give warning to stay away. Once again, she danced off, aloof, haughty, yet as restless as he was.

He followed her, but she turned on him again, and he halted a few feet away, boxing her in an area near a gate. Her scent reached his dilated nostrils, and his hide shuddered and jerked, and he shook with fury. The mare attempted to trot around him, but he shifted and dipped, and followed her movements in a dance of passion.

Then in a show of unyielding masculinity, he locked his forelegs, and his wild eyes followed her movements. She, too, stopped to stand quite still. Every observer clearly heard the heavy breathing of both animals.

Suddenly, she ran around him and teasingly snorted, but she did not go far. Instead, she turned and waited while he advanced, slowly and deliberately. She turned her back to him once more but did not move away. He sniffed her hindquarters, and nudged her a little at a time, until her head was against the fence. She raised her tail high to expose herself, ready and awaiting the stallion.

The big sorrel neighed loudly and reared, exposing his huge erection, while she waited patiently and quite docilely. Then he reared again, silently, and lunged toward his target, while she braced her forelegs for balance. His powerful forelegs circled her back and sides; she whinnied loudly, and it turned into a screech.

The stallion grunted and worked, and the mare stood braced against the onslaught and the weight of the heavy horse. Obediently, she cooperated until his seed embedded deeply into her womb.

A hush hovered over the crowd, until one by one the onlookers ambled away, not speaking. Rafaelo walked away toward the creek, lighting a thin cigar as he did so. Sarah and Annie linked arms and strolled toward their homes probably going to put their supper on the table.

Ricardo and Cynthia stayed and gazed at the handsome stallion and pretty mare, and dreamed not of the foal that would come, but of each other. She felt slightly stunned by the sight she had witnessed, and her own body responded with swollen breasts and genitals, and a tight sensation low in her belly.

Without a word, Ricardo snatched up her hand, and he began to walk with long strides toward the main house, dragging her along behind him. He reached up to the brim of his hat and tugged it low on his forehead, but he never looked at her at all.

Cynthia, herself, was dazed and followed as fast as she could walk to keep up with her husband's long gait. She knew he had one purpose, one thing on his mind. Neither did she speak nor did she object, because this was what she longed for, as well. An entire week had passed. He had avoided her, and she made certain he understood to stay away. Now their minds and hearts were in one accord, and without voicing their feelings, they knew.

Consuelo was cooking supper, and she turned when the pair entered the back door, ready with a smile to greet them. She stayed quiet, though, and turned back to the stove. Cynthia kept her head down in embarrassment but continued to follow her husband down the hallway and into their own rooms.

The only thought she had, besides the next few minutes, was a hope and prayer Felicitas, for once, would mind her own business and stay asleep or quiet or something. Heaven help the woman if she raised any sort of ruckus in an attempt to gain attention. Surely, Rafaelo, her own husband, would come into the house soon and see to her.

Ricardo pushed Cynthia forward into the

bedroom, but he did it with a gentle, if not firm, hand. The sun had not set but would in the next half-hour. He turned to look at her and without a word, threw his hat on the chair, and began to unbutton his shirt.

Cynthia thought to undress in her private area, but as soon as she turned, just a little to walk away, her husband lunged forward, grabbed her upper arm, and spun her around to slam her into his body. He braced his legs and pulled her between them, with one arm around her back and the other on the back of her head. His lips came down on hers, hot and wet, and he devoured her with a long, breathless kiss. She threw her arms around his neck, stood on tiptoe, and kissed him with more fervor than she had ever known how to display. Every ladylike thought she ever had flew out of her head, and in their place, came hot, lustful fantasies about what he might to do her.

He paused long enough to quickly unbutton the front of her dress and push it off her shoulders. One big, dark hand pressed to her breast, but he stopped again to lower her chemise, and then he held the bare swollen flesh in his hand. Now fully exposed, she looked down at herself, and then, back to him. His head lowered slowly and he kissed the top of the plump breast, and he ran his tongue down to the nipple. Reverently, he placed his lips over it, and sucked in his cheeks, pulling the hard, brown pebble into his wet mouth.

Cynthia's knees buckled. Ricardo caught her, swept her off her feet, and turned to the bed. Instead of placing her there, he put her down, and took time to rip the entire top coverings off the bed and sling them away to the floor. Now, all his attention was on her. He reached for the remaining buttons on her dress, and pulled her arms from the sleeves. She assisted his struggle, for he tried to remove his own shirt and her dress as well. Together, they worked feverishly to divest the other of clothing, as well as, their own.

At last, they were down to her pantalets, but impatience won out for the moment. He sat her down and leaned over to begin the kissing all over again. Her arms encircled his neck and pulled him down with her to the bed. For a moment, they gazed at each other and both laughed a little at their wildness and aroused state. However, the humor did not last long.

Lovemaking began in earnest, as he kissed her mouth, her eyes, her neck, and ear. She returned the favor, and kissed his cheek, his cleft chin, and the hollow of his throat. She laid her hand upon his face and looked into his black eyes, made even darker with desire, and they seemed to bore into her soul, and even her heart.

"Ricardo," she whispered. "My dear husband. Make love to me."

That's exactly what he had in mind. The blood rushed through his veins and down to his member. Just like the stallion by the scent of his mare, Ricardo burned with the desire to mate with his beautiful, soft, ladylike wife. For one brief moment, he thought perhaps he was too forceful, too base in the pursuance of his goal. But the thought escaped his mind, and all he could comprehend was that her smell was so amazingly arousing he wanted nothing except to force himself inside her hot, wet warmth, and bury himself physically and spiritually into this female who belonged to him.

Before they could appropriately continue the act, Cynthia rolled away enough to remove her pantalets, and he removed his last piece of clothing. As one, they rolled toward each other, and once again, took up the goal of seeking satisfaction.

Ricardo straddled her, but instead of entering

her, he leaned down and kissed her sweet, moist mouth. Cynthia gasped as he kissed and sucked and licked. After a few moments of insane ecstasy, he spread her legs with his knees. At once, without a moment's hesitation, he thrust forward into her deepest parts, and moved in and out with great deliberation.

After a few moments of intense, forceful movements, she stiffened and bowed her back and gasped. He would have smiled to himself, but he was too intent on his own satisfaction. He climaxed and sucked in his breath. At last, they stilled at the same moment, both now breathing hard. He laid his head on her shoulder and held Cynthia tightly.

The act was so intense and strong, Ricardo closed his eyes. Both dozed for a while, perhaps an hour. When he opened his eyes, they were in the same position, and he watched her as she also stirred and woke. The room had darkened and they could hear no sounds in the house. For several minutes, they looked into the other's eyes and did not move. The joy was too great, the satisfaction too wonderful to disturb the wellbeing both enjoyed.

"I'm hungry." Cynthia finally spoke.

"Yeah, me, too," agreed Ricardo, "but I think we've missed supper."

"I really don't want to dress and go to the table. Is that too selfish?"

"Uh-uh. One of us could go get something, though."

"Yes, one of us could, but one of us isn't going to get dressed."

"And which one of us would that be?" he asked, as he rolled to his side and propped up on his elbow to look into her smiling face. "I think I get the picture here."

"Do you?" she said with a teasing smile.

"Okay, okay. I'll bring a tray. Better light this

lamp first."

"What time is it?"

He looked at the clock on his side of the bed. "Nine."

"I hope you can find something."

Ricardo pulled on pants and boots, and slipped into a shirt but did not button it. He smiled at what he found in the kitchen and returned to his wife with a tray in hand.

"Well, that was quick," she exclaimed as she sat up with the sheet wrapped around her torso and secured under her arms.

He chuckled. "Consuelo was in her room, and Father was nowhere to be seen, but there on the stove were two plates filled with our supper, and here was this tray on the table with knives and forks and napkins. She knew, God bless her, she knew we wouldn't come to the table."

A blush crept up her neck and cheeks. "Now, I'll be embarrassed to face her in the morning."

Ricardo adored how she looked, all tousled and with cheeks blooming pink. How could he ever have been angry with her? Surely, she was not capable of neglecting his mother in any fashion. Sure, she had never been required to take care of anyone, and it was certainly all new and unfamiliar to her, but hadn't she done her duty? As far as the other women, well he had known Annie, Sarah, and Consuelo for most of his life, and never had they failed in their daily responsibilities, as far as he knew. His mother had never complained about a thing where they were concerned.

So, why was he so quick to believe his mother and Starr? Would Starr have some ulterior motive to make Cynthia look bad? He knew she was jealous and a bit angry with his wife, but she had quickly gotten over it, hadn't she? Females. Women were a mystery, at least most of their actions were. Why couldn't they be more like him and most other men he knew? Simple feelings and forthright speaking. That's what he dealt with best.

"Ricardo? Are you finished with your plate? You seem to be daydreaming."

"Huh?" He looked up at her and grinned. "Just thinking. What's on your mind?"

"Something not as pleasant or enjoyable as this evening has been, but I need some help. May I talk business a little?"

"Sure." He took their plates and utensils and placed them on the tray on a table next to the door. "Let me get my boots and shirt off." He kept on the pants and rejoined her in the bed. When both were comfortable and propped up on soft, fat pillows, he asked her again about her problem.

"It's Tom O'Dell." In as few words as possible, she related the incident in the schoolroom.

Ricardo frowned, linked his fingers over his stomach, and leaned back his head. "Hmm, I don't know what to make of it. Tom and his family have been here two years, now. When they arrived, they had a wagon but few household goods. They seemed to be wandering and just happened upon our ranch. Usually, a man needing a job won't drag his family all over the country, hoping something will materialize. I'm not saying it doesn't happen, but he had those four little ones, and it appeared they had been on the road a long time. All of them were very thin and hungry."

"Is he a good worker? Does he follow orders well?"

"Yes, to both questions. He's quiet but kind of cold and unfriendly, and he doesn't mix with the other men at all, either. And now that I think on it, none of the family has been off the ranch since the day they rode in. Everybody wants to go into town when it's his turn, especially the women. But not

209

them."

"What can I do about it? Remember when I talked to you about the school, I said you should have some say if the children attended, as if you were the head of a school board or something like that? But he's made it perfectly clear that his children won't be coming back."

"How does Irene feel?"

"She was very happy about the school, because certainly she has little time for home teaching. The main reason was she knew such little herself, she really didn't have the ability. And the girls, Hortense and Mary, are very excited about school and learning. They've been late both mornings, and I wondered if something was wrong."

"I don't know what you want me to do, exactly. Talk to Tom? What? Suppose he puts his foot down. I'm not sure I should force him."

"It's a sticky problem, isn't it? I just hate so much to think the girls might not return to class. I think they will be very disappointed."

"Suppose I talk to him in the morning, alone? That way, we won't embarrass him. You'll know by noon if the girls showed up or not, and we can talk at dinner. Will that work?"

"For now, yes, but I feel very strongly Tom should allow the children to attend, and perhaps he should be forced to."

"I'm not certain I can do that, sweetheart. Let's see how it goes in the morning."

"Okay. Whatever you say. And thank you."

Chapter Nineteen

Felicitas sat in front of her office window, holding the curtain back so she could watch the road for Leonard Sterling. Thank goodness, Cynthia was busy at the school, and Ricardo and Rafaelo were at the corrals.

The banker should have left town early this morning, if Paulo had correctly issued her request to arrive at the ranch well before the noon hour. She let the curtain drop and slumped back in the wheeled chair. With her elbow propped on the arm, she closed her eyes and rubbed her temple. The pain would not go away.

Hearing the distant sound of a horse, she leaned forward again to look. Good. Leonard rode to the front of the house. Maybe she could conclude her business and he would be gone before anyone except Consuelo saw him.

While the housekeeper answered the door, Felicitas wheeled back to her desk. She glanced over the ledger and stacks of paper to make certain everything appeared neat and orderly. Certainly, she needed to look business-like and in charge. She straightened her spine, even though it hurt, and smoothed her hair on the sides.

When Leonard entered the office, he hesitated in the threshold of the door and looked at her. *What is the fool doing?* Quickly she lowered her splotchy, knobby hands to her lap, and once again tried to sit straight.

With his hat in one hand, Leonard walked

forward with his other held out across the desk.

"How good to see you," he said.

She decided to forego the handshake. "Sit down, Leonard. I don't wish to look up when I talk to you. Did Consuelo offer refreshments?"

As he sat, he answered, "Yes, but I'll wait until I conclude our business."

"Well, this certainly won't take long, and it would be in the best interest of both of us if you could ride out before anyone sees that you're here."

"But...what's going on, Mrs. Romero? It's highly irregular for me to make personal calls. I do all my business at the bank."

"As much money as we have in that bank of yours, you might be a little more gracious about making a personal call."

He cleared his throat. "Yes, well. How can I help you?"

"You know I'm the financial overseer for the Double R."

He nodded. "That's the impression I've always had, yes."

"My husband and my son buy supplies and animals, but they don't have a hand in paying for them. I take care of all that."

"You mean, for example, when Ricardo went to buy horses, you had the money transferred for him. He didn't actually touch anything or know exactly what you did."

"That's right. Neither of them care spit about money. So, here's what I want done, Leonard. Remove Rafaelo's and Ricardo's names from the bank signature cards. Only my name should be there—*my* signature. Can you do that for me without any fuss?"

Leonard sat up a little straighter and cleared his throat. "Well, Mrs. Romero, we have laws in Texas, you know. Your husband is owner of this property, is he not? And you two are legally and rightfully married in the eyes of the state and God, aren't you?"

"But this property is mine, sir. It came to me through my family, generations ago."

"I thought it came through Rafaelo's family. That's how I always heard it. From an original Spanish land grant. Isn't that right?"

"How little you know, you nitwit. It's mine!"

"Even so, the money you have made during all these years was earned jointly, wasn't it?"

"That makes no difference."

He shifted in his chair and reached up to adjust his collar. "Well, but it does, ma'am," he told her with hesitation in his voice. "I...I can't remove his name. He's the head of the household. We have certain regulations to follow. A man must make any necessary or desired changes."

"Ohhh, you're not listening!" she screamed. "Just do as I say."

Speaking slowly, he said, "Well, now, Mrs. Romero, here's something else you should think about. Suppose you become incapacitated and you're unable to sign checks and forms, what would happen? The court would tie up all the Romero money. No bills could be paid, and you would begin to have unpaid debts. After a while, everyone you do business with would stop allowing the ranch to purchase goods and supplies."

"All right, then, add Starr Hidalgo. The next time she comes into town, have her sign it. There. That should take care of things."

"Starr Hidalgo? She's not a relative, is she? Has she agreed to do this? Have you drawn up any legal papers? I must advise you, ma'am, this is not an acceptable solution. It would be difficult for her to do that anyway."

"How so? I don't see how it could be a problem.

Her name will only be there in case I'm incapacitated, and Leonard, I will *not* be! Now, do we have that settled?"

"No, ma'am. I just don't think you realize..."

Felicitas banged her good fist on the desk, and even though she did it weakly, she hoped the thickheaded man got the message.

"Leonard, listen to me. If you do not do as I ask, I'll send a rider to San Antonio to locate a banker who will do exactly as I wish, and I will transfer *every last penny to him!*"

She wanted to laugh, because Leonard Sterling looked like he had swallowed a hot pepper and it had gone down sideways. If she transferred the Romero fortune out of his bank, the board of directors might as well close the door.

"All right, Mrs. Romero. I'll do as you ask."

"Fine. Now, go to the kitchen and have your refreshments, and then be on your way."

"Good day, madam." He stood, gathered his hat, and walked out the door.
****

Ricardo was surprised to see his old friend riding toward the working area where the corrals were. The grim look on Leonard Sterling's face alerted him that this was not a social call.

"We need to talk about your mother. Can you fetch your father? He needs to hear this, too."
****

Cynthia looked out the door and the window all morning during classes, watching for the O'Dell girls. Neither of them showed up, and she knew with certainty their father had put a stop to schooling for them. Such a shame, she thought sadly, because both Hortense and Mary were bright and eager to learn. Even though she wasn't a certified teacher, she at least knew enough to teach through the sixth grade. Also, she knew things of the outside world and Texas politics, because at times her father had conversed with her as if she were a boy he was rearing. At other times, he treated her as a delicate female, void of any serious thought, capable only of learning social manners and rules.

She wondered all morning if Ricardo had spoken with Tom O'Dell as he said he would. Noontime was near, and surely, she would find out exactly what had happened.

After she dismissed her students, she walked to the house for dinner, but neither Ricardo nor Rafaelo were present. She waited half an hour and still neither had appeared.

"Consuelo, do you know where my husband is? He's usually right here at twelve noon to eat, along with his father, but I don't see either of them." She stood at the back screen door and watched.

"No, miss. I do not know. Maybe it has something to do with the banker riding out here this morning."

"The banker? Leonard Sterling?"

"*Si.* Mr. Sterling. He came out to talk with Mrs. Romero. But he did not ride back to town. I think he may be with the men."

"Really? Well, how is Felicitas? Did she eat today?"

"No, ma'am. She's not eating. She was very upset. She is asleep now."

"Hmmm. How strange."

"Do you want to eat?"

"No, not if you can hold the meal. Is that fine with you?"

"*Si.*"

"I'll be back in a few minutes."

Cynthia walked toward the row of small houses to the O'Dell home. The children had been on her mind all morning, and she thought to talk with Irene, if she could. Surely, she would have some

215

influence on her own husband.

The house was quiet, and she thought perhaps the family had already eaten and were taking naps or something. But just as she raised her hand and knocked, she heard the clatter and clink of forks and knives on plates but no voices.

Tom O'Dell came to the door.

"Whadda you want?" he asked in a surly, rude voice.

"To speak with Irene, but you'll do. May I come in?"

"No, you *may* not," he mocked. "We're busy."

"I'll wait on the porch until you've finished your dinner, and then I wish to speak with you or Irene. If you need to return to work, I can talk to your wife just as easily."

"Are you deaf? I said no, we're busy. In my book that's the same as saying, we ain't going to talk to you. And one more thing while we're at it here, you leave my girls alone, you hear? Now, go home."

He turned away from the door and left her standing on the small stoop. Cynthia was used to good manners when she talked with other people. Nothing in her experience prepared her for blatant rudeness. She had the verbal glibness to banter back and forth with someone, as long as both understood the rules of the game, or if she felt superior. But she was at a loss at dealing with a man as coarse and uncaring as Tom O'Dell.

As she wandered back to the house, she saw Ricardo and Rafaelo approaching, also. She called out to them, "Hi. Have you had dinner?"

When Ricardo reached her, he looked grim but answered amiably enough, "No, you?"

"No." She shook her head. "Consuelo is holding it for us. Is something wrong?" she asked as they continued to the back porch.

"Maybe, but I'll tell you later. Let's eat first. I'm

starved."

Before Rafaelo sat down, he said, "I think I'll try to get Felicitas to come to the table. Be right back. Go on and eat, though, I'll catch up later."

"Is he okay, Ricardo? He seems sad or upset."

"I'll tell you some of the problem, but we can discuss it more, later tonight, maybe."

"What?" she asked as she forked sliced tomatoes onto her plate and passed the bowl to her husband.

"Leonard Sterling came out today."

"Yes, I heard. What did he want?"

"Mother summoned him, and he rode out even though he doesn't make it a practice. As he says, that's what he has an office for—business. I suppose he realized she couldn't go in, so he made an exception. Anyway, seems she got it into her head that she wanted to be the sole signature on the bankcard to our account. She wanted Father's and my name removed. In other words, she didn't want us to have the ability to pay for anything without her approval."

Cynthia ate a few bites before she spoke, and when she did, it was with great caution. "If you don't know why, I might venture a guess."

"Tell me. Father and I are at a loss as to why she would want that."

"I'm the reason. Somehow, she's decided if you can't spend money that means I can't, and she wants to make me mad enough to leave."

He placed his fork on his plate, leaned back, and crossed his arms. "I can't believe that. Where did you get an idea like that?"

"You don't believe me?" She shrugged, picked up her fork, and resumed eating. "Well, then, probably I'm wrong."

At that moment, Rafaelo reappeared. Without preamble, he sat down and turned to Cynthia. "I've talked with my wife, Cynthia. May I be forthright?"

217

The stern look on his face alarmed her, and she knew Felicitas had laid some blame on her. "Yes, please," she nodded and she folded her hands in her lap.

He cleared his throat, glanced at his son, and then back to Cynthia. "Well, she claims you have looked in the ledger. Did you?"

Cynthia slid her glance to her husband, giving him a moment to speak up if he would.

"I asked her to, Father. Cynthia, didn't I ask you to see if you could do something with the books? Go through the bills and receipts? Maybe figure out how the system works?"

"Yes, you did, Ricardo. And I did as you asked."

"Well," Rafaelo said, "then you obviously saw the balance of our assets, did you not?"

"Yes."

"Felicitas claims you know that we have a fortune, and you've set out to empty our coffers."

Cynthia could barely hold back a gasp. Instead of a denial, or questions about why Felicitas thought that, she pulled herself together to ask calmly, "And how would I do that?"

"She says the day you were in town, you asked Leonard to allow you to sign the signature card, since you were now a member of the family."

Cynthia stood and clasped her hands at her waist. "If you will excuse me, I think I'll go for a walk. The odor in here is becoming quite foul. I need fresh air."

As she walked out the back door, Ricardo glared at his father. "What are you implying? You know as well as I do that Mother made that up."

"Sit down, son."

Ricardo did sit, and he crossed his ankle across one knee, and pulled a thin cheroot from his pocket. Without glancing at his father, he struck a match and lit it. "What's going on?"

"You tell me. Isn't this the second time we've had to question your wife? The other was when you two got back here from town, and Starr told us what happened. Now, personally, I like Cynthia, and I find it difficult to believe any of this. But Felicitas seems to be quite adamant Leonard reported this to her."

"Well, why didn't he say anything to us? He had plenty to say this morning out at the barn. He thinks Mother is having problems with her mind. Why else would she want us taken off the signature card?"

"So your wife won't persuade you to take the money out for her?"

"That's crazy."

"It sounds that way, but we don't really know her, do we? How well are you acquainted with her father, who by the way is also a banker?"

Ricardo stood. "I'm not sure what to think, but I can't believe Cynthia is that devious."

"Well, we can let it go, since Leonard refused to remove our names from the card. But we'll need to check later to make certain hers is not on there."

"Leonard said nothing like that his morning, so I sure can't believe she asked that. You need to get that out of your mind."

When Ricardo walked out and looked around for his wife, he saw her walking toward the corrals and barns. He decided to join her.

Chapter Twenty

Cynthia located the little black Morgan in a stall next to Princess in the first barn. She draped her arms over the stall door and spoke to the sweet, docile mare.

"Hello, sweetie. It's me again. Seems as if you're the only one around here who doesn't eventually turn on me. Nothing much is going right, is it? Hmmm? Oh, about that big red stallion you had the affair with. He was something, wasn't he? Oh, are you going to have a baby now? You are? Well, bless your heart. Just imagine..."

"Cynthia."

Ricardo's deep voice startled her and she gave a little jump, but she turned slowly and coolly toward him in the dimness of the barn. "Yes?"

"Are you okay?"

Cynthia turned back to the stall, rebuffing him, as the little Morgan had turned away from the stallion. She heard him chuckle under his breath.

Turning only her head, she glanced over her shoulder at Ricardo. "What?"

"Now I know how the stallion felt."

This made her smile but only slightly. She was quite hurt by Rafaelo's accusations and questions, and not too pleased with her husband, either. Since she'd walked away from the conversation in the house, she really did not know how her husband responded to his father. He hadn't defended Cynthia against the other charges his mother had made, and perhaps he hadn't this time, either.

"You didn't do it, did you?" He said it as a statement, not a question.

Now she turned to look directly at him. She crossed her arms around her waist and leaned back on the stall door. "Ask Leonard to let me sign the signature card, you mean? I won't even answer that question. Not now, not ever."

"Well, I know you wouldn't do something so outrageous. Believe me, Cynthia, I know you better than that."

"Oh? Do we really know each other at all? At times, I feel quite close to you, but something happens, and all of a sudden, you seem like a different man. Once you're cold, and then you're warm. Once you don't believe me, but now you do?" She turned and crossed her arms over the stall door again, presenting her back. "You've very contradictory, Ricardo. It's difficult to follow your moods, and I haven't learned to understand you."

"Our marriage is new. Give it time."

Once again, she faced him. "Marriage is built on trust, as I understand it. Not that I have much experience. I wasn't fortunate enough to watch a marriage in action over a long period. Some of my friends are married, though, and one of the main things they talk about is trust. Some have it from their husbands, but some don't. This bothers me a great deal."

"This is all new to me, too. I've lived with my parents all my life, and I've never once had reason to doubt their sincerity or honesty, to each other or me. Now, I'm being asked to believe either you or Mother. Father, too, is in that position."

"And he believes Felicitas, doesn't he?"

Ricardo hesitated, slid his hands into his back pockets, and looked toward the open barn door. When he looked back at her, he said quietly, "Yes, he does."

"So, don't you see why? If he believes me, then he must admit that she has a real problem, a problem none of us can handle nor understand. He isn't ready to face it, as I see it. He knows very well that I'm not brazen enough to ask such a thing, nor does he believe I'm stupid enough to go behind my husband's back, not to mention my new in-laws."

"Hmmm, you know, that makes sense. Tell me about your friends. The ones who think their husbands don't trust them. What do they say?"

"They would kill me if they thought I would tell their secrets."

"But they're hundreds of miles away. Come on. Tell me. I'm trying to learn, here."

She cocked her head to one side and studied his handsome face, now so open and honest, and waiting to hear details about women's lives.

"You're funny, you know. Father would never want to know what females thought or said. I'll give you an example, though. One friend, Edna, cannot go to the mercantile on her own because her husband doesn't believe she'll be frugal and choose moderately priced items. She must wait until he can go with her. And this is for food and clothing, and everyday household items. It's ridiculous, and he makes me angry."

"But does she get angry?"

"She's mad all the time. They've been married four years, and he hasn't changed one bit."

"That seems unfair."

"It's not only unfair, it's degrading. She feels as though she's breaking some law or something. She says she loves him, but I don't see how."

"Okay, I see."

"What are we going to do, Ricardo?" she asked matter-of-factly.

He crossed his arms and narrowed his eyes. "What exactly do you mean?"

Cynthia hesitated a long while, as she looked toward the barn door, and down at her feet, and away to the other end of the barn. Finally, she spoke, very softly and very distinctly. "I don't think I can live here, Ricardo. Nothing has been right since I arrived, and I don't see it'll get any better. Never in my life did I think I would walk into a situation such as this. Your mother hates and despises me so much, I can hardly describe it. Your father doesn't believe what I say, certainly. And then, there's Starr."

The mention of Starr's name brought him to attention. "What do you mean? What are you implying?"

"The truth? I realize you and she have been together far more than you or I have. However, what I've seen and overheard makes me truly believe that one day and perhaps soon, she'll seduce you once more. And that, Ricardo, I will not stand for."

"You're being ridiculous, now. You can get that out of your head, because that won't happen. She understands the situation. That's the truth."

"The truth. Then tell me the truth about this. Did you marry me so the ranches would not merge? Your mother said so. She told me to leave now, because you would never love me, and you would eventually turn to Starr."

"That's a lie!" He pointed a long, slender finger in her face. "That's a damn lie!"

"Oh, so, now your mother *is* lying."

"Okay, okay, I get your point. But it's a lie that I would ever turn to Starr, and I certainly did not marry you so the ranches wouldn't merge."

"I hope so. I sincerely hope so, but there's more to it. She was conveniently here when we returned from town. So, when we came home and were told everything that had happened to your mother in our absence, who told us? Starr. We did not hear it from anyone else. I didn't believe it for a minute, but

Starr gave me a warning. Want to hear it?"

"I guess. You've gone this far."

"You said that with suspicion in your voice. Did you realize it?"

"No, I didn't. Just tell me how she warned you."

"So you can say I'm lying?"

Ricardo removed his hat with a dramatic sweep, and slapped it down on the side of his thigh. "Damn, Cynthia! You're making me crazy! Tell me!"

She waited a few heartbeats as she studied her husband. He frightened her a little with his deep scowl and those thinned lips, but she said, "She warned me you would align with her and Felicitas. At least, she as much as said that. Her exact words were 'we'll just see who believes who around here.' Sounded like a threat to me. She grabbed my arm when she said it. Where I come from, ladies do not manhandle each other. Ever."

Cynthia saw the situation exasperated Ricardo, because he blew out his breath on a heavy sigh. Cynthia still leaned on the stall door, so he joined her. She scooted over a little to give him room. As he leaned back, he propped one foot back on the door and hooked his thumbs in his front pockets.

Cynthia kept her arms crossed and looked down at the floor, strewn with hay, and idly swished one foot back and forth in the dirt, making an arc. The barn was very quiet, even though a few stalls housed mares. The little Morgan approached the stall door and shoved her head between them. In a soft singsong voice, Cynthia crooned as she rubbed the Morgan's ears, "What's wrong, you pretty little thing? Do you feel left out? Are you lonely? Hmmm? You're a sweet girl, yes you are."

"Do you miss Little Dixie?"

She shrugged. "Oh, maybe a little, she was very good, but she is old, you know. I used her only to pull my buggy, and she did a good job. Father wanted to buy a bigger, better horse for me, but I wanted one docile enough not to scare me."

"Does this Morgan frighten you?"

"No, not at all. Isn't she beautiful? I don't think I've ever seen a more gorgeous horse. Oh, the stallion you ride and the one...the one from the other day are both quite handsome. But this one, well, she truly looks feminine. A lady."

"Morgans are known for being strong but light—good riding horses."

"Really? Is that why you chose her to...breed?"

She felt a hot blush rising and placed one palm on a cheek. Ricardo smiled just a little as he watched her.

"It is," he told her. "She's the finest of the lot, so she'll produce the first of this line. We think we'll get a prize-winning foal out of her."

"Oh, then she's special."

"She is. Would you like her for your own?"

Cynthia pulled away from the door. She sparkled with excitement and pleasure. She placed her fingers to her chest. "Me? She could be mine?"

"Sure," he said, looking pleased. "She's perfect for you. You could learn to ride, and it would be easy because she'll be cooperative."

"But...suppose she's...you know?"

"With foal? That doesn't matter. All mares continue their role, even though they may be carrying. They do everything the same way, until maybe a month or two before they give birth. With this one, though, we'll not tax her too much. No daylong treks across rocky land."

"How long does it take for the foal to grow?"

"Gestation is one year. And for the first few months, you won't even know it."

"Oh, I would so love to own a horse. One of my very own. I never dreamed I could have her. Thank you, Ricardo."

"Tell you what. I'll assign Juan and Louis to be your grooms. That way, if one is absent or tied up, the other will do as you ask. I'll see that they keep her fed properly and curried and combed. But there's one hitch to this."

Her eyes widened. "What?" she asked firmly. "Is it something I can do?"

"Yep. Every horseman and horsewoman must be able to saddle and unsaddle his or her own mount. There are reasons for that, and if you stop and think, you'll figure them out."

"So, in case she must be unsaddled and there's no one around, I could do it?"

"Yeah."

"And so I personally will know if the saddle is on right?"

"That's right."

"And so I'll become acquainted with her little quirks?"

"Yep."

"And..."

"Okay, okay." He laughed out loud. "I tell you what, you are one smart woman."

She very much wanted to reply saucily, "I married you, didn't I?" This, however, was not the time to flirt or act coy, not when she was truly still angry with him. Another thought came to her—suppose he gave her the Morgan as a bribe, sort of, a toy to make her happy? Surely not.

"May I name her?"

"Of course. She's yours. What will you call her?"

"Lady Midnight. But I'll call her Lady."

"Perfect. I'll use that name when we draw up the registration papers."

Cynthia excused herself to return to the house. As she walked along, she thought of something. *Maybe he believes what I say, for he entrusted the care and ownership of his prized mare to me. That*

must mean something.
****

Late in the afternoon, Ricardo walked to the house to find his wife. He decided since he was trying to make his marriage work, he would need to deal with Tom O'Dell. Clearly, the problem was not going away, and when he thought on his wife's words, he agreed all children should go to school. It wouldn't do to allow one family to ignore the new rules, even if they thought they had a right to choose. Mainly, he thought of little Hortense and Mary, and how disappointed they would be if the other children walked to school every morning, and they had to stay home with their younger siblings. No, it was not a good idea to let Tom O'Dell make his own rules.

He found Cynthia in their bedroom, folding clothes the laundry employees had washed, ironed, and brought to the house. For a few moments, he stood silently in the doorway and watched her carefully smooth his shirts out on the bed, and then with great care, fold them as if they came from the best Chinese laundry. She hummed a little tune under her breath and had a serene look of contentment on her face.

Why, I think she could be very happy here, he thought, as he watched her perform the domestic chore with a pleasant look on her face. One after the other, she smoothed and folded and carried the shirts to his side of the armoire. Carefully, she stacked them, one on top of the other, in perfect alignment, and as neat as a pin.

Then she did something that caused his heart to lurch, almost stop, and begin to beat with a heavy thud. With her back to him, she carried the last of his shirts to the shelf, but before she laid it atop the others, she held it to her cheek, and closed her eyes, and kissed, yes, kissed the fabric. Then, almost

227

reverently, she placed it on top of the others. With a gentle pat to the top shirt, she reached to close one door, and then the other.

When she turned, she saw him standing in the doorway, and he silently pushed away from the frame and walked toward her. Not once did he avert his gaze as he approached her, but when he was near, he placed his warm palms on her cheeks and leaned forward to give her a gentle kiss.

Cynthia seemed to melt when he placed his lips on her warm, soft ones. She kept her arms down at her sides and did not attempt to touch him. Instead, she waited for him to perform whatever it was he wished, and she swayed a little and closed her eyes. When he finished the kiss, she opened her eyes and gazed at him, silently, waiting.

"Thanks for folding my shirts."

"You're welcome."

He gathered her up in his arms and placed his chin on top of her head. With a firm grip, he hugged her to his body, and she willingly and complacently allowed him to do whatever he wished. Swaying from side to side, he rocked her gently, then stopped, pulled back, and smiled down at her. "You look so pretty today."

She arched one eyebrow. "Why, thank you."

"It's a while 'til supper, and I saw O'Dell walk to his house. I thought I would go over and talk with him. What do you think?"

"Do you agree with me, then?"

"Yeah. After I thought on it, I say you're right. The girls should go to school with everyone else. I won't allow him to make the rules around here."

"He'll be angry, you know. He believes since Hortense and Mary are his children, they and his wife will do as he says."

"Fine. I'll deal with him."

"May I make a suggestion?"

He nodded.

"If you wish to go alone, I'll agree. After all, I've talked to him once. You see, he may think you're pulling rank on him, using your position and authority, and he may balk simply because you insist the girls go to school. Suppose I go, too, and we say we're visiting the families one by one—you know, school visits. Just ask if he has any questions. Go at it as though it's settled they will attend."

"In other words, give him a chance to comply."

"Exactly."

"Great idea. So, could you go now?"

"Yes. Consuelo is tending to your mother, and it'll take another half hour. So, this is a good time."

They strolled over to the O'Dell residence as if they walked in the park. At first, Ricardo held his arm out and she placed her hand in the crook of his elbow. After a few feet, he disengaged them so he held her hand, instead. His heart swelled and he felt light as he grinned down at her and tugged her closer.

The O'Dell household was rather quiet for two adults and four children to be there. Ricardo and Cynthia knew all were inside, though, because the yard was empty and they heard muted sounds. Ricardo stepped forward and rapped three times.

Tom O'Dell came to the door immediately, and his face held a look of surprise, which he quickly masked. "Yes, sir? What can I do for y'all?"

"May we come in, Tom? Mrs. Romero and I are visiting the families about school." He looked down at Cynthia. "Would you care to explain, dear?"

"Yes, this is an official school visit with you and Irene. The community leaders often ask teachers to do a home visit, in case you have questions. May we come in?"

Tom appeared stymied, because his boss stood on his doorstep asking to enter his home. The look on his face clearly said he did not intend to talk with them.

"Well, now, you see, we're busy, and we don't have no questions, anyway. None a'tall. Sorry you wasted your time coming over here, though."

"This is how it is, Tom," said Ricardo in a firm voice. "We need to talk to you and Irene about Hortense and Mary attending school. Now, could we please come in? And ask your wife to meet us in your front room."

Ricardo's tone of voice left no room for argument, even though Tom had his mouth open to do so.

"Just a minute. I'll get Irene."

Ricardo and Cynthia sat on a worn sofa, and Tom and Irene were across from them on straight-backed chairs brought in from the kitchen. The four pairs of knees weren't far apart because the room was tiny.

Tom crossed his arms over his chest, sat straight as a stick, and kept his knees far apart. His thick eyebrows sat over heavy-lidded eyes, and at the present, he glared first at Ricardo, then at Cynthia by only moving his eyes. Irene sat primly with her head down and refused to raise her eyes.

Ricardo glanced at Cynthia and nodded, indicating she should speak.

"Mr. O'Dell said he had no questions concerning the school. So, Irene, do you have questions?"

No answer.

"Well, I'll just begin, then. Hortense is in the sixth grade and she happens to be the oldest student. With her group are Rhesus, Maria, and Lizzie. She knows her alphabet very well, and can do simple sums. So far, I haven't heard her read, but I know..."

"Stop right there. Uh, *please* stop there, Mrs. Romero. My children ain't going over to the school.

230

Irene, here, is teaching them at home, and she's doing fine. So, we don't need no report on how much Hortense knows. Now, if you'll excuse us, Irene needs to get supper on the table."

He paused as he looked behind Ricardo. Ricardo turned to see all four children peeking around the doorframe with wide eyes, listening to the adult conversation. O'Dell practically bellowed, "Git back in your room. This ain't no business of yours. *Scat.*"

Irene raised her eyes slightly and looked sideways at Tom. "Tom," she whispered. "Please don't yell."

"Keep your mouth shut."

Ricardo stood and the others did, as well. He looked directly at Tom, and in a quiet, firm voice, said, "O'Dell, we all live here as a community, almost like a town. We expect every child to go to school now that we have one, and your girls will go just like the others. Now, do you understand, or do I need to explain it in a different way?"

A belligerent look increased the scowl and frown on Tom's face. He folded his arms once more over his chest. "You don't have no right to tell me how to raise my young'uns. I work hard for you for damn little pay, and I follow your orders cause you're the boss man. But when you step foot in my house, you don't have no rights. So, I'd appreciate it if you and your missus go on to the next visit, cause we're done here."

"Suppose I told you that you have no choice?"

"What'd you do? Fire me?"

"I wouldn't want to; you're a good hand. I want you to think on my orders, Tom. All you're doing is creating a bad situation for yourself, Irene, and the children."

"No use in thinking on it. One reason they ain't going is because I don't want them doing book learning with no slaves or Meskins. See? That's how it is. They'll learn with their own kind."

"Do you realize that I am of Spanish descent? That's damn near being Mexican. And I'm one-quarter Comanche. Did you know that? If you did, why are you working for someone not *your kind*?"

"It's different with me. I need to make money to feed my family, and I need a roof over our heads. So, what's a man to do? How I might feel about you ain't the point, is it? As long as I do my job, well, then things oughta be just fine. It is as far as I'm concerned. But my family is my own damn business."

"I'll give you two days to think on this. What you're doing is sort of like mutiny on a ship. One man can't change the rules to suit himself, and I'm the one who makes those rules around here. Now, you'd better think long and hard, because you don't want to find yourself out on the road, heading out to find another job."

"Tom, please," Irene whispered as she tugged on his shirtsleeve. "Let's just do as he says. Please?"

Tom shrugged off her hand without looking at her. "I'll do what I want to. Now, like I said before, we got to eat our supper."

Chapter Twenty-One

At three in the morning, Cynthia's eyes popped open wide. She held her breath and listened. Very slowly, she sat up and remained very quiet so she wouldn't disturb her sleeping husband. She stared into the blackness of their bedroom.

There it was again. A screech, a scream, or something. An animal? Or a woman?

"Ricardo, Ricardo!" she whispered. "Wake up! Wake up!" She shook his arm to rouse him from his deep sleep.

Ricardo came awake very quickly and sat up beside her. He curved his arm around her waist and whispered back, "What's wrong? What?" He gave her a tiny shake and tried to peer closely into her face in the blackness of the room.

"I heard something. Listen!" They heard the sound at a distance, but uncertain if it was from somewhere inside the house. "There it is again. It's outside!"

He swung his powerful legs off the side of the bed, and as he pulled on his pants and boots, said to her, "Stay here. That's a woman's scream." He grabbed a shirt and drew it on but did not take time to button it.

"No! I'm coming, too."

Ricardo was already out the door, taking long quick strides down the hallway, soundless as a panther. Cynthia threw on her wrap and pulled on her short boots she had worn yesterday. It wasn't easy without stockings, but she didn't want to take the time to don hosiery. By the time she got to the back door, Ricardo was running toward the small houses where the families live.

Irene. She knew without a doubt the screams came from Irene O'Dell.

She saw Ricardo reach their house, but instead of going inside, he continued to run around it and toward the creek. He disappeared from sight into the darkness. Cynthia had never spent much time in her life running, but she ran now, as fast as she could. She glanced at the back of the house as she passed it, and saw the four children in their nightclothes at the back door, peeking out into the night, huddled together like little birds in a nest. In a split decision, she decided they needed her here, rather than down where the men were. She stopped and turned back to the house, walking quickly and with purpose. She could hear Tom yelling at Irene, and thuds, but then the screams stopped, and she heard Ricardo yell, "Tom! Tom O'Dell!"

Before she reached the children, she could tell by the sounds the men were in a fistfight. *Oh, please don't get hurt, sweetheart. I couldn't bear it!*

"Miz Romero!"

She heard Hortense call plaintively to her. "Yes, darling, I'm coming. I'm right here."

As soon as she was near the children, other families spilled out of the houses. Everyone obviously had heard the commotion and had awakened. The women gathered in a group, huddled together, whispering and wondering what was happening. The men ran toward the creek where they heard thuds and moans and voices.

"Come inside," she said to the O'Dell children. "Come with me to the parlor." There, she sat on the floor with her back to the worn sofa and all four children fell onto her and threw their arms about her neck. "Okay, okay, everything will be fine. Sit down now; sit here beside me. Billy, Sam, come here, darlings." She pulled little Sam onto her lap, for he was only three, and she drew five-year-old Billy to her side. "Hortense, you sit next to Billy, and Mary, you come around here to my right side. There, that's a good girl. Now," she said as she breathed out, "let's see what we have here."

Cynthia talked calmly to them and told them not to worry, that some men, including their daddy, were having an argument, but it did not concern them, and they should be calm and wait with her until it was all over. "Sometimes, people disagree and instead of talking it out as they should, they might lose their tempers. I will tell you that it'll be over soon, and your mommy and daddy will be home, and you can go back to bed. It doesn't concern you at all."

She watched all four children yawn and saw their little heads droop with exhaustion. Baby Sam sucked on his thumb with his eyes closed, and his head burrowed onto her breast.

"Hortense, sweetie, will you help me get the little ones in bed? Then you and I will talk for a few moments."

After fifteen minutes or so, Cynthia had everyone taken care of, and the three younger ones had easily gone back to sleep. She and Hortense sat in the front room on the floor once again in front of the sofa.

"Miz Romero?"

"Yes, darling?" she said to Hortense. "What is it?" She held the little eleven-year-old to her side. They both propped up their knees and Hortense held Cynthia's hand with a very firm grip.

"My daddy hit Mama."

"Oh, he did?" Cynthia asked calmly and softly

"Yes. They talked loud at each other in the kitchen, and then she made us go to bed, and when I was sleeping, I heard a loud noise, like a chair or table fell over, and I got up and looked, and my mama and daddy was in the kitchen and he hit her over and over—in the face. And then she ran out the door in the dark and I was scared, real scared, and I didn't know what to do, because my daddy ran out, too. And...then I heard Mama scream, I think, but I couldn't see them."

"Well, I think your mother is fine, now. Maybe it wasn't as bad as you remember. Have you ever awakened in the middle of the night and thought something bad was happening, perhaps a monster in your room or something like that?"

"Yes! I have. Have you?"

"Certainly, when I was a little girl like you. When I woke up in the morning, though, I didn't see anything bad had happened, so I thought maybe I was dreaming, or it was just that the darkness made everything seem worse. When the sun comes up, everything is always better. Don't you think?"

"I guess." She yawned and slumped against Cynthia. "I'm awful sleepy."

"Well, let's get you in bed. What do you say?"

"Yes, ma'am."

"Okay, up you go."

"Miz Romero?"

"Yes, darling?"

"I like school. I hope I get to go to your school."

"Well, perhaps you shall."

All the noise from the direction of the creek had stopped. Cynthia sat on the back porch step in the dark with Ruth Milford. Everyone else had stayed close to their own homes, and she heard screen doors open and close a few times. It seemed as though the other men and women decided to mind their own business. The Milfords, however, lived in the next house to the O'Dells, theirs being the first in the line. Job Milford had moved off very quickly in the direction of the creek when Cynthia told him what was happening.

"I wonder if I should go get Jake and Sarah. What do you think, Ruth?"

"Oh, I don't know. I just don't know exactly what the right thing is. Maybe when your husband gets back, he'll say so if he needs Jake. We might need to get Annie, if Irene is hurt, but let's just wait and see."

"Okay. I'm so nervous about all this. Why did it have to happen?"

"I wonder what set him off. He's not the nicest person to be around, not a'tall friendly, but I've never known him to beat up on his wife. Heard him yell a bunch of times, but I don't think he ever used his hands."

"Well, it's probably my fault."

"What? How on earth could it be yours?"

"Because I insisted he allow the girls to come to school, and he was completely against it. Irene really wanted them with me because she says she has reached the limits of her own education. She couldn't see how she could teach them anything else. Anyway, I asked my husband to visit with me, and I can tell you, it did not go well. Tom remained adamant. No school for Hortense and Mary."

"Why that's downright awful, a crying shame! So, he beat her up over that. Now, I don't want you worrying none that it might be your fault, because it just isn't. Plain and simple. You didn't do nothing wrong. Not a thing."

Cynthia laid her hand on Ruth's arm. "Thank you, Ruth. You're a good friend."

"And you're a mighty fine teacher. Why, when Lizzie, Julie, and Katy get home, all they talk about is you and school. I think they'd stay all day, if you'd let them."

"Well, that's my plan in September, Ruth. We'll

have school all day, at least until three o'clock. Six hours of teaching and learning is plenty, I think."

"I hear something. I think they're coming."

Cynthia and Ruth waited and peered through the darkness. The first to appear was Ricardo, and he walked alone with long strides. Job came next, holding Tom's arm as they walked. Tom was really beaten up, but she saw blood on the corner of her husband's mouth, too. She remained calm and quiet, though, until he reached the house. Irene was nowhere to be seen.

"Ruth." Ricardo nodded. "I need someone to go back to the creek with me. We can't find Irene. Do you think you might go with me? Maybe Cynthia could stay in your house with the girls. So, if they wake up, they won't be alone."

"Why, su..."

"No," said Cynthia, as she jumped up from the step. "I'll go with you." She turned to Ruth and placed her hand on her shoulder. "You stay with the children. Ricardo, do we need a lantern?"

"Now, Cynthia, it might not be pretty. Maybe I should get Annie or Sarah."

"Oh, no, please. I want to go. I feel responsible. Anyway, remember I stayed with Felicitas out on the range. That toughened me up, don't you think?"

He touched her chin and through the faint light from the stars and smiled ruefully. "Yeah, you sure are one tough lady. Job? Will you stay in the house to watch Tom? I think he has the picture, now. He'll stay quiet."

The lantern made moving patterns along the ground as Ricardo carried it. Every so often, he raised it and called for Irene, and the slash of light briefly illuminated the trees as he and Cynthia walked past. They heard nothing except the *whooo* of an owl and cicadas *shushing* in the trees. On they walked toward the creek until they reached the same location where the encounter with Tom had happened. Ricardo told Cynthia that Irene had picked herself up off the ground and staggered and ran through the trees.

"Irene?" Cynthia called. "Irene, its Cynthia. Tell me where you are. Please." She walked farther into the trees and back, and Ricardo did the same on the other side.

"Here she is, Cynthia! Come over here."

Irene was huddled against the base of a big oak, lying on the ground among the exposed roots and leaves and rocks, curled into a ball, crying and whimpering pitiably. Her thin nightgown was torn and bloody, her hair strewn with small pieces of grass and twigs. Cynthia knelt beside her and reached out to touch her shoulder.

"Irene, can you sit up? I need to see how hurt you are. Can you?"

"Yes." Her voice was meek and shaky, but she sat up and crossed her legs. "Are...the kids okay?"

"Yes, dear, they're fine. All sound asleep, as a matter of fact. Let me look at you, now."

"Nooo! Don't put the light on me, please. I look a fright."

"Just let me have a quick glance. Can you tell if anything's broken?" Ricardo held up the lantern, but not very high, just enough to barely illuminate Irene's body, especially her face. Her eyes were swollen and already turning black and blue. She really would look terrible tomorrow. With her bottom lip split, blood still oozed out and dripped off her chin. A dark lump was visible on one jaw. "What about under your gown, Irene? Do you have any serious injuries?"

"No, I don't think so. He hit mainly...my face, but he hurt my arms, too. Not enough to break or anything but just to hurt me. And one side of my head hurts." She felt up there and brought her fingers away covered in blood.

"Okay, then. Here's what we'll do. Ricardo, I think I should take her to Sarah and Jake's house. What do you think?"

"Good idea. Irene, you don't want the children to see you like this. So, will you go to Sarah's?"

"Yes," she said.

****

The ranch house was quiet, and Ricardo and Cynthia thought neither Rafaelo nor Felicitas woke up during all the commotion. The families' houses were a good distance away from the main one, so now they marveled that they had heard Irene's scream in the first place. They tiptoed down the hallway to their own rooms and quietly closed the door. Together they sank down on the side of the bed and fell back in exhaustion.

"Cynthia?" Ricardo said wearily.

"Hmmm?"

"I'm sorry you've been exposed to so much since you arrived here. I really regret you've had to go through so many things. If only we could start over, things might be different for you."

"Shhh," she murmured, as she placed her hand on his cheek. "You know what? Probably none of this would have happened if I had not come here. Every problem we've had was something to do with me. Felicitas, Starr, and now Irene because of the school."

He rolled toward her and placed his arm around her waist. "You're not thinking of leaving are you? You mentioned that once before, that maybe you couldn't stay here. You wouldn't go, would you?"

"No, of course not, but maybe I've tried to interject myself too much into the working of the ranch. Believe me, it was all with good intentions; but sometimes, good ideas come to naught. Really, I'm sorry."

"No, don't be. Don't even think about giving up. Just keep going on like you have been."

"But what about Tom? Suppose he doesn't obey the rules?"

"I've already been thinking on that. I think I'll probably let him go. He's nothing but trouble, and I don't need or want a man like that on my payroll. Might as well get rid of him."

Cynthia sucked in a breath. "Oh, no, you can't! Don't you see? Irene and the children have no place else to go. What would they do? He would only drag them around the country again. Please don't fire him, please. Work with him. Surely, he'll come around."

"Well, maybe, but don't you worry about it. It'll all work out just fine. You wait and see."

****

The next three days were peaceful, in a sense, in that no particular event happened to upset the balance of the ranch. Cynthia held school each day, but the O'Dell girls were absent for the first two. On Friday, however, they attended with the others, even though they were very quiet and were reluctant to participate. Cynthia felt some sense of success, simply because they showed up, dressed in clean clothes as before.

Irene O'Dell stayed with Sarah for two days until her swelling and bruising abated, even though the black and blue marks were still visible. As soon as they were at least faint, she went home to take up her role as the good mother. Annie stayed with the children and cooked for them during those days, and took care of all the necessary chores around the house until Irene came home.

Tom O'Dell was to stay in the bunkhouse through Friday as a sort of punishment, but also to allow his injuries to heal enough so that he would not frighten his own children. Ricardo kept her informed. The man performed his chores to Ricardo's satisfaction, but he went about it all with a scowl on his face. Ricardo became wary of him, wondering what he might do in the end. Tom never seemed to acquiesce to the rules laid down by his boss. Ricardo watched him with great care.

Felicitas began to improve. She stayed in her wheeled chair all morning and went to her room to rest after dinner. Around two every afternoon she would spend an hour in her study, and then wheel herself to the back porch to watch the goings-on of the ranch for a couple of hours. That was about all she could handle, but Rafaelo was pleased his wife seemed to be on the mend. Cynthia, however, watched her in a different light. Felicitas looked increasingly frail and bent, even though she stayed up longer during the day.

Felicitas would not allow Cynthia to do anything for her and not even come near her. That was fine with Cynthia, for she still saw the hatred from her mother-in-law and had no wish to be in her line of vision. She wondered often how she and Ricardo could continue to live as man and wife in the same house with her in-laws. Now both of them were suspicious of her.

****

Friday night, Ricardo took his wife on a moonlight walk down the road that led away from the house.

"I have an idea. I think tomorrow is the day for you to learn how to saddle your mount. The perfect saddle is waiting for you in the barn. It's been in a storage room, but I had Louis to pull it out and clean and polish it up. You have to ride astride, you know, as Westerners do. No sidesaddle business out here."

"Well, I didn't expect anything else. A few women back home ride astride, but I admit that's very few. Most just ride in a buggy. I do want to learn, though. Oh! I'm so excited."

She turned to him in the road and came to a stop. "Ricardo, I want to say something."

"Okay." He took both her hands and held them down between them. "What is it?"

Cynthia took a deep breath. "I...I want to be happy here, you understand. There are things about the ranch that I truly like, and more than anything, I want to be a part of it. You see, don't you, that it may be impossible. I realize our marriage is still new, but I don't know of any other marriage with so many problems. I'm wondering if I should go home for a while and see Father. Maybe if I'm not around, Felicitas will mend faster and be happier. When she's completely well and on her feet, she and I can deal with each other. As it is now, we're simply not on equal footing. Does that make sense?"

Ricardo's heart beat hard and fast in his chest. Fear. It was fear that she would actually leave here and he would be all alone. With great clarity, he realized finally that he loved his wife, was *in love* with her. He adored her, and it would kill him if she went away. No, he decided, she would not leave.

"I don't want you to go, Cynthia. Please don't talk about it anymore. Remember, we said vows—twice if you remember." He chuckled under his breath and she laughed lightly, too. "I need you here, and you promised before God that you would love and honor me, as I would you."

He took a deep breath, looked up at the stars, and back to his beautiful wife. "I, Ricardo Romero, take thee, Cynthia Harrington, beautiful bride of mine, to be my wife, now and forevermore. In sickness and in health, and during all tragic events, and even when my mother acts harsh, and my father acts like an idiot, and I don't treat you right and you get your feelings hurt, and you have to hunt for beaten up women down by the creek..."

She laughed. "Okay, okay. I'm staying. If you love me, Ricardo, that's really all I need. Well, maybe one more little thing."

"What's that?"

"If your mother would come around. That would make all the difference in the world."

"We'll work on it. Just remember, sweetheart, I love you."

There in the dusty road, standing in a glow of moonlight, Ricardo understood his wife and himself a little better.

Chapter Twenty-Two

"Is she tame, Ricardo? I mean, she won't buck me off or anything, will she?"

"She's tame as a kitten. I bought her from the James Wheeler farm east of Nacogdoches. Maybe you know of them?" He took her hand in his.

"Father dealt with him some, and I saw the whole family in town once in a while. I can't say that I knew them. I believe I'm correct in saying the farm was quite prosperous."

Cynthia and Ricardo continued toward the first barn and the stall where they housed Lady Midnight. "Seemed to me that it was. I liked buying from a good farm, because they usually take real good care of their animals. This little mare especially was well cared for. Mr. Wheeler had plans of his own for her, but he liked the price I offered. Tried to go up more, but I kept him at my stated amount. In truth, I was prepared to pay more if I had to, but he buckled."

"Is that fair and ethical?"

Ricardo laughed. "Why sure it is. It's called 'horse-trading' and each man wants his way. It just depends on who blinks first."

Louis stood in front of the mare's stall. "I fed her good, Mr. Romero. She's ready to go."

Ricardo looped a rope around Lady's neck and she willingly followed him to the other end of the barn. There on sawhorses were several saddles and tack hung all along the wall. "Okay, let's bridle her first. Come over here, honey."

Cynthia grinned. "Are you talking to me or the horse?"

"Come over here and I'll tell you."

She laughed merrily and the delightful sound caused Ricardo to pause for a brief moment and gaze at his beautiful wife. He was still amazed that the prim, proper young lady he had married turned out not only to be willing to learn new things, but to confront problems head-on, however unpleasant or dangerous they may be.

"You bridle your horse first. Now, this is a headstall and this is a bit. See? It's metal, and this is why you guide your mount with as easy a hand as you can. You don't want to make her mouth sore. The reins are attached to the bridle.

"First, work the bit into her mouth, gently but with a firm hand. Like this. Then you slip the headstall over the ears. Her ears hold the rig in place. We can let the reins dangle for now, but you know that they're pulled up on either side of her head—one for each hand. Now, you see if you can do it."

Cynthia stepped forward looking confident. But she moved too fast, and Lady tossed her head and stepped back. Ricardo said nothing, for he knew Cynthia was a quick study, and he would give her time to accomplish the lesson.

She talked quietly and soothingly to the mare, and the horse responded in kind by nickering softly and standing quite still while Cynthia worked the bit into her mouth and the headstall on her head. The entire process took only a few minutes, and she stepped back with pride to look at her handiwork.

Ricardo watched her beam, but he saw her discretely wipe her hands down her skirt to remove the horse slobber. If you worked fast, that didn't happen, but the few extra minutes caused the horse's mouth to fill with saliva.

"Good girl," he said with a chuckle.

Once again, she looked sideways at him. "Was that compliment for the mare or me?"

Ricardo's heart melted. This girl was a jewel. He reached for her neck and pulled her mouth to his. He stood very still and enjoyed the kiss.

"Hello! Anybody here?"

Cynthia broke the kiss, stiffened her back, and glared at Starr.

Ricardo turned. "Oh, hi," he said casually. "We're learning how to saddle a horse. Come on down."

Starr strode slowly forward, making certain her pants-clad hips swayed just the right amount. Her smile was somewhere between a smirk for Cynthia and flirtatious for him. Why had he not seen this before?

"Don't let me stop you. I'll just stand over here and watch."

"May I offer you tea, Miss Hidalgo?"

"No, thanks," she answered bluntly with barely a glance at Cynthia. Her eyes remained fixed on Ricardo's face, studying his mouth, his hair, his eyes, all the while smiling at him. "I've come to talk with Ricardo." Now she looked at Cynthia. "May we be excused?"

"Excused? Certainly, you may be. I'll just remove myself. Take all the time you want." With that, she turned away and began to walk out of the barn at a faster pace than her usual easy stroll.

Ricardo called to her, but she did not reply. He knew she was angry. Truthfully? He was irritated at Starr, too.

****

The house was quiet, and Cynthia walked through the kitchen, wondering where Consuelo was. Usually she found her in the kitchen, at the stove, in the pantry, or out in the vegetable garden.

247

She continued in the direction of her and Ricardo's room, when she heard Felicitas call out to her.

"Cynthia! Cynthia! You come in here, girl! This instant!"

For a sick woman, one who was an invalid and useless, she could really yell. She detoured into her mother-in-law's room.

"Yes?" Cynthia stood in the doorway with her hands clasped at her waist. "What do you need?"

Felicitas sat up in her bed, propped on several pillows, her wheelchair nearby. This time of the day, she usually would rest and take a nap, but today she was wide-awake.

"Was that Starr? Did Starr just ride in?"

"Yes, she did. Only a few moments ago."

"What did she want?"

"To talk with Ricardo. That's what she said." How could a grown woman be so very detestable? Why did Felicitas hate her so? She had done nothing she could recall to irritate the woman, save marry her darling son.

"Well, I wish to speak with her," Felicitas demanded imperially. "Go out and tell her to come in the house and visit with me. Now!"

Cynthia dared to walk closer to her mother-in-law. "Do I hear a 'please' in there somewhere? Do you think I'll automatically jump when you issue a demand? No, Felicitas, I will not, unless you speak to me in a civil tone. I've done nothing to you, and you know it. Why do you order me around as if I were a lowly servant? You don't even talk with Consuelo in that manner of voice. I won't allow you to order me about any longer nor speak to me so harshly. I won't stand for it."

"You will *so*! Now do as I say!"

"No." Cynthia turned to walk from the room. She had had enough of the ridiculous woman. No one in her entire life had spoken to her that way, and no one would now. Period.

Before she walked two steps beyond the door, Felicitas called again. "Oh, all right! I'll speak nicely. Now come in here. Please." The words were softer but the tone was not. Cynthia decided to give her a chance.

"Okay, Felicitas," she said as she stood in the doorway. "What do you want?"

"Tell Starr that I wish to see her. That is, when you have time to go back out there."

Cynthia almost laughed. The woman said the correct words but her voice was sharp and demanding, and her eyes still narrowed and her mouth was in the same grim thin line.

Cynthia leisurely walked out the back door to the barn to speak with her husband and find Starr. When she got to the barn door, her mouth fell open, she gasped, and her world upended.

Starr's arms were wrapped around Ricardo's neck and her mouth was near his.

"Cynthia. Sweetheart." Ricardo pushed Starr off him. She fell in the hay pile at the end of the barn. "Wait! Cynthia!" He ran toward the door.

He stopped at the opening to the barn and stalked back to Starr Hidalgo. "Get off my ranch right now, Starr. You hear me? Go! Do it now. Before I really lose my temper."

She struggled to her feet and stood in front of him, brushing the straw from her pants and from her hair. All the while, Starr kept her eyes on his. "Really, Rick? Do you really want me to go? I think you're overreacting, darling, don't you? I only kissed you, just as we've done countless times before." She leaned toward him. "And don't tell me you didn't like it, because I felt it. I felt you leaning toward me and returning the..."

He turned and stalked down the middle walkway of the barn without looking back.

Starr yelled at him. "You come back here, you idiot! Don't you see? Don't you understand? You think you love her, but you love me! I know it!"

Ricardo walked with long, angry strides, his heart pounded with apprehension, and frustration roiled up through his gut. With all certainty, he knew this was the end of Cynthia's patience with Starr. His wife had made efforts to accept every roadblock or mishap, even his mother's resistance to their marriage and her bad behavior. Nevertheless, when it came to Starr, he knew Cynthia would not forget nor forgive any transgression on his part.

That was just it. In reality, he had not committed any sin where Starr was concerned, but he had allowed her to manipulate him and his mother. Father was almost a nonentity around the place anymore, so he was out of the picture relative to Cynthia's feelings.

Just as he stepped up on the porch, he heard riders on the road. Several of his men looked and waited, to see the visitors. Strange men riding to a ranch were always cause for alarm in this part of Texas, where lawlessness was still a major concern for the officials.

As the two men neared, Ricardo noticed their identical dress of black Stetsons, tan pants and vests, white shirts, and black boots. On even closer inspection, he saw the flash of the silver circle-star badge of the Texas Rangers. These men were not visiting to pay a social call. They looked for somebody.

Ricardo walked to the hitching rails and waited until they brought their mounts to a halt.

"Hello, men," he called. "How can I help you?"

The rangers dismounted and walked forward to shake Ricardo's hand.

"I'm Lieutenant Al Wilson and this is my partner, Sergeant Roy Bennett. We have a problem we need to discuss with you, sir. I will say right up front we're touching base with as many ranches and settlements around here that we can, so you know we're not singling you out."

"Fine. If you don't mind coming in the back door here, we can get you some coffee and refreshments. I'll see what Consuelo has."

All three men tromped through the back door. Ricardo instructed Consuelo to serve the men coffee and some of the peach pie from dinner. Then he excused himself to find his wife.

Cynthia was very busy. She'd obviously dragged her big trunk from the storeroom to the bedroom. She already had the smaller trunk and her hand valise on the bed. When he walked in, she whirled about but stood very still and stared at him. "What do you want?" she snapped.

In a quiet, low voice, he asked, "What the hell do you think you're doing?"

"Don't use that sort of language with me. I've told you that before. And you needn't even ask that question, anyway, now do you?"

Slowly he walked closer and shook his head. Gently he said, "Don't do this, sweetheart, please. You have it all wrong. Nothing happened, and I did not initiate anything with her. You know I wouldn't do that, don't you?"

She turned away and resumed her chore of emptying her side of the armoire. He placed a hand on hers that was atop a stack of clothing. "Please wait. Stop now, so we can talk about this. Two Texas Rangers are in the kitchen with a problem. I've got to talk with them. Will you make an appearance, Cynthia? Please do this for me."

"Go back to the kitchen, Ricardo. I'll be there in a short while. I need to make myself more presentable. I won't shame you in front of visitors."

As he walked down the hall, he stopped long

enough to inform his mother who the men were. She became quiet and asked that he tell her about it later. When he arrived at the kitchen, Rafaelo was there, and they made introductions all around. Before they could sit down to the pie and coffee, Cynthia entered.

Ricardo placed his hand at her waist to guide her forward. "Gentlemen, my wife, Mrs. Cynthia Romero, formerly of Nacogdoches. So what brings you here?"

"We're looking for a man who's been on the run nigh on to two years. His name is Charlie Tanner. His crimes, we believe, include robbery, assault, and murder. We've tracked him for a long time but haven't been able to pinpoint his location. He might not even be in the country anymore. Now, I ask you, sirs, do you have a man on your payroll by the name of Charlie Tanner?"

Ricardo had never heard of him. "No," he replied.

Al nodded. "Okay, fine. Now, he might have changed his name, but we have no way of knowing that. But I can describe him."

Ricardo, Rafaelo, and even Cynthia leaned forward with interest.

"He's a big man, not overly tall, though, with long yellowish hair and a drooping mustache. The last report we actually have of him was close to two years ago down in Goliad County. We think he has a family, a wife, for sure, and a couple of reports said he had a little boy but another said two girls. No one is sure."

"You say he committed several crimes?"

"Yes, sir. This seemed to have started over in Harris County, near Houston; then moved to various locations on down to LaSalle County close to the border. There were a couple more incidents, and the most recent was about nineteen, twenty months ago in Goliad."

Ricardo twirled his coffee cup. "I sure can't come up with anybody by that particular description. We do have several families with children."

"Names?"

"Well, there's Job Milford. He has three little girls. About the most gentle, kind man in the world. There's Jim Davis, but he's a freed slave. We have Juan Garcia with little girls, but of course, he's Mexican. Then there's Tom O'Dell. He has two girls and two boys. He's big, but he sure doesn't have any blond hair. He's practically bald."

"I see. What about Milford and O'Dell. How long they been here?"

"Job Milford's been working for us about five years. He's dependable and almost like family. Tom O'Dell? Close to two years. He drove up here one day in a beat-up wagon and a team of tired horses, and one mare tied to the back. He said he needed work, that the ranch he worked for up near Waco let several hands go because of financial problems."

"Mind if we talk to him?"

"Not at all. He'll be out at the third corral. Now, Milford is out on the range with the cowhands."

"Sounds like we can discount him. Anybody else? If you could come up with several, no one man would feel so threatened."

"Sure. Give me and my father, here, a few minutes, and we'll make a list."

****

The men departed on their mission, and Cynthia resumed her packing. Her emotions still ran as high as they had earlier, so there was no need to hesitate. As soon as she had everything packed, she would go find Louis and tell him he was to drive her into Rico Springs early in the morning to catch the train. She dreaded the coming evening and night, for she had little doubt that Ricardo would allow her to leave peacefully. He would surely kick up a fuss, even though it might be just a little faked. To all appearances, Cynthia believed that he truly did prefer Starr.

The part of the puzzle she did not understand was how Starr and Felicitas could accomplish the merger of the two ranches, if they needed Starr to marry Ricardo. She was married to him in the eyes of the law and God, and nothing could sever that tie. Nothing. Holy Matrimony bound them forever, whether they lived together or not.

There lay another problem. If Cynthia moved back home, she could never remarry and never have her own family. Well, that was just fine. It was not the life she always dreamed of, but then, one couldn't have everything.

Perhaps she could learn the banking business. Her father was not a young man, and there was no reason a woman couldn't run a banking establishment. Was there? Maybe she could start a private school. Yes, that was much more feasible. Already, she had the foundation, and of course, she could have a school.

By suppertime, Cynthia had everything packed and her carrying case was ready. With the traveling clothes laid out, she could pack her personal necessities in a few minutes, just before she left. The one problem was Louis. He insisted on asking permission from Ricardo, but Cynthia refused. She convinced him this was quite acceptable with her husband, as she was returning to Nacogdoches to care for her father. She explained that Mr. Romero had his hands full with the Rangers, and he had asked if she could make her own arrangements. In the end, Louis was satisfied. He told her he would have the buggy at the back door at six in the morning.

****

The atmosphere at the supper table was tense and unhappy. Ricardo and Rafaelo talked half-heartedly about the Rangers' visit but felt they had done all they could. No one on the ranch seemed to fit the description of Charlie Tanner. Cynthia remained silent throughout the meal, but she secretly thought Tom O'Dell was a great possibility. Like the others, however, she could not say there was a good case against him.

Cynthia and Ricardo fought and argued for two hours before exhaustion overcame both of them. Around three in the morning, all hell broke loose. Men began to yell which woke Ricardo. By the time he pulled on boots and pants and grabbed a shirt, Cynthia had also quickly dressed and followed him. He ran down the hallway to the kitchen. Ricardo's men pounded on the back door and yelled for him. Rafaelo had awakened and was in the kitchen minutes after Ricardo.

Jake Oliver and John Sutton burst in the room. Jim Black, Job Milford, Louis, and Mario waited on the porch. All of them wore six-shooters strapped low on their hips, hats in place, and dressed in riding clothes. Their saddled horses waited at the first corral.

Jake Oliver spoke in short, breathless sentences. "Tom O'Dell, we think. Let all the mares out, and the new stallion. All ran off, toward the open range. The stallion pushed them out in front. They're gone."

"By damn!" Ricardo swore. "What about O'Dell? Have any idea which direction he went?"

"Maybe more in the opposite direction. We're not sure. Hard to tell. Didn't follow the mares, though, I wouldn't think."

"Okay. Father, you stay here and see after Mother and Consuelo. You should be the one in charge here. I'll need the rest of you to ride with me. Grab water and any food you can find—bread, meat.

Consuelo, can you lay out stuff here on the table? We'll come by and pick it up."

"*Si*, I have beef, bread, and sausage."

"Let's go to the porch."

As they stalked out, Cynthia caught Ricardo's arm. "What are you going to do?"

He looked down at her hand on his forearm. "You care, Cynthia? You actually want to know. Now, isn't this something?"

"Oh, go on. No, I don't care. Leave."

****

After a short consultation, Ricardo chose Mario to ride with him. The young man was strong and wiry and had good tracking skills.

"What's your guess, Mario? Which direction?"

"South. Mexico. He run for the border, I think, but he will go around Rico Springs so no one will see him. But Boss, I do not know if this is right. It will be hard in the dark."

"We have a full moon, Mario, and that'll give us light. There's not a cloud in the sky. If he rides flat out, the horse will leave deep tracks. There's not that much grass this time of year for him to hide hoof prints. Men, you go with Jake, here. He's in charge. Follow his directions, and John'll help him with decisions if he needs help. I want those mares back. The stallion we can catch later if we have to. If we get the mares, he'll come looking for his harem."

Chapter Twenty-Three

For the remainder of the night, Cynthia walked the floor, fumed, and worried. Foolish, foolish woman. She feared for her husband's safety, but she kept her emotions down as much as she could. She couldn't allow herself to fold in the face of this one disaster. The carefully thought-out plan was still on the table. Once every few minutes she thought she might stay until Ricardo came home, or least when the men returned with the mares. That could be days, though, and she wouldn't wait that long. Now that she had made up her mind, she would stay on course. Neither event was any of her concern anymore.

The thought struck her again that Tom O'Dell was actually Charlie Tanner. Why else would he release the mares and stallion? He had good reason to get away, and forcing the men to ride out after the horses was clever. Not to mention he would be getting revenge on the Romeros.

Six in the morning. Still dark. Cynthia tiptoed down the hallway to find Consuelo. She would be up making a fire or still in her room. A few people around here still had to eat. She wasn't in the kitchen, so Cynthia walked softly on to the woman's room on the far side of the house.

"Consuelo? Consuelo?" she whispered through the crack in the door to her room.

"*Si?* What do you want, *chica?*" she whispered back.

"Breakfast, I guess. I wanted to tell you..."

Both women stopped for they heard a window break somewhere on the other side of the house.

"Oh, my goodness," Cynthia whispered, and she grabbed Consuelo's arm. The women stood in the bedroom, clinging to each other in the dark, and breathing hard. They froze and listened.

"There!" Cynthia said quietly. "Did you hear that?

"A scream? A muffled scream? Or what?"

"Felicitas! She's trying to scream or yell. Someone's in there," Cynthia whispered loudly.

"Where's Mr. Romero?"

"Out with the men at the corrals. Standing guard, but no one's watching the house. Do you have a gun, Consuelo?"

"I do. A small gun, but it is revolver. Six shots." Consuelo went into her room and returned with the loaded weapon.

"Thanks. Now listen. You go out the back door. I know it's hard for you, but Consuelo, you must get to the men. We're going to need help."

"What are you to do?"

"I don't know. Go in there, I guess. I can't leave Felicitas alone. She's too vulnerable."

"I go. But I do not go so fast."

"I know. Just be careful."

Her only thought was Felicitas, to protect her, to keep her from harm. Maybe though, she was already hurt. Cynthia's heart pounded from fear, and sweat broke out on her forehead and palms. She wiped one hand, then the other on her skirt as she tiptoed along the dark hallway, carefully gripping the gun with her right hand. Now, she wished she had learned more about pistols.

No lights were on anywhere, but predawn at least made the rooms slightly lighter. The door to Felicitas' bedroom was open, which was unusual, and she was not in there. The door to the study was closed, which also was not right. It always stayed open unless someone worked in there and wanted privacy.

Now, she heard the muffled voices inside the study. Cynthia paused and listened at the door. A man and a woman. She knew who the woman was, and somehow, she knew the man, as well. It had to be Tom O'Dell. They talked in loud whispers, both trying to stay quiet. Felicitas' voice was fearful, and Tom's was harsh.

"I *said*, old woman, where do you hide your money?"

"No money is in here! I do not have a safe. All our money is in the bank in town. None is here, I tell you! Stop! You're hurting me."

"Okay, okay, just be quiet! You've got to have a stash. We're paid in cash once a month, and it's near the thirtieth. So, I know you have the payroll in here somewhere. Now tell me."

"No!" Her voice was louder, and Cynthia heard a slap, then a moan and a cry. "Don't, please don't. I'm already hur..." Another slap.

Cynthia had heard enough. She took a deep breath and threw open the door. Holding the gun with both hands straight out, she pointed it at Tom O'Dell.

"You leave her alone and step away! Back up slowly to the wall."

Tom's gun was stuck in his waistband, but he raised his hands as she said. He never took his eyes off her.

"Now, back up. Slow. Good, now get your hands up as far you can and freeze."

"Okay, okay, Mrs. Romero. Now, listen. I didn't hurt her. All I need is about a hundred dollars. I haven't done anything wrong—here or anywhere else. But now everybody thinks I have. I just need to get out of here."

"No. We'll stay right here until Consuelo gets back with some men. You just stay still. Felicitas," she asked without taking her eyes off Tom, "are you all right?"

"Yes," Felicitas whispered in her weak voice. She was in her wheeled chair; how she got there, Cynthia didn't know, but it didn't matter.

Cynthia kept her sight on Tom with the gun pointed straight at him. She saw his eyes move toward Felicitas and widen slightly, and he lowered one hand very fast to draw his pistol. Before his pistol was level, a bullet exploded though the air and found its mark. Felicitas held a tiny pistol. A thin waft of smoke rose from the small barrel.

Tom O'Dell dropped the gun he had just pulled from his waistband. His hands lowered slowly, but his eyes remained opened and stared right at Felicitas. He remained against the wall, and a red stain began to form in the middle of his chest. In slow motion, he slid to the floor, never taking his eyes from the woman who had shot him. He crumpled in a very still heap.

Men burst into the room: first Rafaelo, then John and others. Rafaelo ran to his wife who stood...she stood! By the time her husband reached her, her eyes rolled back and she fainted into his arms.

Next, surprisingly, Ricardo ran into the room, six-shooter drawn, on high alert, ready to take on the danger. All was well, though. He quickly took in the scene and holstered his weapon.

"Mother!" He ran to his parents.

His father murmured quietly to his son, as he smoothed the gray hair from his wife's face, and gently kissed her on her cheek, "She is fine. Just a faint. Can you open your eyes, my dear?"

****

The house was quiet at last. When Cynthia went

to check Felicitas, she was asleep and her husband lay on the bed next to her, asleep as well. They held hands.

As Ricardo ate a quick breakfast, he explained that he and Mario had followed Tom's trail only a short while, and realized he had actually turned back toward the ranch. When he finished his meal, he made his way to the barns and corrals to learn any news of the mares, but he didn't speak to her.

Cynthia summoned Louis once more. He loaded her trunks and hatboxes and helped her into the small carriage. By seven o'clock, they were on the road to Rico Springs.

The eastbound train finally chugged away from the depot at two in the afternoon. Cynthia had just barely made it. Louis had driven up, jumped from the carriage, and ran to the ticket office. He pleaded with the ticket master to hold the train until he had Mrs. Romero's trunks loaded, and she was on board. As before when she came west with her new husband, she bought a ticket for a private compartment with a berth.

Now, she sat by the window and watched the scenery pass by, but she saw it all through blurred vision, because tears clouded her eyes.

What am I doing? The only choice I had, really. My husband prefers another woman, and why wouldn't he? Starr can outdo me in everything. Starr is an excellent horsewoman; I can't even saddle a little mare, let alone ride her well. Starr knows all about horses. I know if one is pretty or not, or good-tempered. Starr is a very good lover, obviously, because she and Ricardo had consummated at least a few times—how many, I do not wish to know; I am adequate, at best.

At eight in the evening, the train made one stop. During that time, the conductor's assistant knocked on her door.

"Yes?" she asked as she opened the narrow compartment door.

"I am here to make your bed. Will you be going to supper?"

"Oh, yes. Let me get my reticule and jacket." She shrugged on the dark blue, waist-length jacket over the tucked white blouse and buttoned it. She brushed her hands down the skirt to smooth any wrinkles one might notice. When she had her little bag over her wrist, she walked up the aisle to the dining car, leaving the assistant to his chore.

With a heavy heart and a knot in her stomach, she proceeded with as much breeding and sophistication she could manage. After all, one must at all times project the image of the refined lady, whatever the circumstances. Even if one's heart was breaking. Even if one couldn't eat a bite. Perhaps a couple of glasses of wine would do, but she didn't think she could force one morsel of food down her throat.

"Table for one, madam?" the waiter asked.

"Yes, please."

The waiter, dressed impeccably in his white short jacket and black pants, pulled out her chair to the very small, round table for two. "No one will be joining you?"

"No one."

"Then I'll remove the place settings."

"No need," a deep masculine voice said. "Ma'am, is this seat taken?"

Cynthia looked up into the dark face with the long, aquiline nose and cleft chin. "This seat is reserved for someone," she answered primly and coolly.

"Oh? I don't see anyone else. Perhaps I'll sit here until your dining companion arrives."

"No, I don't think you should do that, sir." She narrowed her eyes.

"Never fear, I'll gladly remove myself if your friend shows up." He sat down and snapped his fingers in the air.

The waiter appeared immediately. "Yes, sir?"

"A bottle of your best wine, please, with two glasses. And a plate of cheese and bread."

"Yes, sir. Right away, sir."

"If you don't leave, sir, my companion will be quite angry." She sniffed and turned her head away.

"Really? I think I can handle him," he said quietly.

In a very few minutes, the wine and tidbits were placed on the table. "May I pour, sir?" the waiter asked as he popped the cork on the bottle.

"Not yet. In fact, take everything to compartment number six."

"What?" Cynthia gasped. "What are you doing?"

"You'll see." He stood, pulled her from her chair, and picked her up with a flourish. The action caused everyone in the dining car to look toward the couple, laugh, then applaud. Ricardo grinned and nodded to the other passengers.

****

One Year Later

"Miz Romero! Miz Romero!"

Cynthia hurried to the kitchen as fast as she could; encumbered by the extra weight she carried. "What? Mario, is it time?"

"*Si*," answered Mario. "Lady Midnight will foal any minute. Boss says to come quick if you want to watch. He said you did."

"Oh, I do! Here, somebody, take Rachel."

Consuelo and Felicitas both stood from the kitchen table and reached for the dark-haired two-month-old with the slight cleft in her chin. The baby smiled, gurgled, and drooled, revealing a deep dimple in one little cheek. Felicitas won out and reached for Rachel Maria Elena Christiana Romero.

"Now, she's not too much for you, is she, Felicitas?" Cynthia asked with concern.

"No, of course not. Granted, she is a heavy *chica*, but I can certainly hold my precious granddaughter. Now, go! You must not miss the birth of our first foal!"

Cynthia gathered her wide-brimmed bonnet that protected her skin from the hot, Texas summer sun. As she ran out the back door, she tied the ribbon under her chin. With great excitement, she entered the first barn. *Everything is happening in one day.*

As she approached the knot of men peering into the stall, her husband saw her.

"You'll all have to step back a little, men. Here's the proud owner," Ricardo said with a wide grin for his beautiful wife. "Hurry, sweetheart, you're missing it."

Just as Cynthia looked, the foal slipped out of its mother's body. In moments, before her very eyes, the mare stood and turned to care for her first offspring. Cynthia clearly remembered the birth of her own child and felt a kinship to the pretty, little mare. *Now, both of us have babies, Lady Midnight. Aren't we the luckiest females on the face of the earth to be so adored? Oh, we'll make such fine mothers, you and I.*

"What is it, Ricardo?"

"I believe, sweetheart, we have a fine colt that will grow into as fine a stallion as his sire."

"Ohhh," she cooed. "How wonderful! And he's so beautiful. And perfect."

"Yep, we did well, that's for sure. In a few more weeks, we'll have more, and later on, who knows? We'll have a fine herd—two good lines. Do you have a name chosen?"

"Glory."

"Glory?"

"Yes, like *Glory Hallelujah*, or *Old Glory*, or..."

"Okay, Glory it'll be," he said with a chuckle.

"Do you know what time it is, Ricardo? Felicitas and Rafaelo need to leave in no more than half an hour to catch the train."

"I know. Father headed for the house a few minutes ago. Let's walk back."

As they strolled along arm in arm, they discussed how the next year might be. With Ricardo's parents sailing to Spain to live for a year, and Cynthia's father arriving for a long visit, their lives would certainly be different. In addition, their new home farther up in the hills, but still nearby, would be finished in another three months. Every day, Ricardo expressed concern over Cynthia's daily workload, now that they had a baby.

"You know, everything will work out fine; I'm sure of it. Look how things worked out for Irene O'Dell—or rather Tanner. She is happier now than she's been in many years. Darling, thank you again for allowing her to remain here. She was so frightened about her future with four small children to rear on her own."

"Yeah, I know."

"She'll be fine. She's very happy to take over the housecleaning job from Elena Garcia, so Elena can take care of Rachel while I'm in the classroom until dinner. Irene works with Juan on the house chores and, that way, she can keep an eye on her two who aren't old enough for school."

"Elena sure is happy, isn't she? She can't say enough about how you selected her to be Rachel's nanny."

Cynthia laughed. "God bless her. You would have thought I had given her a million dollars."

Ricardo stopped their progress and turned to Cynthia. He held her arms and leaned forward, and gently kissed her.

"Remember when you ran away?"

"Which time?" She teased.

"Both. I want you to promise to never, never do that again. I love you so much. I can't live without you."

"The luckiest day of my life was the day I ran away from Father. That was the first time you came after me to make me go home. The second luckiest day was when you followed me to the train to ask me sweetly and lovingly to come back home. What a train ride that was!" she said with laughter and joy in her voice.

"Yeah, I remember that ride. In fact, I won't ever forget it."

"Well, to ease your mind, darling, I'll never run away again. Why would I, when I have everything I've ever hoped or dreamed?"

A word about the author...

As a fifth generation Texan, I love to read and research all aspects of the state. Even though my degrees are in science and education, I find the history, the people, and our ancestors much more interesting topics, which provide endless characters and situations to create love stories. Although my husband and I travel, no place on earth is more precious to my heart than our home in the Texas Hill Country, surrounded by acres of live oaks and whitetail deer. Romance novels are not my only form of reading material, but they are my favorite, and I wouldn't leave home without several tucked away in my luggage. Being a member of Romance Writers of America has provided information, encouragement, and guidelines to help me on my exciting journey. What fun it is!

Visit Celia at www.celiayeary.com

Printed in the United States
212256BV00004B/2/P

9 781601 543691